THE HIGH KING'S PROTECTOR

Book One in The Bruadar Series

C. A. KLIPPERT

THE HIGH KING'S PROTECTOR

BOOK ONE IN THE BRUADAR SERIES

by
C.A. Klippert

The High King's Protector
By C.A. Klippert
Copyright © 2019 by C.A. Klippert

For more about this author please visit caklippert.com
All characters and events in this eBook, other than those clearly in the public
domain, are fictitious and any resemblance to real persons, living or dead, is
purely coincidental.
All rights reserved. No part of this publication may be reproduced,
distributed, or transmitted in any form or by any means, including
photocopying, recording, or other electronic or mechanical methods,
without the prior written permission of the publisher, except in the case of
brief quotations embodied in critical reviews and certain other
noncommercial uses permitted by copyright law.
For permission requests, e-mail ca@caklippert.com

Editing by The Pro Book Editor

Book Blurb by Best Page Forward

Cover Design by Damonza

For Marti

PROLOGUE

In the shadows of a great mountain, nine acolytes in robes of dark red lay dead. They had walked in deep, dark canyons and over rarely trodden paths to worship and give tribute to the Asshai, the God of Midir and Holder of the Mithruim.

As their blood trickled and seeped into the ground, three robed figures continued on the path to the great mountain. It rose before them, a black giant whose peaks reached a fiery red sky.

Prince Loris took off his hood. His hair, a light gold, went past his ears and framed a thin and sallow face. His pale blue eyes reflected the color of the sky.

Something in the mountain called him.

Pulled at him.

Though the fear of what lay ahead made him hesitate, the deep, thrumming voice from within the obsidian peaks echoed in his heart, and he sought to follow it. The closer they got to the foot of the mountain, the more uneven the ground became. The fine roots that lay just below the surface protruded from the rocky terrain. Prince Loris scanned the desolate canyons. There were no trees or vegetation in sight. If he were to make a conjecture, the roots seemed to stretch from the mountain. He'd find out soon enough.

He tripped more than a few times, and though he resented it, his guards helped him get up. They followed the path, and the deeper they went, the thicker the roots seemed to grow. They covered the land with serpentine veins of dark gray. The path led the prince and his companions to the mouth of an enormous cave.

They felt it then—a pounding, like a heartbeat that called to them.

Prince Loris lit a torch to peer through the thick blackness of the cave. He shook his head at his guards and waited for them as they lit their own torches.

They tentatively made their way into the dank warmth that smelled of blood and fire. Shadowy tendrils rose from the ground and walls. The tendrils followed them silently, creeping above and around them.

"Prince Loris," one guard called out. "Maybe you should wait outside while we see if there are any dangers inside."

"No. I've come this far. Follow me and stay close."

As they went deeper into the tunnel, they felt as if something was watching them.

A rustling sound and a stone rolling on the ground startled Prince Loris. The guards turned around and brandished short swords. All they saw were long shadows flickering on the walls.

Suddenly snatched from the ground, they screamed as the shadowy tendrils surrounded their bodies. Their swords fell, but Prince Loris didn't pick them up to free his two protectors. He watched, frightened, as the two stopped screaming and stared at him with unseeing eyes.

He felt it then—something creeping up his legs, his torso, then his arms. It squeezed his body until his breath came out in short gasps. He closed his eyes and let go of the torch. Its fire died, and he was plunged into the darkness. For the first time since he'd started this journey, he doubted whether he would make it out of Midir alive.

As Prince Loris's consciousness started to waver, he whispered three words in a chant.

Deep in the mountain, where the roots were as thick as trees, was an enormous cavern. Cloaked sentinels, trapped within the roots, stood all along the cavern. They guarded the circular hole in the ground where the roots converged.

There, the roots went ever deeper, until they covered everything in an impenetrable web. And in the center of that web, on a thick slab of flat rock, embraced by those roots, lay a sleeping gray-skinned giant. His head was smooth and free from hair, as was the rest of his muscular body. Black lines, thick and shiny like glass, streaked around his body, save his face. Dark dreams marred his beauty. His hands were fists that fought against his bondage. Midir was his, as were the surrounding lands. Yet his dreams held him imprisoned in a vision that enthralled him.

The tendrils crept up to Prince Loris's neck and face. He opened his hand and small white flowers fell from his palm and drifted to the ground. Their ephemeral glow was the only light in the cave. The fear was real, and he fought against it. He cursed Cain for being a coward. Cain should be here. Instead, he was across the waters.

As the flowers hit the ground and scattered dust, the sleeping God of Midir opened his eyes.

❧ I ☙

Leona stared out the window at the horizon that stretched out into eternity. The fog that engulfed the tops of the trees that morning had since blown away, revealing an endless expanse of blues and greens.

She leaned against a pillar, intricately carved with snakes, and waited for the High Historian. Leona wouldn't have been impatient, but it was almost time for her to go back home.

She slapped a hand against her thigh and winced at the dust that flew around her. Leona had on a white, long-sleeved shirt tucked under a leather vest with fur trim. A wide belt cinched the vest at her waist. Her dark green pants were so dusty they looked a muddy brown. Black boots reached her knees, and she dreaded cleaning the caked mud under them.

With skin pale from the winter, her complexion was clear and rosy—a sharp contrast against her dark hair, which was in a thick braid that fell down the middle of her back. At nineteen, the roundness of her face and small stature made her look younger. Her eyes, a deep gray, contained a trace of impatience. She masked it as soon as she heard footsteps behind her.

"Leona," a young apprentice called to her. "High Historian Trevelyn is ready for you."

"Thank you." The first person she saw when she entered the High Historian's receiving room was Doyle, a fellow warrior in the Tribunal. He was standing in the center of the room, his black clothes dusty and his shoulder-length hair disheveled from traveling. She nodded to him in greeting, then bowed to Trevelyn. "Sir."

Trevelyn stood by his desk, a florid man gone wide in the middle. His bald head shone, appearing smooth from the lights overhead. His wide face was tan and unwrinkled. Leona always thought it was because he never displayed any emotion. She didn't how old he was, but he'd always looked the same as when she was first adopted into the Tribunal at five years old.

His white and brown robe stretched to the floor. Smooth, long-fingered hands were clasped before him. He looked at her in that piercing way of his that made her feel as if he were seeing right through her.

"I have a mission for you." He picked up a folded parchment and handed it to her. The wax seal was Mandubrath's, the most powerful kingdom in the land of Bearnas. Curious, she unfolded it to reveal an invitation. Trevelyn waited for a beat, and then continued. "You've heard of Edward?"

"Ruler of Mandubrath and over the last two years, declared High King over its four surrounding kingdoms."

"That invitation you have in your hand is for a Gathering of the kingdoms and Borderland tribes." Trevelyn clasped his hands behind him and walked to the map of Bearnas that was tacked above the fireplace. "There is speculation that he will try to sign the last two remaining kingdoms to his treaty of Greater Bearnas."

"And if they don't?"

"He might declare war. Doyle just delivered this message

from Mandubrath. Edward has requested that the Tribunal send representatives. High Healer Irena and I are to go."

"You wish for me to escort you?"

He must have read the confusion on her face because he explained, "Rikard has offered Normundir for this Gathering."

Leona was finally starting to understand. She was stationed up in Normundir and had been on her way back there when she had gotten the summons earlier from Trevelyn. "All the way up north?"

"Edward has accepted the offer. You will accompany him and make sure he arrives safely. You know the Borderlands well, and the White Queen likes you enough not to give you any trouble."

"Well, that wouldn't be accurate...Not after last year."

Trevelyn slightly inclined his head. "She hasn't tried to kill you, has she?"

"Not yet."

"Good enough."

Leona had more questions, but she only nodded.

"I want you to lead this mission. You will have Doyle and a few others to help you. Be discreet. We want to keep Edward safe but not have it be known we are siding with him. Keep your ears on the ground and eyes on the king."

"Understood."

"You will leave tomorrow morning. Edward will be in Kentigern in ten days. You will intercept his party there and join them. I assume you can manage from there?"

"Of course," she replied.

He nodded. "Be safe."

She and Doyle walked out in silence. They didn't talk until they'd reached the main hall that overlooked the Great Library. They watched the people, most of them supplicants, who flocked from all over Bearnas to see the three pristine white buildings that formed a triangle that flanked the town of Midroska—the High Temple, the Healer's Grove, and the Great Library.

Of the three, Leona most liked spending time in the Great Library. The High Temple was impressive with its wide-open spaces and spires that reached up to the sky. The Healer's Grove was beautiful with its gardens of herbs and plants both inside and outside the building. The Library was the simplest of them all. Even so, its size and grandeur inside was a sight to behold.

Made of white marble found in the Hellig Mountains of the north, the walls and pillars were cold to the touch. Leona stroked the smooth surface of the balustrade, breathing in the smell of old books and incense.

Wide pillars spanned the length of the Library's main hall. Even from where Leona and Doyle stood, they had to tilt their heads up to see the ceiling. All the books and scrolls that the Library was famous for were in the upper level where they stood. Several big sections had long tables and chairs. Ladders leaned against the shelves, stretching upward to the highest tiers of countless bookshelves.

Below them, in the main hall, were exhibits of various artifacts found across their lands and those beyond the sea. Paintings, instruments, clothes, hats, and all manner of things were on display, welcoming the Library's visitors to touch and admire.

In the center of the hall, a sphere made of ixmus towered above everything around it. The black obsidian glass was lit from within with luminous veins of blue. It stood on a pedestal of white gold that was carved with ancient symbols that resembled the mark that Leona and Doyle both had tattooed on the inside of their right arms. The circular tattoo of the Tribunal's Chosen was unique to each bearer, but from a distance, they all looked the same.

People who visited the Library never failed to marvel at the sphere's perfection. Most who came stroked it with a reverence akin to a prayer. Those wearing small round ixmus amulets would take them off and hold them against the large sphere, while those wearing ferum beads stretched out their hands and tried to call on their feru'talent. But nothing resulted, whether people called on powers of ice, fire, water, metal, heart whisperers, or animal sight. She toyed with her own necklace of ferum beads—small metallic nuggets that were half the size of her smallest fingernail. Black thread poked through each nugget and was braided on two thin leather strips that held the ferum beads in place. In the middle of her necklace, a narrow silver tube, as long as her thumb, hung heavily just above her heart.

Leona had seen over and over again. The sphere did what those amulets could not—rendered everyone with feru'talent helpless to use them within the Library.

Warm to the touch, it was whispered that it was made by the hands of the Tribunal's Elders—the Namtar, as they were called back when the lands were young. Though none had ever seen the Elders, all who came to Midroska worshipped them.

Midroska was the town built around the Tribunal's white buildings. Throughout its history, as more people moved within the town's walls, the buildings grew higher and higher —the mismatched additions were a patchwork of wood, bricks, and stone.

Most of those who lived in Midroska served the Tribunal's Chosen and its members who had yet to be sent to their assigned temple. Panhandlers and tradesmen—who sought to earn a profit from those who lived in and visited the town— crowded the streets, especially the town's square.

Leona looked at the people who milled among the exhibits. Rovers were there, loud and boisterous with their children. They lived in the Borderlands—outcasts of society and immigrants of long ago from the great land across the sea —Bahadur. Whispered as the land of monsters, frightening tales were often told about their penchant for human hearts and blood. But, as Leona was told by a Rover—the only things in the Borderlands that had a penchant for blood and human flesh were the wild animals that roamed the foothills of the northern mountains.

Their appearance varied enough so it was easy to tell one tribe from another. Today, the Rovers who visited had skin so dark they looked like burnt wood. Their foreheads had bony plates and horn-like protrusions the color of warm gold. They wore colorful but roughly hewn clothes.

On the other side of the main hall were rich noblemen and ladies who haughtily looked around as servants followed them and tried to prevent those who were poorly dressed from touching their masters.

There were some poor folk wearing better clothes. Leona knew from experience they were the ones who sought to work for the Tribunal's Chosen. She mused at how remarkable it was that there were those who decided to live that life —to live under somebody else's charity, to follow orders wherever that decision might lead them.

She turned to Doyle, who, like her, was watching the comings and goings down below. "I didn't realize Edward was high on our list."

Doyle leaned back from the balustrade. He had dark-brown, wavy hair with streaks of silver that had grown in the past few years. Deep grooves lined the sides of his mouth, while shallow ones had formed on his forehead, making him look older than his forty-three years. He wore his usual colors of black and brown, which matched his dark features. There wasn't anything striking about him that would call attention. In fact, he blended into the background most of the time.

"Edward has been on a quest to merge all the kingdoms and Borderland tribes. He's been successful with the kingdoms south of the Borderlands and north of Varannis. Not bad for his first four years as king. His reach has extended all the way to the eastern and western coasts." Doyle paused and smiled. "But then, you know all that already. And if you don't, you should."

Leona nodded before Doyle continued. "He needs Normundir to win over Arag'nilDarahoff. As for Varannis, well...there are speculations it's only a matter of time until Jannik makes an offer of his daughter to Edward. If gossip is correct and there's truth in it, Edward is also trying to make alliances with the leaders in Bahadur."

She thought of Bahadur—the lands beyond the Gowad Sea. She'd never been there, but she'd heard stories of the strange customs of its people and the enormity of Bahadur's size. "That's ambitious of him."

"He's got the right of it. Young as he is, he has offered a stability that Bearnas hasn't seen in a long time. He's a firebringer, and he's got a reputation in the battlefield as a fighter and a strategist. People say he doesn't merge for power, but for peace."

"That could be for propaganda." Leona said.

Doyle nodded and scratched his chin. "It could very well be. He's also got a reputation for drinking himself under the table. There are stories of him in Bahadur, Leona. Stories of debauchery and excess while his father was dying. Lord Merall took over running Mandubrath right after his father died. Everyone thought he'd be king until Edward suddenly decided he didn't want the crown to go to someone else."

"If he's a drunk, then it shouldn't be too hard to keep an eye on him." Leona remarked. "We should decide on who we should invite for this mission."

"Let's keep it small, shall we? Discretion is key."

From within their own rank of warriors, they decided on Colm, Gawen, and Lance.

Colm was a spry young man of short stature. His cap of ruddy gold hair and bright hazel eyes lent him an air of good-naturedness that made people trust him right away. At seventeen, it was an achievement that the Tribunal entrusted him with important messages. He'd spent the majority of the last two years traveling around Bearnas, and most importantly, he had animal-sight. Colm had the rare ability to see the land through a fraught connection with hawks he had trained. Underneath the relaxed attitude was a quickness and reliability that Leona knew they needed for the mission.

Gawen, a firebringer, was a skilled horsemaster stationed in a healer outpost near the meadows of the Borderlands. He was a big and stocky man. The same age as Doyle, his coarse, reddish-brown hair remained vibrant. In fact, he kept his hair just below his shoulders and sported a thick beard he was proud of.

Lance, with his dark hair curling against his nape, had the sharp looks that reminded Leona of a hawk. He had a carefree way about him and a quick smile he often flashed to charm the women around him. A quick wit, he could talk his way out of anything. Just a year or two older than Leona, he and Leona had apprenticed together, and Lance was one of the few who hadn't given her a hard time. A metalforce, Lance was stationed in the High Temple. Leona liked to think of him as someone who would have done a good job of thieving had he not been chosen by the Tribunal.

The one person who wasn't part of the Tribunal that Leona was going to ask help from was her friend, Belinda. The twenty-year-old daughter of Lord and Lady Carran of Kentigern, Belinda was plump and had inherited her mother's plain looks—ash-brown hair, with brown eyes and a pale complexion that leaned toward sallow. While her mother tried hard to keep her figure and make herself more attractive, Belinda didn't care a wit. She liked staying in the castle's library, content with keeping the records or reading in solitude. She'd confessed to Leona that she fantasized about working at the temple in Kentigern as the historian's assistant, but her mother had not given up the hope that someday she would make an advantageous marriage.

⚜

At first light the next day, Leona and Doyle set out for Kentigern, where the rest of their companions would meet them in the coming days.

Kentigern sat at the border of Greater Bearnas and the Borderlands. Just west of Midroska, it was a small kingdom that relied on facilitating the trade of the goods from Normundir and the Borderlands with the rest of Bearnas.

It was already dark when they arrived. The cobblestones in the narrow alleyway were wet and shiny from the earlier sprinkling of rain. Leona and Doyle made their way to a tavern known to the locals as the Black Bird.

Colm was already there when they arrived. He gave them a small nod and a smile. He had always been a fast one. They snagged a table in the back, closer to the conversations in the tavern. A particularly loud table amused them.

"I hear the High King will travel to Normundir," a raucous man from the loud table announced.

"Hah! Looking for a bride? My Jenny is right here." The fat woman who spoke pointed to her equally fat daughter.

The man beside her slammed his drink down. "Just because your daughter is desperate to marry, it doesn't mean everybody else is."

The whole table rocked with laughter.

"I'm going to the temple to get some sleep. I'll see you

two first thing tomorrow," Leona told Colm and Doyle, both of whom were staying at the inn above the tavern. She had just taken a few steps away when a drunkard stopped her with a hand on her arm.

"Lady, won't you join our table for a drink?" The man looked like he hadn't bathed in days. His matted black beard had crumbs of bread and cheese, while his breath stank to high hell.

She looked at him with annoyance. "No, thank you. Excuse me."

"Come on, don't be a stiff." He pulled on her arm. She slammed him against the wall and drove her knee into his groin. He grunted as he slid down to the laughter of his companions. Doyle and Colm both smiled down at their cups. Leona wasn't known for her patience with stupidity.

The next day, they met at the main square, close to the keep at Kentigern. What the castle lacked in size, it made up with its impressive view of a blue lake and the forest of the Borderlands.

The market in the main square teemed with merchants and folks from the other kingdoms getting their supplies. There was a sense of busy anticipation in the air.

A stocky trader with a host of horses called them over with a whistle.

"Gawen." Leona gave him a small nod in greeting. "When did you get here?"

"Just this morning."

Leona stroked a beautiful brown gelding. "You're not really selling any of them, are you?"

"No." Gawen's eyes turned soft at the horse who was trying to sniff out food from Leona. "I've turned away a few interested buyers already. Told them that they're all reserved for King Rikard of Normundir. A gift from Lord Carran."

"Have you seen Lance?"

"Aye. You know him, he likes to talk to people. He said he'll be at the tavern tonight for supper."

"Can you be there as well? Doyle, Colm, and I will be going over our plans tonight."

Gawen nodded. "Also, Lance left a message for you." He inclined his head at Doyle. "He said you'll find employment with Lord Carran."

Doyle nodded in thanks. "I suppose I should head over to the castle now before I lose my chance."

"Sure looks like everyone's looking forward to the High King's visit," Colm mused at the overly crowded square.

"They see it as a great honor. I need to find Belinda. See what you two find, will you?" Leona didn't wait for a reply before leaving Colm and Gawen. She grimaced at her appearance as she made her way to the castle. It was the best dress she'd found in the coffers of the temple. A deep blue with bright red accents across the bodice and sleeves, it looked, with its low front, like it belonged to a high-end prostitute. Leona tucked a white piece of fabric across the top and vowed she'd ask for plainer and more conservative clothing.

When Leona reached the castle and was told that Belinda wasn't there, Leona gave it some thought and headed back into the main square. She walked around until she saw an old woman she recognized standing in front of a stall. Leona stepped inside and into the back. Belinda was rifling through the fabrics and dress samples, a dreamy smile on her face. Her chubby figure was ensconced in a plain yellow dress, while her brown hair was tied in a low bun.

"Belinda," Leona called out.

"Leona, how did you find me here?"

"I went to the keep first. Since you weren't there and your mother is most likely trying to set you up with every noble she can find, I thought you'd seek refuge in town. In a place where your mother wouldn't think you'd go. I also saw old

Cybil lurking by the food stand outside." Cybil was Belinda's hawkeyed servant.

Belinda smiled and hugged Leona. "And here I thought you had magic."

Leona had always liked Belinda. Leona had met her a few years ago when Belinda showed up at the Kentigern temple needing assistance with the records and books kept there. At that time, Belinda'd thought that Leona was the historian's apprentice. The friendship they formed continually surprised Leona, but she was grateful all the same.

Even though she hated to bring Belinda into this, Leona squared her resolve. She knew Belinda enough that the lure of adventure would be enough to get her on board.

Leona looked around the small shop. "Can you talk right now?"

After Belinda assented, they stepped out of the shop and leisurely walked around the town.

"Will the High King arrive tomorrow?" Leona asked.

"Yes, that's what father said."

"Are you planning to go with them?"

"Mother insists that I should. She thinks I'll meet someone along the way." Belinda grimaced. "At least I'll get to see the Borderlands and Normundir. I've seen nothing outside Kentigern."

"Is your mother going?"

"Good Elder gods, no! That's why it'll make the journey bearable. My brother's too young to go or else mother would come. Can you imagine if she did?" Belinda shuddered.

Leona smiled at her reaction. "I'm sure it's not that bad. The reason I ask is that I'd like to go with you."

"Truly? Is this a mission?"

When Leona nodded, Belinda clapped her hands in excitement. "This is even better. I've always wanted to see what's involved in your missions."

"Oh, Belinda, you're not even going to ask why?"

"I'm sure if you could tell me, you would. Otherwise, I think I'd just be wasting my time asking you a question I know you won't answer."

Leona chuckled and shook her head. "For my cover, I thought it would be best to keep it close to the truth. I'm an apprentice at the temple for the historian. Traveling through the Borderlands and Normundir will help improve my chances of getting a permanent job at the temple. Do you think your mother will let me join you?"

"Of course, she will. I've told her before that you've got my coveted spot at the temple. I'll tell her that this is your one chance to observe in person the royal families. I'll also add that you're too scared to travel on your own, and she'll think that that's commonsense. Nobody will question those motives."

"In other words, she'll probably think I'm really there for the rich and titled men." Leona laughed at that. "I'm sure I'll be one of many."

Belinda stopped and looked at her. "You need different clothes, though. Even I know you can't dress like that."

Leona looked down at her dress and sighed. "Don't worry. I'll have something appropriate to wear."

"I'll see if I can get some of mother's old dresses. You're closer to her in size, but she's bigger than you."

"I'm a poor apprentice, remember?"

"That doesn't say apprentice to me."

Leona looked down at the bright garish slash of red and low bodice. Belinda laughed as they made their way back to the castle.

THE HIGH KING ARRIVED THE NEXT MORNING TO FANFARE.

Leona stood on the rooftop of one of the buildings with Colm and Gawen. They had a good view of the kingdom gates from where they stood. She peered down at the crowds of people that flanked both sides of the road. Streamers of blue, yellow, red, and green danced in a tumble of colors.

Colm was beside Leona waving one of the stupid flags that had been handed out in the main square. Gawen, his arms crossed in front of him, looked annoyed at the smile on Colm's face. Leona took a bite of the apple she'd brought with her and looked toward the castle keep. She could barely make out Belinda with her twelve-year-old brother. She scanned the crowd, looking for Lance and Doyle, but there was no sign of them.

Leona turned back to the gates and had just finished her apple when the horns blared, announcing Edward's arrival.

His guards came riding in first, dressed all in black. Their faces betrayed no expression as they surveyed their surroundings.

Her first glimpse of Edward had her straightening up. She'd been so wrong about him.

Leona thought he'd be florid and flabby, based on his reputation for drinking and womanizing. But Edward was pure muscle. Dressed in all black, he looked taller and bigger than his guards. Tall with unkempt dark-brown hair, he had hooded, dark eyes; full lips; and a strong jaw. A thin scar marred his right cheek from the temple down to the chin.

If it weren't for the scowl and the wicked-looking scar, Edward would have been impossibly handsome. Next to him was his cousin, Conrad, Lord Merall's son. Not as handsome as Edward, but good-looking nonetheless. Conrad waved at the people around them and smiled jovially—exactly what Edward should be doing. Instead, he kept the scowl going and nodded to those who called out to him. Behind them, in a long procession, were various royalty and noblemen with whom Edward had treaties.

Leona couldn't help but think that Conrad was better suited for the job of benevolent monarch. She turned away as soon as Edward reached Lord Carran's castle. There would be festivities and games scheduled for the next two days before everyone left northward.

She went back to the rooms in the temple and found a chest full of clothes. She inspected the dresses and found they weren't all the same size.

"If you don't want them, we can get more," said a booming voice behind her.

Leona turned to see the temple healer, Arlo. A small thin bald man, he shuffled closer to her, his robes swishing on the floor. "Thank you. Where did you get them?"

"Apprentices, mostly. You'd also be surprised at what people leave in the temple once they are healed."

"Do you know if anybody can help me alter some of these clothes?"

"I've already asked the cook to help you with that. He'll be done in the kitchen shortly. Not much of a cook. But he's the only one in here who knows how to do it."

Turek the Cook was a big, bullish man with arms the size of Leona's torso. He didn't look like he belonged in the kitchen. More like a brawler, his scowl betrayed his impatience with Leona's request.

"I have a lot to do, and you want me to fix these dresses? You'll fit just fine in there."

"Yes, I could fit just fine in there, if I wanted to wear a tent."

"Then you should fatten yourself up."

"Believe me, the thought crossed my mind, but I don't have time to fatten myself and get taller in two days," Leona retorted.

His lips twitched. "Fine."

He grabbed the dress at the top of the pile. Leona almost made a move to stop him when he gave her a look. "I washed my hands. And if the dresses smell, you wash them afterward."

Leona had him go outside and called him back when she had the dress on. They both looked in the mirror.

"You can make do. Just wear a cloak on top."

"You didn't say that last time. How am I supposed to run or fight in this if I'm just going to trip over myself?"

"Fine, I'll fix them."

He measured the dresses that Leona chose to take with her. He also grabbed the ones she chose not to use.

"What will you do with those?"

He just pursed his lips and looked at her as if her question were stupid. Then he left without another word. With nothing more left to do, Leona made her way to the tavern where she was to meet with the others. Once inside, the smell of onions and potatoes permeated the air. There was an undercurrent of spilled ale in that mix that made her mouth water. Though it was early for supper, the tavern was starting to fill up with people. Leona snagged a table in the back and ordered some bread, cheese, and ale. Might as well be comfortable while she waited.

⁂

"WELL, NOW, I DON'T HAVE THE FINAL NUMBERS, BUT HE has six guards and a hundred soldiers. About equal are the nobles and servants," Lance told everyone as they sat around a meal in the tavern. Belinda was the only one missing. It would have been too suspicious if someone of her rank supped at the tavern—and scandalous should her mother and father find out.

"Just a hundred soldiers and six guards? With that many people? Is that to make himself appear less threatening?" Leona asked with a frown.

Doyle nodded. "Yes, it's a strategy that could backfire. Traveling with that big of a court makes for an easier target. It might get bigger, too. Edward is unmarried, and the smaller kingdoms are hoping for an alliance through marriage with a king who could become the most powerful man in the land."

"You'd think he'd be warier of the Borderlands. They hate royalty there." Leona shook her head. A big swath of land that separated the north from the rest of the lands, the Borderlands featured no established kingdoms within them. Only the Rovers roamed the land with relative freedom.

Some families had built steads and farmed the same land for years within the Borderlands. Savage power struggles crept up, and whoever was the strongest led the bigger tribes. The balance of power always changed, and, owing to the nomadic nature of the gypsies and tribes, the idea of consolidation had never entered their minds. The gypsies and tribes fought hard for freedom, and freedom they would keep until their dying breaths.

Queen Anva, the White Queen, was the undisputed power who protected the boundaries of the Borderlands, but she was a nomadic queen as well. She came and went as she pleased. Queen Anva, with her court, was wont to travel within the Borderlands, staying as long or as short wherever her whims dictated. She never meddled with the lives of the Rovers and rarely interacted with them. As long as they stayed out of her way, they were safe.

Trading villages ran alongside the major route from one edge of the Borderlands to the other. Edward and his retinue would definitely create a spectacle of themselves.

"I've spoken with Belinda, and I will join her as a distant

cousin." She turned to Doyle and raised an eyebrow in question. "And you?"

"I found employment as one of her guards. I told her father I worked for King Rikard but will be getting married to one of his fine citizens who can't leave her parents and grandparents." Doyle shrugged. "He didn't seem to care much once his soldiers validated my skills, and he thought my knowledge of Normundir might help since we're all going there."

Leona looked at Colm and gestured for him to speak.

"I'll be one of the messengers-for-a-fee." He said it with gusto as he took a hand-painted sign from behind him. Made of two pieces of wood hung from a braided piece of rope, the sign on the front said, "Messenger," and in the back, with red paint, was a hawk.

Gawen chuckled. "Very artistic."

"Thank you."

"Bran"—Colm gestured at the hawk on his shoulder—"is a part of my service. I'll try my best to keep myself always available to my favorite customers." Colm cut a small chunk of meat and fed it to the patient hawk. Its feathers—a hundred different shades of brown—glimmered with a golden glow in the candlelight.

"Lance?" Leona prompted.

"I'll be one of two blacksmiths. It'll be easy enough for me to do simple repairs." Lance flicked a finger and a fork on the other side of the table flew to his hand.

"I really wish you would stop showing off." Gawen scowled.

Leona shared a smile with Colm before continuing. "Gawen? The usual?"

"Yes, a horse trader." Still scowling.

Leona then assigned alternating times of the day for them to communicate so that they established no clear pattern.

They'd be leaving in three days, according to Belinda, and Leona was confident they were as prepared as they would ever be.

The night before they were to leave, Lord Carran held a banquet for Edward and his nobles. Belinda invited Leona, but she chose not to go. She needed the quiet to prepare herself. She lay down on the cot and thought of tomorrow.

An air of anticipation pervaded Kentigern. Although there was drinking and merrymaking in the castle, outside in the tents, the soldiers, blacksmiths, servants, and horse keepers were all busy getting things prepared.

Leona had to play the part now. She'd been through the Borderlands more times than she could count, and she knew the dangers. Discretion was a priority in this mission, and she knew she'd assembled the right people. The skies were darkening and long shadows were cast in the tent. She closed her eyes and cleared her mind. Tomorrow would be a long day.

The next morning found Leona putting on a light gray dress with small embellishments in the form of clever thread work by the temple cook. The dress fit surprisingly well. There was a give to it when Leona stretched her arms. Leona looked at the fabric and noticed the small clever stitches that stretched with the cloth when needed. She looked at the other dresses, and they had similar stitching. Hidden pockets in the dress also ensured she could keep a spare strand of ferum beads—not that it would do her any good. The trickle of ice she'd been able to save up would only be good for one or two usages. It would take her forever to store that much feru'talent again.

Leona opened the wrapped package included with the dresses. She unfolded the dark green riding suit and looked at it closely. The back was long and from that view, it would look like she was wearing a full-length dress, but the front of it was tailored to reach her hips. Leona took the folded black trousers from the same package. The lining on the outer sides matched the green riding suit. She smiled at the pleasant surprise. He worked fast.

She folded the traveling clothes she'd been wearing, wrapped them in the packaging that the cook had used for the riding suits, and put them at the bottom of the chest. Doyle would accompany Belinda this morning, and when he did, the plan was to hand him her traveling clothes to include with her pack—which included a bow, arrows, two short swords, daggers, and other necessities. Truth be told, she felt naked without her weapons. She attached her dagger to her thigh. For now, that should be enough.

She walked to the square to watch Lord and Lady Carran's send-off of Edward and Robert. There was a tangible excitement in the air, and soon the tents were dismantled and packed. Leona looked at the assembling group and thought they were doomed if someone with marginal skill attacked them. Oh, well, her job was to protect the High King and not the court.

Edward's reputation on the field could have made it possible for him to force the hands of the other kingdoms left outside Edward's treaty of Greater Bearnas. Yet, here he was, going to a Gathering to bring unity to the lands. Leona only hoped that the Borderlands would be represented during the talks. Too much distrust bred unnecessary bloodshed, not just between the Borderlands and the other kingdoms, but also within its boundaries.

Lord Carran turned and raised a hand for silence. The square became silent, save for a few who coughed and whispered.

"My lady and I wish you all a safe journey. May you all have uneventful travel to Normundir and accomplish our goals of peace, unity, and a stronger Bearnas at the first Gathering." He bowed to the two kings, and everyone cheered.

Edward nodded in agreement. "Thank you for your generosity, Lord and Lady Carran."

There were more trivial pleasantries between the nobles. Though Edward didn't betray his impatience, Leona saw it when he nodded to one of his guards as soon as the pleasantries were over. His horse was brought to him. When Edward mounted his horse, everyone took that as a sign they were all leaving.

Now it starts, Leona thought.

2

Leona rode with Belinda in a horse-drawn carriage. She was used to riding a horse, where she was in control of the speed and could feel the wind. In comparison, this was claustrophobic. She kept her eyes on the passing scenery in the window, marking their progress by the sun's position and the lay of the land.

"Are you storing ice right now?" Belinda blurted out, looking at the necklace around Leona's neck.

Leona nodded. "Yes. It's habit whenever I have the time."

"Can I see them?"

"Of course." Leona took her necklace off and handed it to Belinda.

Belinda hefted it in her hand. "It's heavier than I thought."

"You've never held one?"

Belinda shook her head. "It just seems rude to ask. It seems too personal. Don't they always have someone's feru'-talent stored in them?"

"Most of the time. It's heavy because it hasn't been used much."

"Is it true that they eventually crumble?"

"With enough use, they get lighter and lighter until they're like air. But then you want to get rid of the beads before then since you can't store that much feru'talent in them."

"Is the pendant praevadium?" Belinda asked.

"Just an ornament from Normundir."

Belinda handed the beads to Leona. "I wish I had something. Anything. I wouldn't even mind being a grower. I hate plants, but I'd take being able to make them grow over nothing."

"It's not always sunshine and rainbows. Having an ability doesn't make things better." Leona looked out the window, wishing she had never been born with hers.

❧

As the sun started its descent, they arrived at the giant looming trees that marked the beginning of the Borderlands and stopped for the night.

"Thank the Elders." Leona left the carriage before Belinda could get off her seat. Leona stretched her arms and back. She took in the pine smell of the forest. The cool breeze was a relief against her face.

Tents were set up amid the giant trees. In the biggest clearing, a long table was set up for the court. Servants laid a slew of food and drinks on the table. It was a big effort not to roll her eyes at the excessiveness.

Belinda sidled up to Leona. "Shall we get something to eat?"

"Not yet. I think we should go for a walk. And don't frown. We've been sitting the whole day." Leona took Belinda's arm and led her in a stroll around the camp.

"I didn't realize trees could get this big." Belinda looked up in wonder at the cathedral-like canopy of green.

"You should see this cave near the Snake River. It's so big, if feels like it can swallow the keep in Kentigern." Leona then told Belinda about the meadows in the middle of the Borderlands where a tribe lived with wild horses, about the foothills of the Hellig Mountains, about the different steads and tribes that made the Borderlands their home.

By the time Leona was done, she and Belinda had taken a meandering path around camp. When they arrived back at their tent, Belinda went to the privy while Leona sat on one of the two chairs laid out in front of the tent. She leaned back and contented herself watching the comings and goings.

Edward was seated at one end of the table. While two servants kept the wine flowing for the noblemen and noblewomen, one of his guards was stationed behind Edward with a bottle just for him. Leona couldn't help but think how paranoid he must be to have his own guard serving him wine.

At Belinda's urging, they got some food and sat near the long table. The sun was going down, and bonfires were lit in the camp. Musicians played lively tunes while Leona tapped her feet to the rhythm.

She kept her eyes on Edward and watched as Conrad stood up and join in on the dancing. Edward stayed back, still drinking. After a while, Leona stood up and turned to Belinda, "I'm going to sleep. Are you coming?"

"Yes, please. I know all I did was sit in the carriage, but I am so tired."

"It takes some getting used to—traveling this long," Leona explained as they made their way to their tent. Among the revelers, Leona caught sight of Doyle with two Kentigern soldiers. She gave him a nod in greeting. He inclined his head in return.

When they got to their tent, Leona changed into her

night shift. When she heard soft snoring, she looked behind her and beheld Belinda already sleeping without changing out of her travel clothes.

The next day, Leona watched in amazement as everything was dismantled and they journeyed on. She couldn't help but think how much easier it would have been if they had simply camped out instead of bringing a castle's worth of people, food, and furniture.

The next few days went in the same manner—traveling all day, then setting up camp well before sunset. Edward was nothing if not predictable, but all the other noblemen and noblewomen became more relaxed. The women became more daring, especially with Edward. Though Leona couldn't hear them, the body language alone looked like an innuendo to her.

After a week of slow traveling, Leona had read through most of Belinda's books and had even written her observations for when she reported to the temple in Normundir. She'd even noted who had what feru'talent—well, those that showed off. Leona was hoping to catch a glimpse of Edward's fire, but saw nothing.

Near the end of the day, they set up camp close to a trading village. The village was comprised of temporary steads and people who had set up their homes and wares to trade with nearby tribes and those who traveled through the Trading Route.

Leona and Belinda joined a group of women who wanted to walk through the village. The apparent leader, Princess Helen, was from the eastern kingdom of Menoa. Her father, Robert, had allied himself with Edward early on when Edward had begun his mission of merging the middle kingdoms. Until now, Robert had had a lot of influence among the other prosperous kingdoms. Helen knew this and made sure that nobody forgot her ties to Edward.

A classic beauty, her creamy skin complemented her long golden hair while dark thick lashes framed her deep blue eyes. The other women hung on to every word that came out of Helen's mouth, while their servants followed closely, silent and attentive.

"Oh, my!" Helen exclaimed. "How dirty this is. And the smell!"

"They should clean this place," one of the women chimed in.

"They're not poor by choice," Belinda said after half an hour of complaining from everyone.

Helen arched an eyebrow at her. "Excuse me?"

Belinda looked down and mumbled, "I'm just saying they didn't decide to be poor."

"What do you know?" Helen huffed and walked away.

Leona took Belinda's hand and squeezed it. "You said the right thing."

Belinda sighed. "That's the reason I have no friends."

"It's what makes you a good person."

They put a little distance between themselves and the others. Leona was entertaining Belinda with a story to distract her from feeling too sorry for herself when they heard Helen's scream of outrage ahead of them.

A peasant woman in front of Helen was gathering a crying child in her arms.

"Don't touch me, dirty child!"

"I'm sorry, my lady. My girl, she thinks you're pretty and your dress. She meant no harm..."

"My dress is ruined."

"I'm so sorry." The peasant woman looked down as she tried to soothe her little girl. "We have nothing to repay you for the damage my daughter has done to your dress. She doesn't know any better. If you're to blame anybody, it should be me."

Even though the thrum of activity hadn't stopped, all eyes were on Helen and her companions. Helen summoned a magnificent smile and looked benevolently at the woman. "I could have you punished, but instead, I will forgive you."

Leona rolled her eyes for the hundredth time since they'd left Kentigern.

"Oh, thank you, my lady. Thank you." The woman nearly wept in gratitude.

"And it's not *my lady*, it's *Your Highness*." With that last dig, Helen left.

The woman gave her child another hug to calm her. She put her down and gathered the bread from the ground. The woman looked at the muddied bread and wiped it as best she could before putting it in her basket.

"It's all right," she told her sobbing daughter. "She's gone now."

Leona, too angry to follow Helen and the others, stood her ground with her fists clenched and her jaws tight. Belinda, who had gone several steps ahead, turned around and looked at Leona with that embarrassed and meek gaze that Helen's companions had shared after the exchange with the peasant woman.

"Leona? Are you coming?"

"I will, but go ahead." Leona stayed behind and waited for all the eyes in the market to follow Helen. She went to the baker's stall and purchased bread. She also bought fruit and cheese as an afterthought.

The woman had picked her daughter up and begun to walk away when Leona stopped her with a hand on the shoulder. "Wait. This is for you and your daughter."

The woman shook her head. "My lady, I can't."

Leona looked down at her dress and wished she were in her usual hunting garb. "Please, take it."

The woman accepted the satchel with suspicion. "Thank you."

Leona held an apple out to the little girl, who was trying her best to hide in her mother's arms. "Do you like apples?"

When the little girl just looked at her, Leona continued, "Don't be frightened. I'm not the scary lady. I don't look like her, do I?"

The girl giggled and accepted the apple.

"I'm sorry, my lady. We can't accept this. It's too much."

"I would like for you to have it. And it's really for your girl."

The woman looked at Leona and nodded.

"She's lovely." Leona briefly touched the deep dimple on the girl's cheek. She must have been three or four years old. Her tangled hair was a riot of light brown curls. Her big round eyes were delighted at the attention she was getting from Leona.

The woman smiled at that. "Yes, she is."

The girl reached over to touch Leona's hair.

"Go on. It's not as lovely as your curls, but I suppose it will do for now."

The little girl giggled again.

"Thank you, my lady," the woman said with a smile of gratitude.

Leona turned away from the woman. She'd just taken a step when she bumped into someone. Someone who felt like solid muscle. Her hand automatically went into the slit in her dress, to the knife strapped on her leg. She trailed her eyes up, surprised to see Edward looking down at her. Still in black clothes, but this time, Leona noticed the sword and dagger strapped to his waist.

"Your majesty," she blurted out.

Everyone who heard her stopped, but nobody deemed to bow. This was the Borderlands, after all.

"Trouble?" he asked.

Leona shook her head. "Not at all."

Up close, Edward was so tall she had to tilt her head back to look at him. His wide shoulders and muscled build made her feel small. Leona wrinkled her nose. His clothes reeked of alcohol already, but his eyes were surprisingly steady. He looked her up and down. "I've seen you with Carran's daughter. What's your name and what house do you belong to?"

"My name is Leona. I'm an apprentice to the historian at the Tribunal temple."

"So, Leona-with-no-family-name, what truly happened here?"

"Is that how you talk to everyone?" Leona asked before she could stop herself.

He raised an eyebrow at her tone. "Do they teach rudeness in the Tribunal?"

"Only when it's warranted," she retorted.

His eyes narrowed as his jaw clenched. Leona watched in fascination as the scar on his cheek flexed with the movement.

"Are you done?" Edward raised an eyebrow.

Leona relented at the annoyance in his voice. "Helen's dress got dirty. She panicked and screamed. But now everything is fine. She went back to camp."

Edward nodded after a while. "It's getting late. You should also go back."

Now it was her turn to clench her jaw. The insufferable man was ordering her like she was some helpless female. "Fine."

He turned away from her, and Leona stood there watching as he walked further into town with two of his guards following him.

3

“Hunting!” Leona exclaimed, incredulous. “These are the Borderlands. What the hell is Edward thinking? Did you try to warn his guards?”

Doyle nodded. “People are getting bored, and these lands are known for big and unusual game.”

Leona paced the tent while Belinda read a book. They needed a plan, and quick. Tomorrow was the hunt, and the whole camp was already busy preparing.

“Doyle, can you coordinate with Edward’s army the moment any suspicion of attack arises? Colm and Gawen will be our eyes from a distance. I’ll keep myself close to Edward.”

Belinda cocked her head. “But how will you keep close to him during the hunt?”

“If I have to act like a complete nitwit, I will. If it’s the one thing that will keep that man safe.” Leona thought about how intimidating Edward looked. It felt ridiculous thinking that he needed any protection.

ON THE DAY OF THE HUNT, LEONA WAITED PAST THE EDGE of the campsite with Colm and Gawen. Hidden behind a thick brush, her horse shifted under her, probably sensing her impatience. She was holding on to the reins of Colm's horse while Gawen was on his own, looking up at where Colm was stationed above in the thick branches of a tree.

It was Gawen who suggested they wait in this part of the woods. He'd scouted the area earlier, and he had a hunch this was the direction the hunting party would pass through.

Colm jumped down as a horn blared, signaling that game had been spotted.

The ground thundered with hoof beats. Louder and louder they came, until the hunting party swept past them. Leona, with Colm and Gawen just behind her, took off in a burst. They trailed after the hunting party, expertly maneuvering through the trees, staying at a careful distance.

Suddenly, chaos erupted and magic flared.

Horses tumbled on cleverly laid-out traps. Wide nets fell from the trees and onto the riders. All around the hunting party, the trees were alive with Rovers brandishing spears and swords. More Rovers were in the trees shooting arrows.

Fire swept across a band of Rovers, and more than half the hunting party was able ride away. A strong wind blew and squelched some of the flames. Leona looked up and saw two of the archers had stopped firing and were focused on the fire. Windcasters. She shot two quick arrows at the archers, and the wind immediately stopped.

A small man dropped down from atop and landed on Leona, dragging her from her horse. She punched him in the face and pushed him away. Another Rover leaped at her back and as she fought him, she tried to see where Edward was.

She frowned when she saw he wasn't doing a good job of fighting. She was expecting more from him. Probably all that wine he drank had addled his brain.

Leona faced the two men. She lunged for one of them with dagger in hand when the dagger was suddenly pulled to the side. One of the Rovers was a metalforce. He pulled on the dagger again and this time, Leona let him, following the lead of her dagger right into his chest.

She caught Gawen's eye, and he signaled he was going to circle around to get closer to Edward. Meanwhile, she caught a glimpse of Colm fighting three men who were nearly twice as big as him.

As two more Rovers surrounded Leona, another set of nets dropped on top of Edward and his guards. This time, the nets were sown with large raw chunks of ixmus. The same nets used by pirates. The ixmus rocks were big enough that anybody touching the net wouldn't be able to use their magic.

When she saw Edward's call for surrender, Leona sneered in disgust and let the Rovers drag her forward. Annoyance flared on Edward's face when he saw her. "Let her go. She can't possibly be of any use to you."

"That's where you're mistaken." A large Rover, a man, leered down at Edward. He was so tall that Leona had to strain her neck to look at him. His dark, full beard was matted, and he smelled like he'd needed a bath for some time now.

Leona finally looked around at the Rovers that surrounded them. They looked like a purely human stead. Gawen was nowhere in sight, but she saw a glimpse of Colm up in the trees.

"Tie them up and take all their ferum," the large man ordered forcibly, then took Edward's left hand and took the praevadium ring from him. "I think I shall keep this."

The Rovers brought them to an aging keep with a sorry-looking fort surrounding the perimeter. An air of desperation permeated the keep. There were boys who looked too young to handle weapons, but they carried them and were walking the perimeter.

She walked beside Edward. Both of them had their hands tied behind them with unwound portions of the ixmus net. Edward gave her a brief but derisive look. "What were you doing there?"

She looked down, contrite. "I wanted to see the hunt up close."

Edward shook his head. "If you're out looking for a husband, joining the hunt isn't the way. Whatever happens, stay quiet and let me do the talking. This isn't a friendly place. Do you understand?"

She wanted to roll her eyes at him, too, but she nodded.

The man who'd been pushing them from behind brought them to the main hall, where the large, robust man waited for them.

"Welcome to my grand kingdom. I just realized that I've been remiss and didn't introduce myself earlier. I am Lord Finbar. At your service." He did an exaggerated bow.

Full of joviality, he gestured for them to come closer. "Surely, this isn't your first time in the Borderlands?"

When Edward said nothing, Finbar continued. "Come now, Your Majesty, at least talk with me before I deliver you. You are worth a good sack of gold to someone."

"That's it?" Edward asked. "I thought I'd be worth more than that."

There was a startled silence from Finbar. Then he guffawed in laughter. "That's a good one." As if noticing Leona for the first time, Finbar stood up and walked to her. "Ah, and who are you? Come now, speak up, milady."

Leona looked at Edward, and Finbar took hold of her chin. "You're to talk with me."

Edward stepped forward, and two men roughly grabbed him by the arms.

Leona looked at Finbar and tried to get his attention. "My lord, my name is Leona. I...I don't have much to offer. I'm afraid I won't make a good hostage."

He leered at her, slowly looking her over from head to toe. "That's not true. You have a lot to offer, dear lady."

Edward looked at Finbar in pure anger.

"Why the animosity, Your Majesty?"

"She's done nothing to you."

"She'll provide me with pleasure tonight. We'll just say she's a casualty of war."

"I'm confused. Are we at war?"

"You're one of them. Putting yourself above others. Thinking you're better than the rest of us."

"This is to make all men equal? How do you propose to do that by capturing me?"

"I want no part in any war—just the gold, simple enough."

He signaled to the man behind Leona. "Take her to my tower."

Leona tried to muster a scream and pretended to try to struggle out of the man's hold. She was taken to a decrepit tower and thrown in a room. The stone walls were a cold gray. There was scarcely any furniture, save for the bed, table, and two chairs. A somber green, threadbare rug lay on the floor.

Leona bent over, took a small knife from inside the lining of her boots, and cut herself free from her ropes. She took one of the folded green blankets and carried it to the window. She unfolded it and hung it on the window's ledge like a banner. As Leona waited, she fingered the knots that tied the curtains to the sides of the window. She didn't have to wait long to see Colm's hawk circling high above. The hawk dove close to the window before flying away.

Finbar soon entered the room and saw Leona standing by the window. "You'll fall to your death if you try to escape with that blanket. Why don't you sit down and join me for a meal?"

Finbar sat down, and she followed suit. A servant soon came in with a tray containing a sparse meal. He noticed Leona looking and remarked, "You don't approve? Come, speak up."

"That's a poor-looking meal."

Finbar laughed jovially. He shook a finger at her. "Doesn't match your rich and delicate tastes? I'm sorry, dear lady, but there's a whole village of hungry folk out there. I can't very well have more if they starve, can I? But then, you don't understand that."

"You'd be surprised by how much I understand."

"You're a feisty one. I like it. Now, tell me about yourself. I need entertainment while we eat."

"I'm more intrigued by you." She leaned forward and didn't bother to act like the insipid girl he thought she was.

"Well, now. Ask away, my dear, so we can get to know each other."

"Why don't you tell me why a seaman—or, shall I say, a *pirate*—like you is landlocked and leader of this keep?"

He narrowed his eyes and looked at her with surprise. "How did you know?"

"Your manner of speaking, the way you carry yourself, and the ixmus nets."

He sat back and looked amused. "This is a delight. You're a fair lass. I can tell already that you would pleasure me well."

She kept her silence and looked pointedly at him.

He smirked and lifted a hand. Wind rushed through the room. It twirled around her hair and made the fire on the hearth flicker.

"Impressed?" he asked her.

"I've seen better."

His smile got wider, and the wind the whirred faster and

whipped Leona's hair up. She laughed, delighted at the display.

"Can I?" She gestured at the wooden box he had brought up with him.

He slid the box to her. "What feru'talent do you yield? I saw your ferum bracelet."

"Ice." She rifled through the ferum beads that Finbar's men had collected. Necklaces and bracelets. The rare ring stood out—one or two beads of ferum threaded through a thin piece of leather.

"It won't do you any good here."

"It's not much anyway." She finally found Edward's ring and took it out. The thick band, made of rare praevadium, was heavy. She could almost feel the magic swirling in it. "What do you do if they're filled with magic?" she asked Finbar.

"There's a light wielder living in the caves of Matahui. If he's still alive, we'll give him a share of the ferum in exchange for his services."

"I've heard he can only do a trickle at a time. You'll be waiting for a long time to sell these."

Finbar gaped at her in surprise. "How do you know about him?"

"I have my ways."

He frowned. "Well, we'll make do. We always do. What's a pity is that we're not on that bed."

He made to stand up, but Leona stopped him. "I need to ask you something."

"I'm sure it can wait, my fairest one."

"Would you risk your people's lives when Edward's army attacks your keep? Is the gold worth all that death?"

"Yes!" he said vehemently. "Those people you talk about are desperate and starving. In case your delicate eyes didn't see, we have nothing here. Nothing." He pounded his fist on the table. "The gold will help us get provisions to get the hell out of this place and buy our way elsewhere."

"Listen, then." She gestured to him. "If you surrender, your people will be spared. If not, their death will be on your shoulders."

He looked at her with suspicion. "Those are bold claims. Since your king's in the dungeon, he won't be able to rescue you."

"I have my hands untied." She stabbed him in the leg with her knife.

Finbar stood up and grabbed hold of her leg, but she maneuvered her body by flipping up and kicking him in the chest. He staggered back against the wall and looked aghast at her. "What manner of woman are you?"

She grabbed the spear, swung it full force at his head, and knocked him out cold.

Two men barged into the room, and Leona quickly incapacitated them with the spear. A sound from the window had her raising the spear and lowering it when she saw who came through the window. "Colm! Did you climb up?" She looked down at the ground outside the window and back at him again.

He grinned. "I thought it was better this way. You've been busy."

"Hurry, help me tie them up."

Colm knelt beside her. "Doyle is with Edward's army, and they are waiting for our signal. Gawen and Lance are"—he looked out—"making their way in."

"Can you stay here?" She inclined her head at Finbar. "I have to free Edward before anybody gets the stupid notion to use him as a hostage."

"Go ahead. I don't think any of them will be waking up anytime soon."

She stuffed as much of the ferum beads as she could in

her pockets and walked out into the hallway. An old servant woman was shuffling away when Leona grabbed her. "Don't scream. I will hurt you." She held the knife against the old woman's neck. "Where did they take King Edward?"

"They took him to the dungeon."

"His guards?"

"They're with him."

"I'll take the knife away, but if you do anything, I will hurt you. Don't make the mistake of doubting me. Now, take me there. Tell anyone who stops us you're taking me to the dungeons."

The old woman nodded and led her through the dank staircase and into the main hall. There were men there eating and drinking. They called out for the old woman to bring Leona to them. The woman just shook her head. "Milord said to take her to the dungeon, and I'm to hurry back. You don't want me to tarry and tell him it was because of you fools, now, would you?"

That quieted the men. Leona and the servant went down into a sorry excuse for a dungeon. It was rank, and the entrance was narrow and small. Two men slouched against the wall. The old woman called out. "You there, dinner is served, and you dillydally."

"I told you to bring me the food," one of the guards demanded.

The old woman pointed to the doorway. "You get it yourself or you starve."

He swore at her before he walked away, leaving one guard.

The guard looked up in interest as Leona approached him. He scratched his crotch and gave Leona a toothless grin. "What have we here?"

Leona returned the smile. "Why don't you come and see?"

The instant the guard stood up, Leona grabbed his head

and struck it against the wall. She grabbed the keys from his belt and motioned for the woman to lead her forward.

"How long before he comes back?"

"He'll jest with the cook before coming back down."

"Why are you helping me? You could have said something."

"I've seen my fair share, as I've traveled these lands my whole life. I may not know a lot, but if a Tribunal warrior"—she paused and looked at Leona sharply—"is here, and a king is in the dungeons, then it's only a matter of time before we're all under attack. I hope you remember this kindness."

Leona opened the door and cringed. It stank to high heaven. It was exactly what Edward deserved after going on that hunt. She found him with his guards, seated on the cold, hard ground, chained to a pole running against the wall.

"What are you doing?" He looked at her incredulously.

She knelt beside him and freed him from his manacles. "Isn't it obvious?" Leona handed him his ring. "Here."

She stepped aside and freed one of his guards, who helped the others. Leona gave them the ferum beads. "I didn't know whose was whose."

They heard a scream and the sound of footsteps. Edward motioned to the door. "Lead the way."

"Your work?" He gestured at the guard slumped near the door.

"Yes." She led them to the main hall. Standing over the men who had been having supper earlier were Gawen and Lance.

"It's about time you two got here," Leona said.

Lance saluted her. "There were some...unforeseen obstacles. All handled and nothing to worry about."

That's when she registered the sound of weapons clashing outside.

Lance made a grand, sweeping gesture with his hand to Edward and his guards. "We've delivered your army."

Edward told his guards to go outside. Before walking off with his men, he looked at Leona. "I assume everything is handled in here? Even Finbar?"

Leona only nodded.

"You and I will talk later." It was a warning not to disappear.

⁂

WHEN FINBAR WOKE UP, EDWARD WAS IN FRONT OF HIM. He swore before shutting his eyes again. Finbar opened his eyes again. He looked down and saw the knife on his thigh. "Aaargh. Take it out!"

Edward obliged and took the knife out swiftly. He nodded to the old woman, the same servant who'd helped Leona earlier. She promptly poured spirits onto the wound and staunched the flow of blood with wads of cloth.

Finbar's eyes watered. "Holy hell. Fuck your arse." More expletives followed.

"Are you done yet?" Edward asked.

"You've beaten me. What else do you want?"

"You said I was worth a sack of gold. I want to know who you were planning to sell me to. I have other questions, but we'll start with that."

"Can I at least be comfortable and have a drink?"

Leona stepped from behind Finbar and handed the old woman a goblet of water to help Finbar drink.

"You! You infernal woman." He jumped out of the chair, but Edward's guards held him down. "You did this. A venomous snake. Just like all women."

"She was only doing what she needed to do. Now you are dealing with me." Edward crossed his arms and relaxed his stance. He had cold eyes that betrayed no emotion, but Leona could feel the simmer of anger.

"I don't know exactly who offered it, but I overheard there was a reward for your capture. A big one if you are alive and whole."

"Where did you overhear this?"

"I was headed east to barter with some of the bigger tribes, but something was wrong. The steads and tribes were all gone. Mind you, the closest stead to us is about a half a day's ride away. Some of them have packed up their belongings, and the others, well, it seemed like something bad happened, and they left everything behind. It gave me and my men a bad feeling, and we followed their trail."

"What did you find?" Edward asked him.

"We found an army of Greyfolk and men from one of the coastal tribes. We didn't go further east, but from what we heard, there are ships coming from Bahadur with more reinforcements. Then we heard the High King of Greater Bearnas was going to the North for a Gathering and there was a mighty reward for your capture. I figured you would be worth gold enough to buy our way down south."

"Why not go deeper into the Borderlands? Closer to the White Queen?" Edward challenged.

"Ha," Finbar scoffed. "She lets us be, whether good or bad. If we go west or north that would bring us closer to the Greyfolk. No, thank you. South is where I'd like to take my people. But for that, I need gold. You know how suspicious you folks are of us."

"Why didn't you join them? You said there were Rovers among them," Doyle asked.

"I'd rather go down south than join in with the Greyfolk." Finbar spat on the floor after he said that. "They're big, ghastly things. Swindlers. All of them."

Leona couldn't help it. She had to speak up. "The Greyfolk keep to themselves for the most part. They don't even go past their borders unless it's for the trading season. They've kept the peace with everyone else for this long, and their Elders have always chosen peace over war, even among their own tribes. They haven't been able to cast visions in hundreds of years. I know they won't do anything unless they feel threatened."

"Still can't be trusted. They'd sooner feed men like us to the dogs than treat us like equals. Just like those people from Bahadur."

Edward leaned back. "You've been to Bahadur, then? Perhaps Breven?"

"I may have spent some time out in the sea. Back in my more youthful days."

"The truth, Finbar."

"Fine. Aye, I was captain of a ship. Not my own, mind you. I had...investors. We had some bad luck, and I lost my ship when a storm hit us. I didn't think I'd survive, for I lost a good many sailors that day. We couldn't go back. We'd lost the cargo, and I took that as a sign it was time to come home. My mother, see, she still lived here when I left. I would send her money when I could. I loved her, but I needed adventure and to be rich, aye." He turned around and looked at Leona. "I'm telling the truth, so don't you dare stab me again." He took another gulp of water. "When I came back, my poor ma had passed away, and they were needing a leader for this stead, so here I am."

Edward merely nodded at his story. "When were they planning to ambush me?"

"We intercepted you a day earlier than their plan. They were going to ride into your camp in the middle of the night, make sure that your camp got split up into different groups, and then capture you in the chaos."

"Just like you did." Edward said.

"Well, we don't have as many men as they do, but your chosen day to hunt helped us out," Finbar explained.

"How many were there?"

"They made it sound like they could have your whole camp overrun and still have more than enough men to spare."

"Were they going to take my people?"

Finbar shrugged. "It was just you they wanted. I told my men to steal anything of value, then to leave everyone alone."

"We're done. Everyone, leave." Edward motioned for the servant to leave and for Finbar to be taken away. He then turned to one of his guards. Like Edward, he was dressed in black, with the insignia of a hawk embroidered on a small leather patch on his tunic. Long and lean, he was slightly taller than Edward. His dark-brown hair was almost black and loosely framed his narrow face. His light-blue eyes twinkled with amusement at Finbar's parting gesture at Leona.

Edward issued the order quietly. "Alik, tell Gage and Jon to report back as soon as they're done with Finbar." When the door closed behind Alik, Edward turned to Leona. "I'm not done with you yet."

Leona hid her irritation and stayed where she was.

Edward stood up and stalked toward Leona. He hadn't changed his clothes, and the dungeon smell still clung to him. His tunic and pants were bloodstained, his dark hair mussed. He looked dangerous with the barely contained rage simmering in his eyes.

He grabbed her right arm and before she could stop him, he pulled her sleeve up to expose the intricate and circular tattoo on the underside of her arm. "Tribunal." He sneered. "What are you doing here? And your real name this time."

"I'm here to ensure that you make it to the Gathering. And Leona is my real name."

"What else?"

"Those were my orders. I don't ask questions of my superiors."

He let go of her arm. "Who else is with you?"

"Four others. All warriors. Doyle, a whisperer. Colm has animal sight. Gawen, a firebringer, and Lance, a metalforce."

"And you?"

"Ice. I'm a norther," she replied.

"So few," Edward said as he walked to the fireplace.

"I was told to be discreet."

"You think it was foolish of me to travel north without more soldiers."

Leona said nothing.

Edward scowled at her. "I would have preferred to travel without the court, but this was a journey of goodwill. Had I traveled with my full army, everyone might have misjudged my intention and thought I meant to take the North by force to unite the kingdoms. That's not the message I want to convey, especially in the first Gathering. I wish to have more of them in the future."

"Instead, you do the complete opposite and traipse across the country as merry as can be."

His eyebrows raised at her bland tone.

"With all due respect, Your Majesty, that was careless."

"You question my decision?"

"I am just telling you how I see it."

"The Tribunal shouldn't be so secretive. You could have come forward and told us your suspicions of danger."

"Discretion was the aim," she reminded him.

"Your precious Tribunal doesn't want to look like they're siding with me."

"I wouldn't know that."

"How did you get Belinda to agree to take you with her?"

"I was assigned at Kentigern to help the historian. Belinda and I became friends. This was a favor I asked her."

"How did you take Finbar down?"

"He was easily distracted. He saw what he expected to see." She let it go at that.

There was a knock on the door. Gage handed him a note.

He was Captain of the Guards, and, like the others, he wore black from head to toe. With dark-brown skin and closely cropped black hair, Gage sported a light beard peppered with some gray. There was something about his face that drew Leona to give him a second look. A trustworthiness and strength to it. He carried an authority about him that told Leona he took his job seriously.

Edward inclined his head at Leona. "We're done."

Leona chafed at the sudden dismissal but left the room.

❧

THAT EVENING, LEONA FOUND HERSELF RUSHING BACK INTO the main hall of Finbar's small keep. It was claustrophobic and dark in the setting sun. Perfect. It matched exactly how she felt.

"You're sending your men to scout." Leona said without waiting for Edward to acknowledge her.

He didn't bother to look at her, instead he kept on looking at the maps in front of him. "When I have need of you, I'll send for you."

"You're not even going to hear me out? We know the Borderlands."

"What could you possibly add to what Finbar already told us?"

"Colm can commandeer his hawk's sight. And Lance knows the Borderlands like the back of his hand. They should go with your men."

Edward finally straightened up. He crossed his arms and regarded her. "And then what?"

"How else can we better protect you?"

Amusement flashed across Edward's face. "And how can you protect me? You freed me but my soldiers were on the ready. I haven't seen any proof that you can do any better."

Leona never knew she could feel this need to strangle someone so strongly. "We have people, use us."

Edward finally nodded. "Tell Colm to look for Niall."

"I heard there are two scouting missions."

"My, my, my. My men seem to be chatty around you. Fine, Lance can go with them." He gestured for her to leave before turning to the men who entered the hall.

❄   4   ❄

Colm, Lance, and Edward's guards left to investigate Finbar's claim of empty steads. It was a little over a day's ride to the kidnap point where the Greyfolk and Rovers waited.

The eastern coast, however, was at least three days' ride, and Colm didn't want to leave anything to chance. He'd brought his hawk, Jumper, to scout those far distances. The ferum beads around his neck had enough feru'talent in them to make sure that Jumper would make it back to him alive.

As the hawk flew to the east, Colm and one of Edward's guards, Niall, arrived at the first stead and found it exactly as Finbar had described. There were signs of struggle, but the stead was empty. They followed the trail left by its inhabitants and captors. Soon they arrived at a campsite of Greyfolk and Rovers.

The Rovers outnumbered the Greyfolk by at least twenty men. They were weathered men and women whose leathery, tanned skin marked time spent out in the sea. There were a few Rovers who looked like they belonged in the central regions of the Borderlands, with their pale, tattooed skins, while the others had the dark skin that verged on black, with thorny protrusions on their foreheads.

Though they all looked different, the Rover garb was unmistakable, made of the coarse fabric common in the Borderlands. Rough to the skin, it provided warmth when needed, and it didn't let water soak through. There were Borderland tribes who had mastered the craft of creating the fabric with squared and striped patterns that were sought after during trading season.

The Greyfolk stood a head taller than the Rovers. Their skin, just like their namesake, was gray and had the texture of stone. Their faces, like those of the other Rovers, had the same features—except the men had no hair on their bodies, while the women grew coarse hair they braided into intricate knots. Not needing any armor, they wore leather tunics and trousers that had slits on the sides. They favored the cold of the northern mountains and found the warmth of the Borderlands uncomfortable. Their strength was unmistakable, and their choice of weapons showed this—big broadswords and hammers made with such impeccable craftsmanship, it was hard to believe the rough hands of the Greyfolk had made them. Known as the Folkvar in days of old, they were one of the ancient and great races that used to rule the lands.

Because of the Greyfolk's size, girth, and preferred habitat, they bred their horses to be large and able to weather the cold. Not only were they big and plodding, but their bodies were covered with a thick layer of fur. They were not fast, but they could easily travel along the mountainside with their sturdy hooves.

The Greyfolk and Rovers soon left their campsite. Colm and Niall followed them for a time before something up above caught Colm's attention. A black raven flew along the treetops. The Greyfolk leader looked up and pointed. They all cheered, which was very unusual for the Greyfolk.

When the Greyfolk and Rovers passed a row of trees, they disappeared from view.

Niall blinked. "Did you see that?"

"They're still there. Just hidden from plain sight."

"How?"

"I'm not sure. You must follow me." Colm's eyes became glassy, as if a milky layer covered them, and his skin took on a blurred sheen.

They arrived at a site near the route they would have taken with Edward and the court. Niall couldn't see anything that would have alarmed him, but Colm insisted that they hide their horses by the trees and go on foot.

"There's too many of them. At least a hundred Greyfolk. There are others with them, clothed like Rovers, but they don't act like them. I'll take one last look before we make our way back," Colm said as he and Niall followed the Greyfolk and Rovers.

Niall narrowed his eyes and tried to see what Colm was seeing. But he still didn't see anything. Everything around them looked like a normal forest. An empty one with no Rovers or Greyfolk.

They stayed quite a distance away from the wide path, and Colm stopped when he noticed something on a tree.

"Lance and Simon were just here." He pointed at a notch on a tree. They circled around until they heard a low whistle. Lance waved them over to the hiding place he shared with Simon.

"You saw?" Lance asked Colm.

He nodded. "A group of riders were concealed in front of us. And you?"

"We nearly walked into them. If it wasn't for that raven circling above, I wouldn't have thought to check for concealment."

"Do the ravens see them?" Niall asked.

"Yes," Colm replied. "When one is around, they always seem to be attracted to anyone that is concealed."

Niall was about to ask more, but Lance put a hand on Niall's shoulder. "Maybe next time, we'll explain some more, eh?" Lance turned to Colm. "When will you bond with your hawk?"

Colm looked out into the distance. "Soon."

෨෪෩

FOR THE FIRST TIME IN DAYS, LEONA WAS COMFORTABLE. She didn't have to pretend anymore that she wasn't a warrior of the Tribunal. She was wearing her own clothes, traveling gear that comprised hunting trousers, high brown boots, a fur vest, a plain white shirt with long sleeves, and a thick leather belt that held a dagger. She waited in silence with Edward in the keep's main hall. It had surprised her when he set up temporary residence away from the court.

"They distract me," he told her, reading her expression.

Leona knew it was none of her business, yet she'd hoped that he would be generous in his decision to the people of this stead. She'd observed him as he walked around the stead. Edward had none of the disdain that others in the court had for the Rovers. He talked to them as she had seen him talk with the lords and ladies in his court; even treated them equally, save for the pity she'd seen him quickly hide when he first saw the children working the keep.

Edward turned his attention to Finbar when he entered the hall.

"Milord." Finbar bowed and winked at Leona. "My great thanks for not putting me in the dungeon."

"Just like you did with me and my guards?"

Finbar gave him a quick smile. "Had I known this was

how things would unfold, I would have offered you the best room in my keep."

"I want you to do something for me."

"I hope it has nothing to do with my neck between a noose."

"What if I offered your people a place in the outskirts of my kingdom?"

"What sort of payment would you expect from me?"

"You say you and your men have experience on a ship, and I need more people with...shall we say, your specific experience."

Finbar raised an eyebrow at that. It was more than generous, and they both knew it. "When do I start?"

"You won't ask about payment for services rendered?" Edward asked.

"You spared my life and offered a home to my people. Seems like you're a man who's got his head straight on his shoulders. You'll pay me, I've no doubt of that. And if I, or any of my men, cross you after this, well...we'd be the ones to pay for that. Am I right?"

Edward nodded. "Order your people to gather their things. They will travel with my men when they are ready. As for you, your service starts today."

"What would you have me do?"

"Tell two of your men to spread the word to the other steads and tribes. They are welcome in my kingdom should they wish to leave the Borderlands. As for you, I want you to talk to those who were going to ambush me. I want their leader. I want to know why there are ships from Bahadur coming here. And why they want me."

"And how am I supposed to do that? Just walk in there and invite them for a drink?" Finbar raised both hands up and his brows went up comically with them.

"Tell them I'm at a secret location and you won't reveal

where I am until they take you to their leader and give you payment." Edward gave him a torn insignia from one of his tunics.

"You'd like for me to deal with the Greyfolk? I have to confess I do not have any experience with them."

"As you said, they remind you of the people of Bahadur. I'm sure you can improvise. You'll leave as soon as the scouts are back."

⁂

COLM, LANCE, NIALL, AND SIMON CAME BACK WITH DIRE news of a concealed army of great number.

"They're blocking our route to Normundir." Lance didn't mince words.

"There were hundreds of Greyfolk and Rovers. All of them were under concealment," Colm added.

"Explain," Edward demanded.

Niall stepped forward. His golden hair grew long about a face that leaned toward the younger side with his wide brown eyes and round face. "One moment we were following a contingent of Rover and Greyfolk riders, and the next, they vanished. Like they weren't there at all."

"Didn't you send your hawk out before you left to scout to fly to the coast? Did it show you anything?" Leona asked Colm.

"Yes, I looked through his eyes, but only for a moment since we were so far from each other. There are ships on the eastern coast of the Borderlands and an army camped nearby. Like the others, they too, seem under concealment."

"How are you able to see them?" Edward directed the question at Colm.

"We've been trained since birth, milord. It's not an easy thing. It's a gift given to the chosen warriors of the Tribunal.

And it's not something we really talk about in the open..." Colm explained.

Doyle spoke up. "When a person or a thing is under concealment, they can see everything as it is happening, but they can't affect us until they come out of that concealment. I don't know how it's possible to conceal an army, for we have been trained to do it for small amounts of time, and we are only able to do it for ourselves." Doyle paused and shook his head ruefully. "There's this other thing...if they're not trained, then there's a Source that enables them to be concealed."

"What's the Source, and how do you destroy it?"

"They," Leona interjected. "The Source will be people. They are what feeds the power for concealment. We don't exactly know how or why, but there are books in the Great Library in Midroska that talk about this. It's an old magic that comes from the Elders."

"The empty steads and tribes?" Edward asked.

"Perhaps," Leona answered him truthfully.

"If they are the Source, how do we break them free of this? Are they still alive?"

"I wish I could tell you more. We can find the answer in Midroska."

"I'll go," Lance volunteered. "It will be easier for me to keep myself away from enemy eyes."

"Go with Finbar. Help him find the concealed army before going to Midroska," Edward told Lance.

Lance nodded. "If that is what you wish."

"It might be wise to go back to Kentigern," Leona interjected.

Edward rubbed the back of his neck. He turned away, thinking as he did. "I don't want to risk any more lives. It's me they want."

"What are you suggesting, milord?" Doyle asked with suspicion.

"I'm suggesting that my guards and I separate from everyone. They go south, back to Kentigern, and we go west to Central Valley. Rikard has indicated that the route there is patrolled by his men."

Leona was already shaking her head even before he finished. "We'll go with you wherever you go, but Central Valley is too far, and we haven't scouted that area. I think we should go back with everyone else."

"And risk more lives? More than half the people in my court don't fight. The men, women, and children from this stead also travel south. Do I also risk their lives?"

"But what's to stop them from being attacked as well?" Leona challenged. "They don't fight, like you said."

When nobody said anything, Edward inclined his head. "We ride for Central Valley before first light. Finbar will plant the seeds when we leave tomorrow."

5

At first light, they rode westward to Central Valley. The trees whipped past as Leona led them through the forest. She stroked her horse's side. "A little more," she whispered.

They rode until sunset, when they came into a glen. Colm took first watch while Leona and Gawen stayed with the horses. She smiled as she listened to the men admire Doyle's fighting style. The Tribunal's Chosen were trained to fight at a young age. To use speed to their advantage, to waste no movement, and to find their opponent's weaknesses and use those against them. There was another way of fighting they had all been taught—the technique of Fading. Just like the concealed, they were still there, just a slight step somewhere else—invisible to everyone. A skill that couldn't just be learned; it was a gift imbued by their Elders.

"You fought well out there," Corbin remarked to Doyle.

Corbin cocked his head, and a lock of black hair fell onto his forehead. He looked at Doyle with a furrowed expression, an expression that he must have had often enough that it left permanent lines on his forehead and in between his eyebrows.

"Well, thank you," Doyle acknowledged him good-naturedly.

"You want a go?"

"Right now?"

"Yes. I mean, unless you're tired."

"Tired doesn't mean a thing unless you want to lose in a fight."

The men provided a clearing for them. Corbin was skilled but cocky. They circled each other, Doyle looking calm as he waited for the boy to make his move. Corbin attacked low, and Doyle responded accordingly.

They traded a volley of strikes until Doyle turned the tables, sidestepped, and in a deft move took hold of Corbin's sword and held it against his neck while his sword's tip was on Corbin's stomach. The fight was over before Corbin could process it.

"Well met, milord. Well met," Corbin said with a grin as Doyle helped him up.

"You got me good there." Doyle rotated his shoulder and grimaced in pain. They then proceeded to pat each other in the back as they cataloged their pains and praised each other lavishly.

"Men," Leona said under her breath, amused.

Gawen, who stood beside Leona, smiled at that. He nudged her. "Just think of it as you women admiring dresses. Oh, wait, you actually would think that unbearable." He grinned at his own joke.

"Funny, Gawen." She gave him a sarcastic smile.

"I wish you and Doyle would spar again. I don't think I've seen anybody, other than you or Jeremi, beat Doyle that way."

"It was luck when I beat him. He tripped. At least Master Jeremi knew what he was doing."

"And he was also your teacher. So, it doesn't matter. You beat Doyle, and it hurt his ego. That's enough for me." Gawen inclined his head toward Colm, who was seated on one of the big branches up above. "You heard his hawk died?"

Leona nodded, her expression grave. "Jumper was a favorite of his. Colm told me his ferum beads ran out of feru'-talent. We'll just have to give him some space."

The next morning, they rode fast and hard. The Hellig Mountains were coming ever closer, gray and forbidding, their peaks white with ice and hidden in the clouds.

Central Valley lay just ahead. On one side the foothills of the Hellig Mountains stretched out. On the other side were the outskirts of Normundir, marked by the thick pine trees the region was known for. It was a long and winding valley that ran alongside a tributary of the Silver River. Colm pointed up, and Leona saw ravens flying above them. She gestured, and they stopped.

"What is it?" Edward asked.

She squinted up at the sky. "Ravens. It could mean nothing. Doyle and I will have a look."

"I'll go with you."

"We have to go on foot," she warned Edward.

Edward got off his horse. He gestured at Gage and Alik, who did the same. Leona nodded as she and Doyle got off their horses. "You must stay behind us."

Leona led them through the trees and through a trail overgrown with bushes and roots. Soon the valley came into view. The sun shone silver on the river. It was a beautiful sight, and Edward was about to move forward to inspect it when Leona stopped him with a hand to his chest. "Don't move."

"What do you see?"

"At least three hundred soldiers. They're camped by those

trees, close to where the river narrows." Leona looked at Doyle. "How is this possible?"

He shook his head. "Lance will find out. We have to leave before anyone sees us."

They took the same trail back, but Doyle suddenly stopped and drew his sword. Leona took her bow out and shot an arrow. A split second later, a boom sounded from the valley, and Greyfolk soldiers appeared in their midst. Leona's arrow found its target, and one of the Greyfolk howled in pain. She immediately went to higher ground to shoot at the Greyfolk rushing at them as Doyle and the others fought them off. She ran alongside a higher ledge, shooting her arrows, aiming at the soft skin in the Greyfolk's necks and the inside of their arms.

One of the Greyfolk broke through and threw a dagger at the ledge where she stood. He wielded a bludgeon as he ran for her.

Leona dove, the dagger barely missing her. She fell to the ground and rolled to her left. She threw her bow and drew her sword when the Greyfolk man attacked her. Quickly getting on her knees, she evaded the blow with her sword and used his weight, sliding to her right.

As the Greyfolk's momentum brought him forward, she got on her feet and unsheathed her other sword. He took the broadsword from his back and faced her. He rushed to her, and she raised one sword up to defend herself from the broadsword when another sword came in between them. Edward grunted as he pushed the fighter off and told Leona to go.

She and the Greyfolk both looked at Edward in momentary disbelief. The Greyfolk recovered from his surprise and attacked Edward. It left Leona by the wayside. She was tempted to leave him and let him deal with it on his own, but duty won out. She took her bow and arrow, sighted, and shot at the Greyfolk's neck.

Leona and the others fought as they headed for their horses. Soon they broke through the trees. One of the Greyfolk took a big, curved horn and blew. The sound blared into the valley. Doyle threw his dagger at the Greyfolk, but it was too late. A boom sounded, and the ground shook. Another boom and then another, until the sound came faster and faster.

Leona reacted quickly. She ran toward the booming sounds and stopped. Waited. A huge monster of a mountain troll broke through the trees. Its lumbering mass was fast and deadly. Edward, Gage, and Alik attacked it, but to no avail. It swiped at them as if they were nothing. Leona let out a shrill whistle, and the mountain troll noticed her. Its matte-gray body was pure muscle, and its head was the size of a boulder. Leona sighted, and her arrow shot straight and true.

Thwack. It hit the creature right in the eye. It was only a superficial wound, and as it growled in pain, Leona ran and leaped up the creature's body, swinging herself upward and onto its back. She took her two short swords and swung both horizontally on the creature's neck, almost severing the head. As the creature fell, she jumped off, rolled, and tumbled gracefully, landing on her haunches. She didn't even spare a glance as the creature fell behind her.

Leona stood up, wiped her blades on her pants, and sheathed them as she walked off.

They heard the rumble of horses as they jumped on their own. They raced for the main tributary of the river. Leona led them to a bridge that spanned the wide width of the raging waters. Narrow wooden planks lined the knotted ropes. They shifted every time the wind blew.

"The horses won't be able to go there!" Gawen shouted above the roar of the river.

The rumble got louder as the soldiers at Central Valley neared them.

Edward grabbed Gawen by the arm. "We have to leave the horses."

Gawen shook his head. "You all go. I'll take the horses."

"Gawen. Don't do this," Leona said.

"I've a few tricks up my sleeves. You go, and I'll lead them away from here."

When Leona hesitated, he pushed at her. "Go! I'll be fine. Naglfar isn't that far from here. I'll lose them there. Easier for one man to hide than all of us."

Leona nodded at him. "Take care of yourself."

"You as well."

"Thank you for all your help." Edward offered his hand.

Gawen took it in a firm grip. "Take care, milord."

Leona crossed the footbridge, followed by the others. When they reached the other side, Gawen was long gone. Doyle cut the ropes tying the footbridge and watched it be pulled away by the raging waters.

They hiked through the trees and away from the river. Leona's thoughts went to the fight earlier, and she gritted her teeth. Insulting, that's what it was. She didn't see Edward going in between any of his guards while they were fighting, did she? Leona couldn't remember the last time she'd been this angry. She couldn't even look at him.

The thick trees slowed their progress. The leaves were a dense canopy above them. They only slowed when they couldn't hear the river anymore. They found themselves by a rocky stream, and ahead of it was a clearing underneath tall trees. Big boulders were strewn across the forest floor. Moss and ferns grew on them like green feathers.

Colder now, the palpable change in temperature had the men putting their cloaks on. Leona, used to the cold, didn't bother putting hers on. She laid out her map on the ground and crouched down with Colm and Doyle.

Leona was calming down when the devil himself walked over and joined them.

"Leona."

"Yes, Your Majesty?"

He gestured to the map. "Is there a way through the mountains?"

She nodded with reluctance. "It's dangerous. I would advise against it."

"Shemal Pass," Colm said.

"That's where the treasure hunters go, don't they?" Gage looked at Leona for confirmation.

Leona shook her head. "That's the Bruadar. It's built alongside Shemal Pass and it's where the Greyfolk Elders and warriors are tested by the guardians of the Hellig."

"Has anybody gone through it other than the Greyfolk?" Gage pushed on.

"As luck would have it, we have someone here who's journeyed through Shemal Pass." Doyle cocked his head at Leona.

"With a Greyfolk guide," she said. "It wasn't easy going through. That's not an option we should take lightly. If"—she stressed the word—"we get to the other side, Normundir is still quite a ways away, and we'll still be in Greyfolk land."

"Why were you sent there?" Edward asked.

"The High Priest was curious whether Shemal Pass was safe for the Tribunal to use."

"Why you?" Edward prodded.

"Why not me?" she challenged back.

"I'm not implying anything, if that's what you're thinking. Would they follow us there?" Edward asked.

"I don't think so. If they have Greyfolk with them, they won't go there with an army. It's sacred to them, and it's dangerous ground. What are you thinking?"

"How far is it from here?"

Leona cocked her head to the side, thinking. "The trail isn't far. Since we have no horses, it might take us a while."

"And Normundir?"

"It's over two days' ride from there. I don't think it's a good idea."

"It's the only way, and you know it," Doyle interjected. "We can't risk going through Arag'nilDarahoff. Not until we know where the Greyfolk's loyalties are."

"We'll have to risk it," Edward said with finality.

Leona nodded and looked around the camp. "Tomorrow, before sunrise, we hike up the Hellig toward Shemal Pass. It's a long and hard trek going up the mountain. It's a narrow trail, and anybody who thinks of following us can easily be found out. Going through the pass"—she paused—"is not simple. There's something in there that lives, and if it finds you wanting, it will test you for it. It will play on your greatest desires and fears. If you've conquered those two things, then there's nothing for you to fear except the trolls and wild animals that live in the mountains."

"How long is the distance?" Niall asked.

"I was separated from my guide. I was there for four days. He was there for three."

"What did you see?"

"It's as if you're in a dream and everything around you is not quite how it truly is. Don't believe everything you see. Even in sleep you will be tested."

Leona straightened up. Bothered by what had happened in the fight and where they were headed tomorrow, she needed to get away. Without saying another word, she walked off. She found a nearby clearing with a small stream. The soothing trickle of water did little to her mood. Edward was like an annoying thorn she needed to keep and care for. She shouldn't let him bother her. After this mission, she wouldn't have to deal with him.

The rustle of footsteps had her turning. She scowled when she saw Edward walking into the clearing.

"What do you want?" Leona asked, even before she could stop herself.

"I'd like to apologize."

"That's rich of you."

"I was caught in the moment and didn't think you could..." He gestured to the short swords that peeked over her shoulders.

"Fight?" Leona finished for him. She stalked toward him. "You think the Tribunal would assign someone incompetent to protect you?"

He scowled at her. "I don't need protecting."

"Is that why we're in this predicament?"

"Now you're insulting me."

"No, now I am." Leona didn't know why she did it, but she pushed him. At his shocked look, she shoved him again, stronger this time.

He leaned down, his face so close to Leona's that she could feel his breath. "Are you challenging me?"

"You said you haven't seen proof of what value we can bring." She whipped out her short swords.

"I'm not going to back down just because you're a woman."

"I'd call you a coward if you did," Leona taunted him.

Edward took his sword out and stepped back. "Let's see what you're made of, then." He quirked an eyebrow, waiting for her to make the first move.

Leona stood still, both swords on the ready as she regarded him.

Edward suddenly lunged at her. Leona brought both swords up. The clash of metal on metal was jarring on her arms. A flash of his dagger followed as he swiped in an arc toward her face.

Leona twisted away from him and then it became a dance of swords and dagger. He was strong. And quick. Quicker than he should be. Her muscles sang in exertion. Even with cool air, sweat dribbled down her back.

And still they fought.

Their blades sang as hers led a trail up the edge of his sword. Leona let one of her swords drop and punched up, catching his chin.

Edward stepped back and spit blood. Leona leaned down and grabbed her sword. With an unholy light in Edward's eyes, he unleashed on her. Leona parried back against the onslaught. In the corner of her eye, she saw Doyle and others watching them from the trees that bordered the small clearing. She paid them no mind. Edward, with his quick and unpredictable moves, was a challenging force.

Suddenly, flames exploded from him. It was instinct that had Leona fading into the shadow world. Edward's form and his flames became mere smoke that blurred until she couldn't tell how he truly looked. The trees, the clearing—all black and gray shadows in that other world. The tattoo on her right arm throbbed. Louder and louder, until she could feel its beat in her whole body.

She appeared just off to Edward's right. Somehow, even with the split-second disappearance, he was ready for her. He swiped with his leg and tripped her.

Her back hit the ground with a solid thump. Edward was on top of her before she could catch her breath. He took her wrists and slammed them on the ground, forcing her hands to let go of her swords.

Edward smirked. "Good. But not good enough." He stood up and turned his back on her as he sheathed his sword.

Leona sat up. Her back aching. "Where'd you learn to fight like that?"

His shoulders stiffened. "It's none of your business."

"Fine." Leona stood and dusted herself off. Surprise flashed across her face as Edward leaned down, took her swords, and handed them to her. "Maybe when you can beat me, I'll trust you to protect me."

Leona rolled her eyes. Insufferable man.

❧   6   ❧

They rose before dawn and hiked up the foothills of the Hellig Mountains. Leona led them through the copse of trees that lined the lower lands. They hiked until the trees thinned and cold seeped into their bones. Every step led upward, and every step was heavier than the last. Soon, no one talked, and all they could hear were the sounds of their footfalls and the rustling of leaves above them.

The trees eventually disappeared, exposing them to the brightening sky. The trail narrowed, and soon they were walking in a single file. They were as high as the tops of the trees, and the grass before them was a brilliant green.

The sun was low on the horizon when they reached their destination.

"We're close," she said to them. "We need to climb between those boulders."

Once they reached the boulders, the landscape transformed. Where once it had been green and inviting, now it was stark and rocky.

There was a huge, flat clearing of stone and granite. Past

the clearing was a wall that stretched straight up into the sky. In the middle, a narrow sliver, dark as night and forbidding, showed the entrance to Shemal Pass.

It was guarded on both sides by imposing blocks of stone carved intricately with figures from Greyfolk legends. In the front were two figures. The man held a staff and a broadsword. The woman held both her hands out. In her left, she held a wide bowl filled with gray and black sand. Her right hand was outstretched in a welcoming gesture.

Leona told the others to stay as she walked alone to the entrance of the pass. Fear lived in that darkness, a fear alive, as was the black heart that beat in the mountain. She pulled her gaze from the blackness and focused on the water gushing from up above.

Jaworek had been with her the last time she had been here, giving her courage, teaching her the ways of his people. She firmed her resolve and stopped when she reached the woman. She glanced back at the entrance. The Bruadar was on the other side, its presence heavy. Once the centerpiece of the Greyfolk, the sprawling castle was carved into the mountain's face. It was said that the Greyfolk's gods had once lived in the Bruadar. That those benevolent gods who once fulfilled wishes became monsters that terrorized all those who ventured inside.

She'd seen the Bruadar, of course. It gleamed golden, a beacon that called out to all who made their way through Shemal Pass. Her guide had told her to avert her gaze and to keep as far away from the Bruadar as they could.

Leona brought herself back to the present. It felt as though something was pulling her in. Leona reminded herself that it was from the air being sucked into the narrow passage and nothing more.

A soft breeze fluttered and teased her hair. The breeze became louder and louder until the wind howled around her.

And now they spoke. She closed her eyes and listened.

The Greyfolk were a patient race, made of stone. They had eternity with them. In the midst of the howling wind, she picked up a hoarse voice, growling. She couldn't understand what it was saying, but she knew what to do. She reached out with her left hand and placed it on the bowl.

She didn't know if she needed to do this. The last time, she had been ordered by her guide to put her hand in so that the mountain could see, hear, and feel her intentions. Leona did it now, more to communicate with whatever it was that lived here.

The sand moved beneath her palm. She saw tendrils of sand and stone snaking up her skin. It tightened around her hand until it enmeshed her skin. Her hand felt like it was in chains, tightening until the pain was almost unbearable. She bit her lip and fought against the throbbing pain.

The wind continued to howl, but the growling voice was more discernible.

"Leona of the Tribunal." The voice was the sound of eternity. It spoke, dragging each word from its bowels, deep within the mountain. "What do you seek?"

"Safe passage for me and the men who follow me."

"You bring men of flesh."

"They haven't been trained in the ways of the Folkvar."

"We seek to weed out those who are unworthy." Leona felt a cold wind blow from the darkness and through her. "Enter if they are true and have courage. For all who pass must be tested."

The chain of sand and stone unwound from her hand and scattered on the bowl. She rubbed her hand. The pain still lingered, like needles under her skin. She turned and gestured for Edward and the others to do as she did. One after the other, they put their left hands into the bowl of sand. After they were all done, they entered the dark path.

Whispers surrounded them, beckoned them. When they walked into the narrow path, the darkness was so thick it blinded them. Leona lit the torch that she and Colm had worked on the night before. Its dim light showed a wall of rough gray stones and a path made smooth by countless Greyfolk who'd ventured into the pass.

Dust swirled in their wake as they walked the long and narrow path. The air smelled dank, like water that had been sitting for too long. The silence was broken by their breathing and footsteps.

On and on, it went. As the path wound itself ever deeper, the walls on either side of them became shorter and shorter. The longer they walked, the brighter it became, until the expanse of the pass lay open before them.

"Welcome to Shemal Pass." Leona gestured.

Vast grasslands with patches of trees and streams lay in front. The peaks of the Hellig Moutains rose around them. On the east, something carved and massive shone on the mountain face.

"That's the Bruadar. We steer clear of it." She pointed at a great distance ahead where the two peaks met. "That is where we go."

They all gave one last look before heading down into the grasslands.

They made camp near a stream and ate their meal. Colm rubbed his eyes. "The light is different here," he observed.

Leona remembered thinking the same thing. Even the day was bathed in twilight. They were quiet for a time, vulnerable in their exhaustion.

Gage was the first one who broke the silence. "I don't like this place. Something evil lives here."

Alik drank what water he had left. "I believe every place has a story that marks it for eternity."

Colm spoke up. "The Bruadar has a wealth of different

legends. One of them has it that a thousand years ago, the Bruadar used to be a house of treasures. Not gold nor gems. Treasures of the heart. People from near and faraway lands made the journey here. The Greyfolk demanded great wealth. For three days, they had their heart's desire. Be it to be a king, have their ailments go away, or have their true love in their arms. They had it all."

Niall put a hand up. "How did they get what they want? How is that possible?"

"The Hellig Mountains have unexplored magic. Magic that the Guardians of the Hellig Mountains selfishly guard. In exchange for wealth, the Guardians will have their amusement with the whims of men. It was said they've lived an eternity in the mountains, watching the cycles of life pass them by. Rarely was it that men traveled this distance, and the Guardians have grown a liking for the dreams of men, for it was a respite from the slowness of timeless eternity. There are people who leave unscathed from their dreams. Those were far and few in between. Most go back wanting more."

"What happened?" Alik leaned forward.

"They kept coming back until they lost all their wealth and they had nothing. Eventually, they wasted away while the Greyfolk kept firm and held tight to their wealth. The Guardians were amused by those who paid to have their dreams come true. But there came a time when the blood outweighed the gold, and it twisted them, for the spirits of those dead stayed in these mountains. Their screams of torment changed the landscape of this place. No longer was it a palace of pleasure and treasures. The Greyfolk tried to keep it open, but the spirits followed them, and eventually all the wealth disappeared as if whisked by a hand. Misfortune followed the people of this land."

They all gave the Bruadar a glance and felt a collective dread pass through them. Doyle shook himself out of the mood. "A fine tale you tell, lad. Now, you'll have all of us awake instead of resting."

Colm shrugged. "I heard it from Romek." He turned to the others. "What did you see, Leona?"

"We followed the ancient test that the Elders and warriors go through. Jaworek and I weren't allowed to bring provisions or any weapons. That first day we arrived here, we didn't sleep. We looked for water and made weapons." She remembered the fear, how naked she'd felt without her weapons. Even when they could make do with their makeshift weapons, she'd still felt vulnerable.

"There were shadows that followed us, and sometimes we'd see them at night. There are animals here that I've seen nowhere else. The wild dogs are especially vicious here. There were creatures we fought near the other side of the pass. They looked like us...but evil. They were fast, strong, and nothing we did would hurt them. I got separated from Jaworek. He made it to the trail that led out of the pass. I got stuck on the other side and had to climb up a cliff side"— Leona pointed in the distance—"and there was nothing below but a river. I didn't have it in me to go, and so I jumped. Blind faith, hoping that I wouldn't end up drowning after that ordeal."

"What happened when you returned to Midroska?" Doyle asked.

"Caiaphas and Trevelyn were pleased. They sent two others afterward."

"Who were they?"

"Threis and Rimel."

"Oh," Doyle said.

"What did they see?" Alik asked.

"We don't know. They never made it out," Doyle replied.

After a beat of silence, Colm stood up. "Well, then. I'll take the first watch."

Leona bid everyone goodnight and found herself a small patch of soft grass where she plopped herself down. The magnificent peaks of the Hellig Mountains were just above the clouds. Beautiful and terrifying.

What Leona didn't tell them, or the Tribunal, was that she'd gotten something from Shemal Pass during that last visit. Something she suspected belonged to the Bruadar—a leather pouch filled with small grains of crystals of different colors. When she looked at it in the light, there was a black dot within each one. She had gotten it while she and Jaworek had been battling with the creatures. One of them had rushed at her, and as she'd plunged a sword in its chest, in a moment of sanity, it had hissed to her, "This is the racht of all who came before. Keep it secret. Keep it safe."

She thought about that pouch, the only secret she'd kept from the Tribunal. And then of tomorrow. She dreaded being here. Leona looked down at her clasped hands as her stomach churned. Fear was a bad taste in her mouth.

A pair of booted feet appeared in front of her. She looked up at Edward and along with the fear, she felt the surge of annoyance. Especially when he raised an eyebrow. "Care to spar?"

"Not tonight."

"Scared?" he challenged her.

"I'm just not in the mood."

"Fighting's not about mood."

"I know that." Leona stood up and stalked away from Edward. He grabbed her arm in a grip. Leona moved quickly, slamming her body against his, unbalancing him. She followed with a quick punch that he countered away with his forearm.

Edward slammed a hand against her shoulder. Leona jumped away, not before she felt the bite of heat. She looked down and saw a small part of her vest was singed. So that was how he was going to play this.

With his next blow, his fist red hot with flames, she countered with ice. He smiled and shot flame at her. Leona twisted and dodged the other flames he shot in succession. She faded into the shadow world and appeared just in front of Edward. She slammed her hand against his neck, but he quickly caught her hand in his.

"Are you going to freeze me?"

Leona was about to retort when she felt something she hadn't felt in a long time. Feru'talent surged through the connection of their hands. Power that wasn't hers. His ring was against her skin, and the feru'talent contained in there made her gasp. Too much. She couldn't control it. The blast of flames threw him in the air.

"I'm sorry." Leona rushed to him and patted his clothes down with what was left of her ice. She couldn't look him in the eyes.

"You're a light wielder," Edward said with a tinge of awe.

"A grabber, you mean." She winced as she corrected him. "I'm really sorry. I didn't mean to. That hasn't happened in a long time. I didn't even think I could anymore."

He shook his head. "Don't apologize. You use whatever you can to your advantage."

Uncomfortable, it was her turn to shake her head. "Not like that, though."

"What do you mean?"

Leona looked up at Edward. The scowl was still there, but was that concern as well? "Nothing. We need to get some rest. Goodnight, Your Majesty."

Leona looked down at her shaking hands after Edward left. She didn't know why it had come back. She didn't need it. Never wanted it. A gift that steals and hurts others was a curse.

Knowing she wasn't going to sleep that night, she looked up at the sky, at clouds that glowed with the moon. The fear that came over wasn't because of this place. The fear that stole over her was from her shaking hands and the feeling right before that surge of feru'talent had blasted from her.

AS NIGHT PASSED OVER THEM, TENDRILS OF SAND AND stone slithered from the ground until it found skin. As it tightened its grip, the dreams came. And so the test of Shemal Pass began.

Colm dreamt of flying. Always, when he joined his vision with his hawks, it felt as if he were shedding the weight of his skin. In that moment, everything was exhilarating. But death followed if he wasn't careful.

In his dream, he was looking over the Silver River and over Shemal Pass. His ferum beads were nearly empty. He fought the panic down, but he still needed to see if there were enemies in Shemal Pass. When the ferum beads ran out of feru'talent, he braced himself for that break in connection. But the shared vision persisted. His hawk, which should have died, soared on. Alive.

Colm woke up feeling watched, the dream forgotten. He started when he saw a figure cloaked in blackness. It stood in the shadows by the edges of the trees.

He rubbed his tired eyes and looked up again, but it was gone. He never fell asleep during his watch, and he felt guilty that he wasn't paying attention. Remnants of his dream came back. He was flying, and he had his hawk with him. He tried to remember the details but couldn't capture them.

In Niall's dream, he walked the halls of the castle in Mandubrath. Everyone congratulated him. He was perplexed and kept walking toward Edward's receiving room.

"Congratulations," Jon called out to him. "It's well deserved."

Niall was confused, but he shrugged and just gave his thanks. Edward had sent a message he wanted to see him as soon as possible. When he arrived, Edward was standing by the balcony with his kingdom behind him. Its rose-gold colored stones and magnificent beauty shone in the dimming sun.

"You called for me, milord?"

"I wanted to make it official. You're my new captain of the guards."

"I...didn't think you thought I would be ready."

"You're young, Niall, but because of you, we got safely through the pass, and the Gathering was a success. It wouldn't have been possible without you."

Niall couldn't quite remember what he did. He then saw a vision of himself leading Edward and the other guards through a trail going northward, adjacent and close to the Bruadar. The wild dogs came, big and savage. In the vision, he was the only one who knew their weakness. The shadows in the distance of the Bruadar tried to lure them closer, but it was because of Niall's cleverness that they were able to stay on the track and get on the other side of the pass.

The dream was so real that when Niall woke up it took him a moment to remember they were still at the beginning of their journey. His hand was a little sore, and he rubbed it.

The tendrils of sand and stone held Jon's hand as he remembered his grandmother, who had told him stories of speaking to the dead. As a child, he'd nagged her to describe how it was done. His grandmother would always reply that it all started with a flower—one that only grew in the next life. But every now and then, when the moon is blood red, it would bloom in their world. Its color was the same as that moon, and it was as big as the palm of her hand. She called it the flower of Omri.

In his dream, he saw her take the flower from a tree she called the Old Man of the Forest. She showed him how to prepare it by grinding the petals until they turned to a thick paste. Then she took a small scoop of the paste and smeared it on a shallow metal bowl on top of the fire. She took water steeped from fragments of the dead's bone, hair, and skin. Slowly pouring it on the bowl, she continued to mix it with the paste. Round and round, she mixed until it became red and thick.

"This will let you talk to the dead, Jon. Only a little at a time."

He looked down at the cup, not quite sure if he should drink it. In all the years his grandmother had told him of the ritual, he'd never actually seen her do it.

Jon took the cup and drank. It tasted bitter and made his eyes water. He choked and coughed, waking himself up. The dream escaped him, but he thought of his grandmother, who had raised him as a little boy. His hand ached, and he massaged it with his other before falling right back to sleep.

He woke up to a clear morning. There was not a cloud in sight, but the sun shone under a muted light. There was a quality of stillness that made it feel sacrilegious to talk above a hushed tone.

As they started their trek, Jon thought of his dream. He only remembered snatches of his grandmother. His hand still ached a bit. He blamed it on the hard ground. He must have slept on it.

"Twilight is my favorite time of day," Alik commented.

"I wager that when we get out of here, it won't be your favorite anymore," Niall said.

"I'll take that wager. A pint at the Red Pony."

"Alik's stubborn, so I'll take your wager and say he'll still favor it."

The others followed suit, and even Colm threw a wager out there. Leona could only shake her head in bewilderment.

They walked at a fast pace, always wary of their surroundings. Though it would have brought them sooner to the other side of the pass, they stayed on the farthest path from the Bruadar.

Niall was displeased with the idea and expressed it to Gage.

"We can still avoid it, but we don't have to be frightened of something we know nothing about," Niall told him.

Gage shook his head. "You heard what Leona said. We steer clear of the Bruadar."

Niall sneered at that. "There's nothing here. Look around you."

"What's gotten into you?" Gage stopped and turned around.

"I don't like questioning the decisions that have been made during this journey, but I think it's time I did."

"And what would you have done?"

"We wouldn't have gone here, and we would have handled the journey through the Borderlands differently."

"There were reasons behind those decisions, Niall."

"Well, I'm tired of risking my life for these stupid decisions. You're our captain, and you've done nothing but risk the king's life." He pushed at Gage.

Gage looked angry, but he resisted the urge to push back and instead just stood there. "You think you can do better?"

"What's going on here?" Edward asked. He gestured for the others to go ahead.

When it was just the three of them, Niall spoke, beseeching Edward. "I don't think it's a good idea to add another day or two to just avoid the Bruadar, but nobody ever listens to me."

"What would you suggest?" Edward asked.

"Instead of leaning west, we can go on a parallel path along the eastern face of the mountain. It'll shorten our travel time."

"Leona said it's not safe," Gage reminded them.

"We've only known her for a few days. How do we know to trust her? She's been here, yes. Only once. She doesn't know if there's a better path, and I'm saying I looked at the lay of the land before we headed down yesterday. The path alongside the Bruadar looked the same as the one we're on right now."

Edward put a hand on Gage's shoulder without taking his gaze off of Niall. "How do you know?"

"Trust me, milord. I wouldn't lead you to danger."

Edward nodded. "We won't venture that close to the Bruadar, but we'll go northward."

❧

Leona glanced back at Edward, Niall, and Gage. She wanted to stay back and see what it was that Niall and Gage were arguing about, but Edward was clear about wanting their privacy. She turned back to the path, but just like the others, her pace slowed. After a short while, Edward caught up to her. One look at him and she knew it wasn't good.

"Out with it," she snapped.

Edward raised an eyebrow at her tone. "We're going too slow in this direction. Niall saw path along the side of the mountain below the Bruadar. It should cut down our travel time."

"Absolutely not. Haven't I made it clear that the Bruadar is dangerous?"

"We're not going in there. Isn't that what you warned us against?"

"I think we should stay on this path," Leona insisted.

"We're going to run out of food."

"We can ration it."

"And what if we have to fight? We won't have enough strength. We stay at this pace, and we won't have enough in us to replenish our ferum."

Leona huffed a breath. Edward made a good point, but all the same she'd rather stay on the long and winding path. "You've made up your mind. You have, haven't you?"

He inclined his head. "I thought I'd give you a chance to vent."

Leona gritted her teeth in annoyance. "If you weren't..." She stopped herself before saying something she'd regret.

"If I wasn't what?"

"Nothing. But your idea has merit. As long as we don't go any closer to the Bruadar, then I'm fine with that plan."

"Look, we'll steer clear. You have my word." Without waiting for her consent, Edward left her side.

❧

NIALL SHOWED THE OTHERS THE TRAIL HE'D SEEN, AND they followed it for a time. Morning blended into noon, but nothing looked different. It was a silent trudge when they heard a growl and saw movement in the tall grass. Something jumped out and landed in front of them. A wild dog, big as a man; its fur was a muddy brown with bands of black. It howled, and its pack appeared behind it—their teeth bared, their eyes feral.

Doyle stepped forward from Leona's side. He extended a hand, his eyes squinted in concentration. The leader of the pack stopped growling. It took a step back.

"I don't know if I can hold it back," Doyle muttered. "Not like Gawen can."

The wild dog shook its head as if clearing water from its fur. It stopped and lifted its head. It bore death in its gaze. The wild dog barked, and the whole pack leapt for them.

Fire from Edward and Alik erupted, a wall that blasted at the wild dogs. Wind from Niall fed the flames, making it bigger and stronger.

The wild dogs barked in pain, but they leapt through the fire. The first line of wild dogs howled as their fur caught fire. Burning flesh tainted the air and gave the dogs a macabre look. Leona and Colm shot arrows at them, but nothing stopped their attack.

Gage gestured at them to run as he, Corbin, and Simon threw a round of knives using their metalforce. Corbin caught his knives back and ran alongside Edward, who shot his fire at the nearing wild dogs.

They managed to kill a few before arriving at the edge of a swamp filled with mangrove trees. Alik yelled for everyone to go in the water. He and Edward burned the brush and mangrove near the edge of the water. They spread the fire until the wild dogs were no longer visible. One of the wild dogs jumped right through. Burned, it splashed in the water; its blood was a bubbling red as it died.

They waded through the swampy land until they put some distance between them and the wild dogs. It was no easy thing, trudging through the water. Things swayed beneath the surface. It startled Doyle when they first brushed against his leg. It almost made him jump until he realized they were plants, long and wide grass drifting with the water. It made it even more difficult walking through the water, for it dragged at their legs. The cold water was past their knees, getting deeper and deeper.

"I hope your men know how to swim," Leona told Edward. She jolted when she felt something brush against her leg.

"Did you feel that?" Edward looked down. "There." The water was teeming with shadows, swimming just below the surface, brushing against the long grass. Leona looked ahead at the distant shore.

They were waist deep, and every step was an ordeal. The creatures underneath the surface of the water were solid, strong, and slippery. As big a man's head, now and then one would break from the pack and swim toward them in a flurry of speed and bump against their legs.

The water was rising to their chests, the shore coming ever closer. Niall screamed as one creature bit his leg. Sensing the fear and tasting his blood, the other creatures pounced on him. Fishes with dark, round bodies, small fins, and long, sharp tails, they had long, sharp teeth with heads contorted unlike any other fish they had ever seen.

They jumped out of the water, savagely pouncing on everyone. Jon whipped the water around them, trying to dislodge and expose the fish. But even with fire and weapons, there were too many of them.

Alik and Jon were holding onto Niall when he was dragged underneath the water. The creatures were piling on top of Niall, the water a splashing frenzy. Jon tried to get to Niall while Alik fought off the creatures who were attacking Jon.

Edward and Doyle pulled Jon and Alik away. "There's no use. Let go," Edward ordered them.

Leona and Colm were the first to make it to shore. They dragged themselves out and helped the others up.

"Dammit!" Doyle exclaimed. He looked at his mangled pack and tried to see what was left inside.

"All our food's gone." Corbin threw what was left of his pack on the ground.

They finished salvaging what they could, which were mostly cloaks and some skeins of water, and their weapons.

Afterward, they spent hours, wearily trudging, their clothes wet and cold. Making their way up to higher ground, where the trees were aplenty, the trail still gone from view, Corbin stopped and exclaimed, "We've been here already."

Looking up at the sky, the clouds hid the sun, and they couldn't tell in which direction they were headed.

"We're lost," Alik said.

Colm looked up at the sky. He'd seen a black raven fly past their camp this morning. "I have an idea. I saw a raven this morning. Maybe it will let me in."

"Have you done anything like that before? Ravens? And without imprinting?" Doyle queried.

"Well, no. I've tried it with another hawk, not mine. It worked, but it required more feru'talent. Ravens share the same sight as hawks do. I could try. Even a glimpse might help."

"What's the worst that can happen?" Edward asked.

"I wouldn't see anything, and we'd have a disoriented raven flying around."

Edward nodded at him. "We'll hunt in the meantime." Edward looked in question at Leona, but she shook her head. "I'll stay with Colm. He'll be blind on the ground."

Once Edward and the others left and it was just the two of them, Leona and Colm sat on the ground. They sat facing each other. Leona watched Colm as he closed his eyes and turned into himself.

Sweat beaded on his forehead, but his whole demeanor was relaxed, as if he were meditating. Leona looked up at the clear sky. No sign of any ravens above the sparse canopy of trees.

"It let me in! I can see where we are," Colm said with wonder.

A raven, with its wings outstretched, circled high above them. Another raven soon joined it.

"This is wonderful," Colm exclaimed. "I can see through both their eyes."

"I don't think that's a good idea. Let go of the other raven." Leona switched her gaze between the ravens and Colm. A smile played on his lips, his face upturned to the sky. Whatever he was seeing must have been amazing.

"Don't worry, Leona. I can handle this."

The squawking above got louder. She looked up as dozen ravens circled like a funnel above them. More squawking teemed from the trees around them.

"Colm, what are you doing?"

He suddenly stood up. His face contorted with effort. His hands squeezed his head. "They're everywhere!" he screamed. Colm opened his blinded eyes, milky gray from the shared sight. "I can't stop them."

The circling ravens dove from above and surrounded them in a violent flutter of wings. There were hundreds.

Beaks and claws scratched at them. Madness reigned in the forest. Leona shielded Colm from the ravens that were bent on attacking him. For every one that Leona shot down with her arrow, more came. Soon, she and Colm were surrounded. She swiped at the ravens with her sword, but they still came.

Colm writhed on the ground, screaming, clutching his eyes with his hands. The more he screamed, the more frenzied the ravens became.

Leona hit Colm on the head with the butt of her sword. The ravens dropped from the sky and fell dead around them, the ground littered black with their bodies.

"What the hell," Edward said. "Are you all right?" he asked Leona.

"Yes." Something trickled on her cheek. She wiped it away and saw it was blood. "It's nothing." She knelt down and shook Colm. "Wake up. Come back to us."

"You hit him good," Doyle said from Edward's side.

"I didn't want to do it twice."

Edward looked around at the carnage. "Let's get him out of here."

When Colm came to, his head was pounding, and his eyes were a bleary mess. He tried to move his head, but all he could muster was a groan.

"Here." Leona propped his head on her leg. "Have a drink of water."

"Thank you." He moved to sit up, but Leona stopped him. "Do you remember what happened?" she asked.

"I remember seeing through the eyes of all the ravens, and it drove me mad. I couldn't do anything to stop them."

"Did you see anything before the madness?" Leona prompted.

He nodded. "I saw where we are."

Edward knelt by Colm. "Can you get us out of here?"

"I think so."

Edward put a hand on Colm's shoulder. "When you're ready, we'll follow your lead."

Colm moved to stand up, albeit shakily. He led them out of the forest and up into a clearing above the trees. The Bruadar was close enough they could see its face carved onto the mountain.

"We're closer than I thought." Leona looked at the Bruadar with worry.

"Will that be a problem?" Edward asked her.

"I hope not. We might as well try to find camp and forage for food."

"I have some birds with me," Corbin said with a smile and showed his pack, full of raven carcasses. "Gage also grabbed more than a few."

Colm looked about ready to throw up, but he nodded. "Might as well."

❧ 7 ☙

That night, tendrils of sand and stone crept once more on the ground until they found their quarries.

Simon, Corbin, and Doyle dreamt of the Bruadar. As Simon saw the endless treasures it kept in its bowels, Corbin saw the greatest sword created by Kal-Dinakshe, the great blacksmith of the Greyfolk, lost amidst the treasures of the Bruadar, waiting for its next master.

Doyle dreamt he explored its vast and countless hallways. He'd read about the Bruadar, or the Pleasure Palace, as some had been wont to call it in the olden days. There were objects of power that could help the Elders in their quest for the greater good. They couldn't rightfully claim their place of power in the lands. They didn't have their full strength. He felt pride he'd been allowed that knowledge, that they trusted him.

In his dream, he touched the golden walls and tried to find his way. A voice sang to him. A siren's song whose notes shimmered like gold motes in the surrounding air. He was in a great hallway. Shadows filled the big windows on either side of him. Water streamed alongside the windows on the path.

He heard something hiss and turned around. Something twinkled from the grand doorway ahead of him. He ran to it, and music filled his ears as he got closer. He walked through the darkness of the doorway, and a flash of light bathed him in its brilliance.

Alik smiled in his sleep.

"Hurry," Leona called out to him. She held out a hand, and he took it. He followed her gaze to the Hellig Mountains from the Borderlands, their peaks and crags beautiful against the orange sunset.

"It's beautiful!" he exclaimed. "Just like you."

She laughed at that, and he remembered memories he didn't have—memories of them meeting in Kentigern, of being together. He reached for her hand and drew her close. "From the moment I met you, I knew there was something special about you."

"Other than the fact I'm from the Tribunal?" she teased him.

"Well, that's an added complication, but there's something about you that makes me...whole."

"Alik, this can't be. I have my orders to be with your king."

His countenance darkened at that. "Why can't someone else do it?"

She shook her head. "I have my responsibilities, and so do you." She touched his face. "I wish things were different. I want to be with you, but Edward comes first."

He gave a frustrated sigh. "Duty and love. We shouldn't be made to choose."

"Rest easy, my love. Perhaps we'll find the answer tomorrow."

He slipped into a dreamless sleep, and the tentacles of sand stayed with him.

Simon woke from his dream. It was so real he couldn't sleep anymore. He got up thinking to relieve Jon from the watch. Simon walked as quietly as he could through their camp. Jon was seated, his side facing Simon, his back against a large boulder.

"Jon," Simon called out in a loud whisper. But Jon didn't seem to hear him. Jon stood up. Slowly, as if in a trance. Simon called out again, louder this time, but Jon walked away.

Wondering what was wrong with Jon, Simon followed him. They walked quite a ways away from camp. Far away enough that Simon started to feel uncomfortable. He hurried his pace to catch up to Jon, but he couldn't quite catch up to Jon, even when he was almost running. Jon kept walking, his pace unhurried, but Simon could swear the distance between them was stretching.

He looked back toward camp. It seemed impossibly far away. He could barely see the boulders that marked it. He turned back and called to Jon as he struggled to catch up.

Simon followed Jon to a desolate grove of twisted trees long dead. Their color was a muddy gray. The ground was dry with dust, and every step spurred more dust to fly in the air. Never had he seen a forest devoid of life. Simon touched a tree; it was cold like marble. Ahead of them was a giant tree that reached up to the heavens. Simon looked at it in wonder. Its white trunk, impossibly wide, was gnarly and twisted with age. Leaves hung on vine-like branches all around the tree.

"Jon," Simon called out.

Jon turned around, surprised. "Why are you following me?"

"What are you doing?" Simon asked.

"This is the tree my grandmother used to tell me about." Jon touched its trunk. "The Old Man of the Forest. I thought it was just a story. Look over there. Do you see a red flower?"

Simon looked where Jon was pointing at a flower, bigger than the palm of his hand, on one of the branches. "What is that?"

"It's the flower of Omri. It could give the power to converse with the dead. Don't you want to know if there's life beyond death? Isn't there someone you'd like to talk to?"

"Will it show me where the treasure is in the Bruadar?" he said jokingly, thinking of his dream.

Jon climbed up the tree. He reached out and plucked the flower from its perch. He climbed down and showed it to Simon. It glowed like rubies under the moonlight. Suddenly, the ground under them shifted. Jon lurched and almost lost his balance.

"What the—!" he swore.

Thick roots lifted violently from the ground and grabbed at them. Simon and Jon fought them off, hacking with their swords, trying to get away. The ground shook around them, and dust flew. A root caught Jon by the ankle, lifted him up, and slammed him to the ground. Jon dodged away from another root that sped at him and hacked at the one that had his ankle in its grip.

Big roots surrounded Simon, and he deflected their attack using his sword. Jon saw more skimming the ground going for Simon's legs. Jon freed himself and struck the ground as serpentine vines rose to wrap themselves around Simon's feet. Jon swung his sword and freed Simon.

They stood back to back. Dust was a brown haze that covered everything around them. The roots became like shadowed snakes, waiting to pounce on them.

"If we head through those roots, I think we can make a run for it." Jon said, out of breath.

"Throw the damn flower, Jon. You have to. It might be our only chance."

Jon took the flower from his pocket. The roots, sensing the flower, shot at them. He threw the flower toward the tree, and they made a run for it as they hacked at the roots that attacked them. They leaped through an opening. Jon pushed Simon forward and sliced at a root that almost knocked Simon's back.

"My thanks, once again."

The creaking and violent thrashing abruptly stopped. They turned toward the hazy shadow of the great tree. They made a move to step away when a root came out of nowhere and wrapped itself around Jon's waist. It tightened painfully, and he screamed as Simon hacked at it. More roots came out of the dusty haze and wrapped Jon in their deadly embrace.

Leona awoke from the heavy fog of sleep. She couldn't keep her eyes open. Her body was sluggish. She'd heard a commotion, somewhere far away. The scream pierced through the fog of her consciousness. She fought to wake up, pushing herself up to her knees. There was that scream again. Louder this time. There was dirt around one of her hands. She shook it off and was instantly alert.

Everyone in camp was still asleep, starting to stir. She shook Doyle awake. When he wouldn't wake up, she slapped his face. When his eyes opened, she told him to wake the others. She ran for the screams and saw that Edward was already there.

Roots covered both John and Simon in their twisted grip, squeezing ever slowly and hardening into stone. Their screams were the screams of pain and helplessness. Where they hadn't hardened yet, Edward and Leona were able to hack through them.

Edward freed Simon, but there was no saving Jon. His bones were crushed, and blood gushed out of the gaps between the roots. Leona helped support Simon's weight as they took him from the tree.

As they put more distance between themselves and the tree, its roots settled, and all was as it had been. Colm pointed at a close distance where their camp was. "Look over there."

A hooded figure shrouded in shadows hovered in the trees.

"I saw it last night," Corbin said.

"It's a guardian of the Hellig Mountains. A Watcher," Leona informed them. "It has been following us since the beginning."

"Why didn't you tell us?" Doyle demanded.

"Because it won't do anything to help us. They watch and pass judgment on everyone who takes this path. That's what they do."

When they glanced again, the figure was gone.

"How is he?" Edward asked.

"He isn't doing well," Doyle said grimly. "Do your men have enough in their ferum?"

"No. They're running on empty. I need to replenish mine as well."

Suddenly, they heard a boom, and the ground beneath them rumbled.

"What was that?" Alik asked.

Another boom.

"Run!" Leona screamed. She grabbed her bow and notched an arrow.

A mountain troll crashed out of the trees. Leona whistled as it came bounding toward them. It ran for her, and as she shot an arrow toward it, she jumped. The mountain troll, fast, caught her midair and slammed her to the ground. Alik slashed at its legs. As the mountain troll roared, Leona slung her bow over her shoulder and unsheathed her twin swords.

The mountain troll fell on its knees and tried to grab Alik. This gave Leona the opening to strike the mountain troll from behind and kill it.

When it fell to the ground, Leona gave Alik a quick smile of thanks. For a moment, he confused his dream with reality.

After a moment of silence, the ground thundered as two mountain trolls sped toward them.

Fresh from his victory over the first troll, Alik attacked with vigor. In the corner of his eye, he noticed a troll behind Edward. He could have easily stepped in or warned Edward, but something kept him where he was. He had a flash that if Edward died, there would be nothing between him and Leona.

The troll rammed into Edward and slammed him onto the ground. The troll struck again, but Edward had his sword up. He rolled under the troll and struck at its knees. He merely nicked it, but that gave Edward a chance to get on his feet. He slammed fire against the troll, blinding it for a moment. Edward reared back and threw his dagger at the troll's eye.

Alik looked at Edward, dazed. He shook his head from his stupor, willing himself to return to reality. He jumped into action as the ground rumbled, and more trolls appeared in their midst.

Edward, Leona, and the others ran through the trees, slid down the hill, and scrambled through a wide stream. All the while, the thundering footsteps inched closer and closer.

"There!" Corbin pointed at a moon-shaped doorway. Covered with vines, it was carved into the face of a stone wall.

"Go!" Doyle yelled. "Leona and I will hold them off." They protected the doorway as everyone raced inside. Leona and Doyle made it inside just as three trolls rammed themselves against the stone wall.

Inside, small rocks tumbled from above with the impact. Leona put a hand against the wall, gauging its strength. The wide tunnel seemed strong, but each time a troll rammed against the wall outside, the sound of small rocks raining on the ground still alarmed her. Water ran in a stream in a deep groove under her feet.

The trolls' massive frames were too big for the doorway, but one of them extended its arm through the doorway and tried to swipe at anything it could get its hands on.

After a few more futile attempts, the troll withdrew and lumbered away.

Leona broke away from the wall. Gravel crunched and water seeped under her feet as she risked a peek outside. She jumped back when another troll pummeled the doorway.

Warily, Doyle and Leona watched for cracks. When they found none, they walked toward the back where Edward held a small ball of firelight that lit the tunnel. Simon was propped on the ground.

Doyle and Leona leaned against the wall and watched as Edward and Colm knelt over Simon, trying to mend his injuries. Simon's leg was bent the wrong way, and his breath wheezed with every breath. He coughed and spat blood out.

"Milord," Alik called out to Edward, remorse etched in his face. "May I have a word with you?"

Edward nodded and stood up. He let the ball of fire rest just above Simon and Colm. Edward and Alik walked to the steps at the long end of the chamber. The narrow stairs were roughly hewn. Water trickled down a deep groove carved in the middle of the steps.

Alik was the first to speak. "I want to apologize. I froze when I should have done my duty to protect you."

Edward laid a hand on his shoulder. "Leona warned us. I think we all underestimated how this place could twist us."

"I'm ashamed to say I was weak, and I thought only of myself out there," Alik insisted.

"Now you know how the pass tests all of us. Be vigilant, even in your thoughts."

Alik nodded, still looking guilty.

"There's no room for self-pity, Alik. I've always treasured your service. I still do."

The mountain trolls eventually gave up. As silence ensued in the chamber, slivers of light from the brightening sky entered, illuminating parts of the chamber. In a small nook carved from the rock was the petrified body of a Greyfolk.

"What now?" Colm asked.

"We have three options," Doyle said. "We wait the mountain trolls out, or we battle with every one of them."

"Or we go up those stairs," Gage said.

Doyle looked at Edward in question. "What shall it be, milord?"

"Let's wait them out for now."

Doyle gave Simon the last of his water and helped him eat the little food he had saved. "That's the best we can do. Try to rest now." He patted Simon's shoulder once more and stood up. He sat by Leona on the steps and looked at the dead Greyfolk.

"How long do you think he's been here?" Leona asked.

"A long time. Who knows what could have driven him to hide here or why he stayed?"

They both watched Edward as he talked with each of his men.

"I suppose I shouldn't let this get to me." Doyle rubbed his hands on his face. "I've been through worse and seen carnage that haunts me still, but having people plucked off one by one is difficult."

"Don't despair, my old friend. We'll get out of here."

"Who are you calling old?"

"You. For you are wise." She teased a smile out of him. "We can't let hope die."

"You're right," Edward said as he joined them.

Leona looked at him. "You've had men die, and I'm deeply sorry for that. It's on me for leading us here."

"Don't." Edward raised a hand. "I'm not blaming you."

"I'm blaming myself."

Doyle was about to speak when Edward silenced him with a look. Doyle sighed, but he stood up. Before he walked away, he looked at Leona squarely. "You called me wise, then heed my advice. Don't blame yourself. We all decided to come here. You didn't force us. I thought I taught you better than that."

"He's right." Edward sat next to where Doyle was.

"I hope it's not my arrogance that's telling me we'll get out of here," Leona said.

"My father used to tell me that once a leader goes to war and all his troops are in the middle of it, there's no room for doubt or regret. At that moment, he or she needs to do the best they can to ensure success." Edward leaned back and closed his eyes for a moment, as if reliving his father's words. "I didn't realize how true his words were until the first battle I led. In the middle of the fighting and seeing my people die, I wanted to pull back, but I couldn't. We were in the middle of it already."

Edward paused and turned to Leona. His gaze was clear, but intense. "Your instinct told you we'd make it out of here. We're in the middle of the battle. There's no turning back and blaming yourself is only casting doubt on that decision. Don't blame yourself for my men's deaths. They swore their lives to protect me. They're here because of me and my decision to come here."

"You put too much on yourself," Leona reprimanded him.

"As do you."

She looked away from Edward. "I don't know how you do it."

Now it was his turn to sigh. "We all have a load we bear. This happens to be one of mine."

"Then let me share your load. They're not my people, but their lives are also intertwined with mine right now."

Edward didn't say anything, but he held out his hand. She looked at it for a moment before she laid her hand on his.

୧୬୨

BY MIDDAY, THE MOUNTAIN TROLLS WERE STILL OUTSIDE. Leona and Edward had ventured into the tunnel to see where it led and if there were any other escape routes, but there was only the one stairway that led up into a larger tunnel.

Hoping that they would outlast the trolls, they stayed put that whole day. That night, more trolls came. They rammed themselves against the doorway in intervals. Cracks formed under the repeated pummeling. Chunks of rock from the doorway had fallen after the last assault.

Leona stood closest to the doorway, a hand clenched on her sword. She looked back at Edward in question. He stood by the stairway, his fire a small ball on his shoulder, dimly lighting the tunnel.

"We have to leave," Edward finally said. "The doorway won't hold."

Everyone followed Edward's lead. Gage and Corbin supported Simon up the stairs. Deep grooves where the water flowed in the middle of the stairs made it hard on Simon's broken leg.

"What do you think is up there?" Doyle inclined his head up the stairway.

"The Bruadar," Leona gravely replied.

The steps and walls around them were cracked and missing in places. Moss seeped through and made the steps soft and uneven. The path led them up and into a larger tunnel. Beyond the narrow strip of landing they all stood on, water was a black mirror that filled the surface of the tunnel.

Leona skimmed the wall with her hand. A small square receptacle was carved just above her head. From it a straight narrow groove, as deep as her fingers, lined the wall. She asked Edward to see what would happen if he touched it with his fire. The receptacle lit up in a strange white glow that pulsed. The light spread in a straight line along the walls. The tunnel was carved out of yellow- and orange-colored stones with veins of white crystals that spread out like spiderwebs.

Gage took his sword and dipped it in the water. "It's deep. I wouldn't want to swim in that. What if there's something in there? Those creatures that killed Niall could be lurking under that water."

"Maybe we don't have to." Colm pointed at a makeshift raft. It lay on its side by the wall. The raft was made with different pieces and sizes of wood—as if it was randomly brought together. The craftmanship was sound, though. "Must have been built by the Greyfolk downstairs."

"Do you wonder why he came back?" Gage asked.

Alik laid a hand on Gage's shoulder. "There's more of us. And we can all fight."

At Edward's nod, Doyle and Colm dragged it onto the water.

One by one they got on. With eight of them aboard the raft, there was only room for Simon to sit down. Everyone else stood shoulder to shoulder. Colm took the long paddle, and they drifted along the tunnel. The silence made them wary. After drifting along for a while, they entered a bigger tunnel. The light from the walls winked out, leaving them in the dark until Edward used his fire to light the way.

The tunnel forked in three directions. With little deliberation, they went for the middle tunnel. Eventually, they saw dry ground and docked the raft.

Gage and Alik helped Simon off the raft while Colm and Leona steadied it. As they walked along a wide corridor, Edward's fire cast long shadows that flickered around them. Narrow streams of water flowed on both sides through carved channels. The walls were filled with intricate carvings of figures and faces that seemed to watch them. The corridor took a sharp turn to the left and there, large pockets were carved out of the walls. Rows and rows were on both sides with black statues facing their path. All of them were the same. As big as a child, their legs were crossed and their knees bent. Some had their arms around their legs, while others had their hands on the stone they were seated on.

Leona reached out and touched a dent in the wall. She rubbed her fingers together and smelled the gritty blue powder. She called out to Edward and had him touching his fire against the dents on both sides of the wall. They sparked and the light quickly spread in a thin line all along the wall. The corridor took on a golden hue, illuminating a grand doorway at the far end.

A black onyx statue turned its head. With its eyes closed, it opened its mouth in a wide scream. No sound came out.

Leona yelped in surprise. Edward steadied her with a hand on her back. Leona heard the curses from the other men as they saw the same thing happen with the other statues.

Those that didn't scream turned their heads to follow their progress.

After a while, the number of statues became few and far between. There were still windows carved into the walls at long intervals, but there was nothing in them except darkness.

It was through one of those windows that Leona saw a frightening sight. Black-skinned children stood, huddled with their backs toward the window. They peered through the windows along the length of the corridor and saw the same.

The grand doorway loomed ahead of them. A murmur of low voices beckoned them. Through the impossibly high doorway, the blackness beyond was thick. Even with their torches, they couldn't see anything.

"Let's not go in there," Leona said.

Edward nodded. "Let's go back to the raft."

Doyle slowed his pace and watched as they retreated. Making up his mind, he made his way toward the doorway.

The corridor and the grand doorway had been in his dreams. He'd seen descriptions in the Great Library. The temptation was too hard to resist, and he gave none of his companions a thought as he entered the darkness.

8

"Where's Doyle?" Gage asked as they boarded the raft.

"He was just behind me." Leona turned to Colm. "Have you seen him?"

Colm shook his head. "I wasn't really paying attention."

"Let's look for him," Leona told Colm.

"I'll go with you," Edward said. "Gage, Alik, and Corbin will stay here with Simon."

"Leave me here," Simon croaked. "I'm just slowing you down."

"Absolutely not."

Simon coughed as spoke. "You need them with you. I'd feel better feel better if they were."

Edward regarded Simon for a moment. "Then we all go together."

They walked the length of the corridor, but Doyle was nowhere to be found. The grand doorway lay before them.

Leona entered first. "Doyle!" she called out, extending the torch forward. Leona looked behind her, but a thick fog obscured her sight.

They reached a wall and followed it until it forked to the left and right. Leona turned right and walked until the path forked again and led them into a pocket. Leona backtracked and realized something. "We're in a maze."

"How are we going to find Doyle in this?" Gage swatted at the fog, and it swirled around his fingers.

Leona and Colm climbed one of the walls. When they reached the top, they peered over the blanket of fog. The maze stretched out into the expanse in a pattern of squares.

Colm started in surprise and would have fallen if not for Leona. The statue of a horse stood in front of him. There were other statues, all hazy, along the tops of the maze walls.

"Doyle!" Leona called out. The fog thinned, and still there was no sign of Doyle. Colm walked along the tops of the walls, calling out for Doyle.

Leona heard something faint above her. It called out again. This time, she recognized Doyle's voice.

"Go back!" Doyle screamed.

Leona looked in disbelief. Doyle stood far above them, standing on the ceiling like a bat and gesturing frantically at her and Colm.

They could barely hear him, but his next words were clear enough. "Go back! Leave me!"

With no warning, the wall shifted and disappeared from under them. Leona tried to grab onto something...anything to hold on to. Edward's fire winked out, and there was nothing but blackness in the dizzying fall.

Leona hit the ground hard and landed on her back. She grunted while the others swore.

Fire came back, and with it, light. Leona glanced at Edward. She knew he was expending his feru'talent, and she worried that he'd have none left and they'd be left in darkness.

"Are you hurt?" Doyle crouched down at her side.

She grimaced but shook her head. "Just winded."

Doyle helped her get up to her feet.

"Where are we?" she asked him.

"Look up."

Leona did as he said, not understanding what it was he was pointing at.

"Keep looking."

She squinted, and it came to her. "How is this possible?"

What she mistook for patterned squares carved above them was actually the maze they had just been in. The doorway they'd entered from was one of the rectangular holes that lined the ceiling.

She turned at a pained moan. Simon lay on the ground, with Edward and Gage kneeling by him. Gage lifted Simon's head from the ground and gave him some water. Simon took a small sip, then coughed violently. He wiped his mouth, and Leona saw his sleeve covered in blood. When he caught his breath, he shook his head at the offer of more water. "Leave me. I'm no use to any of you."

Edward shook his head. "That's not an option." He and Gage took Simon by the arm, lifted him up, and supported his full weight.

"I tried to see if there are any footholds on the walls, but it's too high," Doyle said.

Leona looked around the big chamber. It looked like a receiving hall in the Bruadar's grand past. The walls were painted with pictures of the forest, people, animals, and mountains. Some paintings were too faded, but she could see Greyfolk in grander garb than they usually wore and creatures that Leona didn't recognize.

They walked along the great hall. Their footsteps echoed loudly in the silence. Unbeknownst to them, up above, shadows slithered from the doorway they'd come from. They crawled, watching them with eyes that gleamed black.

In the middle of the hall, a great pillar stood. A spiral staircase hugged it, leading up to a landing above.

The landing was a feat of craftsmanship. It seemed to float with only the one wall and pillar supporting it. A balustrade surrounded it, and Leona could just imagine the view it offered. A wide doorway at the end of the hall was their only way out.

A large iron sculpture of a warrior, dull in its age, knelt in front of the pillar, a sword in front of him. The sword's hilt held three rubies, a large round one and two that flanked center, shaped like diamonds. The warrior's other hand held a long rod with a ball and chain.

When they approached the pillar, the warrior flicked his sword up to prevent them from passing.

"I am the guardian of this chamber. There are those among you who seek the treasures of the Bruadar." The deep voice came from the statue.

Edward spoke up. "We seek passage through the Bruadar. Nothing more."

"Lies. Your thoughts betray you." The statue stood up and towered over them. It struck at Edward, but Edward had already rolled away on the ground.

They all attacked the statue as one. It was fast and its blade true. Doyle jumped on the warrior's back, looking for a weakness in its helmet, but the warrior threw him off. It swung the ball and chain at Doyle, barely missing him as the ball gouged the ground.

With their weapons proving ineffective against the warrior, Leona and Doyle focused their efforts on disarming the warrior. Its hand glowed red as Edward, with a leap, stabbed his blade into the warrior's hand. Its fingers melted. The rod with the ball and chain dropped with a clang. When it landed on the ground, Doyle took the handle in both hands. He struggled with its weight. He focused then, his skin taking on that translucent sheen.

Doyle swung, and the ball smashed into the warrior's leg. The force knocked its leg off. The warrior collapsed on the ground, and with another swing, Doyle smashed the warrior's head. His sword crashed with a resounding clang that echoed around them.

"Let's go." Edward gestured toward the staircase. Simon, with Colm and Alik supporting him, went up the staircase, followed by everyone except for Corbin, who bent down and took the sword. He looked in wonder. He'd recognized the sword from the moment he'd seen the warrior. The same as the one in his dreams. He held it up, surprised at how light and how perfectly it fit in his hand.

"Corbin!" Edward yelled as he ran down with Gage behind him. The statue lifted itself and, using its other hand, took Corbin by the neck and squeezed until his neck broke.

The warrior threw Corbin's body to the side and started for the stairs. Gage dragged Edward up, and they ran to the landing above with the statue dragging its leg as it used its hands to climb up the steps. They made for the wide doorway ahead, and once through, Doyle and Gage struck at the chains holding the door open.

The big and heavy door fell and secured the entryway with a loud boom.

The warrior banged against the door. The doors held true against the barrage. Once the warrior had gone, they backed up and explored their surroundings.

Narrow white pillars lined the long corridor. There was light here, and the air smelled fresh. Ahead of them, through the pillars, was a circular courtyard built of a warm white stone. It was carved in peaceful lines that eased the mind. Above the domed ceiling was a porthole that let the moonlight in.

In the middle of the courtyard was a delicate but majestic tree with a canopy made of twisting white branches. To the far left was a waterfall. The water tumbled from a fissure in the rocky wall and ended in a small clear pool surrounded by a shore of fine white sand. The rest of the courtyard floor was a colorful mosaic dulled by time.

Their footsteps played with the dust as they walked around the courtyard.

Gage and Alik walked the corridor to explore while Doyle and Colm looked at Simon's condition. From his expression, Leona could tell that it wasn't good. Edward nodded at Doyle, who gave Simon a drink from a blue vial for the pain. From the amount he gave Simon, there was no hope.

Simon didn't last through the night. He died in the company of his king and comrades.

From the ground, tendrils of sand and dirt rose to embrace Simon. They did it tenderly, even lovingly. Gage and Alik made a move to stop it, but Edward told them to let it be. It was abhorrent to them to let the Bruadar claim him. However, if there was a place they should leave his body, this seemed the best—quiet, peaceful, and in its own way, beautiful.

Eventually, everyone but Edward drifted off to their own spaces. He stood in front of Simon, alone, unmoving. Leona didn't know why, but she pitied him.

She walked up to him and stood by his side. "I'm sorry."

Edward opened his fist and handed the object he was holding to Leona. "Here. He was a metalforce."

Leona shook her head at the ferum necklace. "I can't."

"If he'd known what you can do, he would have liked for you to have it. Take it, Leona. It's useless to all of us with feru'talent still in them."

"I don't even know if I can do it again. That was the first time it has flared in years."

"You've never struck me as a coward," Edward said.

"Are we back to trading insults?"

"You're scared. That's why you're hesitating to take the ferum. That's why you haven't used your feru'talent in years. I must have really pissed you off for it to come out."

She rolled her eyes and grabbed the leather-bound necklace from his palm. "There. Happy?"

"Do you feel anything?"

Leona closed her fist. The fear was bile in her throat that she pushed down. She focused on the beads, but she couldn't feel anything. Not even when she tried harder. Strange that after all these years, she thought she'd just be able to summon it on a whim. "No. I told you. That was a fluke."

"What happened, Leona?"

"I hurt someone. I used their own feru'talent against them, and I couldn't stop." Her voice trailed off. It was a shameful thing she'd never told anyone. Everyone in the Tribunal knew, of course. But nobody else. "I would rather fight fair."

"That's not fighting fair. That's throwing away your advantage."

"You can be a prick, you know that?"

Edward leaned his head back and closed his eyes. "I know. It doesn't change the fact that you're afraid of what you can do."

Leona scowled. "I'm surprised you didn't say that I'm stupid."

"I don't have to."

Leona crossed her arms and frowned at him. "Can't you spare some compassion?"

"It'll just make you weak. Aren't you supposed to protect me?"

"Arrogant bastard," she muttered under her breath.

That made Edward smile. "I heard that."

"You were meant to." And with that, Leona walked off.

❧

GAGE HAD BEEN AWAKE FOR SOME TIME, KEEPING THE watch. He'd been replenishing his ferum, but truth be told, he was tired. If he was smart, he would save his energy, but he felt naked without power in his ferum beads.

A stream of light from up above illuminated the tree, and it made him think of sunlight and of his home. Gage closed his eyes. Even if this place drained him of hope, it wouldn't be able to drain him of his duty. Unbidden, his thoughts went to his long-dead wife, Alisa. He thought of going home to the comfort of her arms. Oh, how he missed her so much that it hurt.

He looked up. He swore he heard something.

"Gage, sweetheart."

He saw her then. His Alisa.

She was walking by the waterfall. Her dark curly red hair was as he remembered. She looked at him with the green eyes he loved so much. He had once told her, while in courtship, that she needed no jewels because her eyes would outshine them. She'd laughed and told him he didn't need to buy her jewels if he couldn't afford them. That was before he'd become one of Edward's guards. He had been a soldier with no rank and nothing to offer, but she'd still agreed to marry him.

When he'd become one of the guards, it had been the proudest moment of their lives. When she'd gotten sick, she'd made him promise that his life would not stop if she died. She'd told him she'd always be there, even after death.

With tears in his eyes, he walked to her as if in a dream. Maybe he'd died, and she was here to fetch him.

"My love." She held her arms out to him.

"Oh, Alisa." He took hold of her and kissed her with all the yearning from all the years that separated them.

Leona didn't know what woke her up. Her mind still foggy from sleep, she looked around and saw Gage standing by the waterfall. Leona rubbed her eyes. Gage was kissing a red-haired woman. On her back, snakelike tentacles unfurled and spread wide behind her.

Leona jumped to her feet. "Gage!" she called out as she slowly walked toward him.

Gage turned around, the woman's hand tucked in his. "Leona?" He looked at her in confusion.

"Let go of her and walk away."

"This is my Alisa."

The woman smiled at Leona.

Just as the tentacles moved to grab Gage, Leona pushed him away. The woman's face became distorted as a snakelike tongue came out of her mouth. She screamed, and her eyes became a horrid red and black. Her hair streamed behind and around her face as the tentacles reached out for Leona.

She captured Leona in their grip. Doyle and Colm, now awake, notched their arrows, but Leona was in front of the creature, and they couldn't risk shooting her.

Doyle focused on the creature, whispering under his breath. The creature stilled. Its grip loosened. Leona leaned her head forward and snapped it back as she kicked backward. The creature, caught by surprise, let go of her. It gave the men a clear target. Doyle threw Leona her sword, and she turned around to swing at the creature as the men shot fire and arrows at it. Leona cut through some tentacles. It screamed and writhed in pain. As the creature retreated, one of its tentacles snapped at Leona.

Leona flew from the impact and hit the rocks by the waterfall, landing on the sandy shore that sucked her up. She tried to grab for anything to stop her descent, but the quicksand grabbed hold of her, and before she realized it, she was neck-deep.

Edward jumped and tried to grab hold of her hand, but it was too late. She was gone.

Doyle grabbed a rope and wrapped it around his arm. He jumped into the sand. When he was up to his neck, he felt a tug at the rope pulling him back.

"She's gone." Doyle's calm voice was betrayed by the storm that raged in his eyes.

"She's gone," Doyle repeated unbelievingly.

Doyle pulled himself out of the sand with Colm's help. Their eyes turned to where Leona had slept. Her things were neatly laid on the ground. The only thing missing was the twin of her short sword—the one Leona had been holding when she was dragged into the sand.

He knelt down and handed the sword to Colm. Everything else, he neatly stuffed in her pack. There would be time later to sort through them.

"Should we leave her things?" Colm ventured. "It'll weigh us down."

"She didn't have a lot. We'll take them with us," Doyle countered as he made his way to his own space. He tied her pack to his own. When he looked up, he found Edward staring at him. Doyle couldn't tell what the king was thinking and after a while, Edward turned away. He looked at the rest of his men, who waited for him. "Gather all your things. We're leaving."

❀ 9 ❀

Leona fell to the ground, coughing and gasping for breath. She looked up from where she'd fallen and remembered the horrible feeling of being sucked under by the ground. As heavy, wet sand scratched her face, she stubbornly closed her eyes and stopped struggling. For a moment, something touched her hand and she tried to reach for it, but it slipped through her fingertips.

She kept sinking, and after what seemed like an eternity, right when she accepted the inevitable and would have drawn her last breath, her legs were free and she hit the ground.

Leona gulped a big breath of air and coughed when she inhaled sand. She pounded on her chest until the coughing fit was over. Turning onto her back, Leona tried to calm her fast-beating heart. It was so dark, she could have sworn her eyes were still closed. She quelled the fear that crept into the edges of her consciousness.

Leona picked her sword up and slowly stood up. The walls were damp; the earthy smell was strong. There were drops of water that continually dripped from the ceiling. Tap-tap-tap they went.

Blinded, she groped the walls as she slowly walked. The sound of her breath was unusually loud and jarring. A dim blue light suddenly glowed beneath her fingertips. Leona blinked. She tapped and where the tips of her fingers were, blue light glowed.

Leona stopped and took the ferum beads Edward had given to her. She wrapped them around her wrist. Metalforce. That's what they had. The beads felt strange on her skin. Cold and foreign. She tried to feel the feru'talent within, but there was nothing. If he hadn't told her, she wouldn't even know what was in them.

She continued walking, trailing her hand on the wall, the blue light glowing in her wake.

Grabber, a whisper behind her said.

Leona turned around, sword in hand. There was nobody there.

Stealer. Killer, another whisper said. Leona whipped around at the voice, but all she saw was blackness.

The Bruadar was playing with her mind. That's all it was. Even though she thought that, the whispers bothered her. Hours passed and they taunted her, keeping her company. She'd gotten so used to the tunnel that when she walked into a big open space, just the change in the sounds told her she was somewhere different. The drips of water echoed loudly. Her eyes sought to find the walls around her, but the blue glow only went so far.

The whispers intensified until they felt like a roar in her head.

"Leave me alone," she finally said out loud.

"She finally answers," a teenage boy's voice answered.

Leona followed the voice. Her sword was clutched in her hand, ready to strike.

A bright white light flared above and to her left. Her eyes

teared up, but she refused to look away. She turned her head and saw a lanky figure emerge. The boy sneered at her. "Took you this long. Still think you're above everyone, don't you?"

"Gavin? But..." Leona shook her head, disbelieving who was in front of her. "You're dead."

"Because you killed me."

"I'm so so sorry." Leona's voice broke.

A bright light flared to her left. Another boy appeared. The same one. He even wore the same clothes. "I wanted to be a warrior. I wanted to serve."

"You took what I was and killed me," another boy added.

"I was a son," another said.

"I loved to read," echoed a voice from behind her.

"I helped in the library when nobody was looking."

"I was scared just like everyone else was."

"You took my future away."

Leona turned around in a circle. The eight boys that surrounded her looked exactly how she remembered him. Everything about that day, every detail was clear in her head, as if it had just happened. She'd lived with it every day for four years now. "I'm sorry. I wish I could take it all back."

"That's not enough," they told her in a discord of voices. "I was ordered to give you ferum beads. Grabber. And you took my life. Everything. You're a thief, a murderer. This world would be a better place without you."

"I haven't..." Leona trailed off. She was about to say that she hadn't been able to use her feru'talent, but that wasn't true. She'd grabbed Edward's fire.

"Who will you hurt next?" the boys asked.

"I don't know," she whispered as images of that day assailed her.

Leona's sword dropped on the ground with a clang. One of the boys stepped up behind her, swiped the sword away with his foot, and kicked her on the knees. She fell to the ground, her hands catching herself.

"A life for a life," they all said.

She saw the flash of a sword on the periphery of her vision, but she didn't care. Being a grabber was something she'd always hated. She'd almost started to like it when she'd been trained by another grabber. But when she'd accidentally killed Gavin, it had devastated her. Not to mention all the apprentices who'd hated her—they'd become frightened after that.

Through the flash of silent acceptance, she heard Edward's sneering voice telling her to use whatever advantage she had. She thought of the few in the Tribunal, like Doyle and Colm, who she trusted. And she thought of her birth family, who would certainly be upset if she just gave up.

Gavin was dead. She'd been atoning for it every single day. She couldn't let him kill her. Not now. But then, she'd been dying inside, one piece at a time, since that day.

Leona closed her eyes and felt the touch of metal from the ferum beads. Just a whisper. She could barely hold on to it. She imagined how it had felt when Edward's fire flared in her hand. She tapped into the ferum's power. Bile rose in her throat, but she fought it down. The seed of power began from deep within her gut. It expanded until she felt it in her head and her hands. Leona reached for the sword, willing it to come to her. It moved a fraction. She tried again, the nausea growing stronger with the effort.

The sword flew to her hand.

Leona stood up and raised her arm as the boy behind her attacked. The clash of swords echoed sharply. Moving as one, all the other boys rushed toward her. Leona parried the attacks, looking for an opening. She kicked one of them, stealing his sword and pushing him into another boy. Leona ducked and slid in between two boys. Outside of the circle, she looked for an opening. Any doorway that would take her out of there.

The bright lights above dimmed one by one. A shadow in the far end of the chamber looked like the door she'd come from. She ran for it, fighting all the while, unwilling to kill Gavin all over again.

One of the boys landed on her back and tackled her on the ground. She punched him on the face and pushed him away from her. Leona rolled away, but another boy caught her legs. She looked toward the doorway, then back at him, and kicked at his hands.

The boy screamed at her, "Wonder why this place glows? Or why the walls are wet?"

Leona heard the unmistakable roar of water. To her horror, water rushed through the doorway. She kicked at the boy again and this time, he let go. Leona got up to run to the doorway, but the water that poured in became a strong torrent. She looked behind her, and the boys were nowhere to be found.

The darkness descended on the chamber as the last of the bright lights disappeared. Leona strapped her short sword to her waist and felt along the walls. Blue light glowed under her hands.

Leona fought the panic away as the chamber quickly filled with water. She half swam in waist-deep water that was quickly rising. The torrent swept her in its wake. She tumbled in the water as it rose above her head. She was buffeted around violently until she thought she would not be able to breathe.

When she popped up to the ceiling, she took a few breaths. The water kept surging up until the whole chamber was underwater. She swam, trying to stay close to the blue lights that glowed on the walls. But the water's current was strong, and she had to fight every surge that came for control.

She lost it when it pushed her against a wall. It knocked whatever breath she had out of her, and suddenly she was pulled into a tunnel. With her lungs burning from the effort, she swam upward. When her hands encountered rock, she kept on swimming forward.

With her muscles wavering and the desperate need to breathe her sole focus, she blindly groped along above her. She discovered a pocket of air and hungrily took it in. She swam again and encountered more pockets of air, but they were far and few between.

The tunnel narrowed and the current of water flowed forward, carrying her with it. She let the current sweep her until she saw a sliver of light ahead. Thinking it could be another pocket of air or even the outside, she struggled until she grabbed onto a small ledge. She pushed herself and swam upward until she finally broke the surface.

A tall circular wall surrounded her. Leona took in big gulps of air as she looked up. She was still in the cave, but there was light coming from...somewhere. She took hold of a rock protruding from the wall and started her climb up. Once she reached the ledge, she pulled herself up and over, landing on blessed dry ground.

Leona looked up, and though her arms shook, she put her hands up.

Greyfolk surrounded her with spears and arrows pointed at her.

"Peace," she weakly said. "I come in peace."

Leona got dragged up. She heaved a breath and had to gather herself. She was so cold and her legs so tired. Her clothes and sword were inexplicably heavy.

"Leona?"

She looked up in surprise. "Artuk?"

The Greyfolk was one of the tribes leaders that had allowed Jaworek to accompany Leona through Shemal Pass. He gestured at the others. "Put your weapons down. She is a friend of the Folkvar."

When they let her go, she nearly slid to the ground, save for Artuk, who took her by the arms.

Artuk ordered the others to grab blankets. He took her to a small fire and sat her down. As she was still freezing, the fire was comforting, and the blankets wrapped around her returned some of her body's warmth.

"Sorry for that reception. We expected nobody to come from the well," Artuk said.

"Why would anybody?" Leona humorously asked.

Artuk grunted. "It's good to see somebody from the outside. It's just you, then?"

Leona nodded. "I got separated from my companions. Do you know where we are?"

"We are underneath the Bruadar. Still in the mountain, but not under it."

"Do you know how I can get back inside the Bruadar?" Leona asked.

Artuk raised a hand. "How did you find us?"

"I didn't know you were here. We were trying to cross Shemal Pass when we ended up in the Bruadar."

Artuk grunted again, and this time Leona could see the disapproval in the way his eyes narrowed. "Come with me."

Without waiting for her to answer, he led her through a series of tunnels. Leona kept her silence. She knew from experience it was futile to engage a Greyfolk in conversation when they weren't ready to talk. Better to stay silent than to say something foolish, Jaworek would remind her.

The narrow tunnel they've been following abruptly ended, and she now understood why Artuk said nothing. She wouldn't have believed it if she hadn't seen it with her own eyes.

At least a thousand Greyfolk were camped in the large cave. There were children, women, and even livestock. Makeshift shelters were scattered around haphazardly. There was a small lake on the far side where she could see children playing and women washing clothes.

The air was too warm and stifling with the odor of bodies cramped in the enclosed space. Shafts of light entered through the ceiling of the cave.

Where the sunlight hit the ground of the cave, some enterprising Greyfolk had transplanted crops.

"Why are you all here?" Leona asked.

"Traitors." Artuk grimly looked around him. "Our own people betrayed us. Many joined when the call from Bahadur came. With their own words, they came to us and said the sins of our forefathers aren't theirs to pay. When the Elders heard this foolish talk, they ordered them to rid themselves of their prideful thoughts. But the poison had already spread in their thoughts and now lived in their blood. They believed it was their task to regain the glory of our days' past. They were promised the highest honor, but first, they needed to pay the price of blood as a sacrifice to their false god—the one they call the Asshai—to ensure victory." Artuk paused and shook his head.

"How?" Leona already dreaded the answer.

"They killed all those who didn't join them. Their greatest sacrifice was when they killed the younglings of our tribe. They were in the forest to learn about our lands when they were slaughtered. By our own people."

"What happened after they attacked the children?"

"We fought them, but by then, they'd proven their zeal, and they had a whole army behind them. They attacked our tribes. We were too slow to whisk our other children and

Elders away. They had us trapped. The Bruadar was our only hope."

Leona held her hand out to Artuk, and he laid his palm against hers. "I'm sorry about the children. Apparently, the Guardians of the Hellig Mountains still care for your people."

"But now, we are also trapped. We haven't found a way out. The cave opening we went through mysteriously disappeared. It's been over a moon since we've been here."

"How have you survived this long?"

"We've eaten our horses and caught some critters living in these caves. Bats are still plentiful, but we've had to hunt deeper and deeper. The Elders had a sack of grains as an offering to the Guardians. We weren't going to eat that, but now, we've given it to those with young ones."

They arrived at a chamber where the Elders of the tribes sat in a circle. Standing behind the Elders were the warrior leaders of the tribes.

They looked like they were arguing, but Leona couldn't understand what they were saying. The guttural inflections of their language were sometimes too low for her to hear. She waited patiently with Artuk until one of the Elders acknowledged her. The Elder motioned her to step forward.

They all quieted when Leona stepped in the circle. She made the Greyfolk sign of respect to the Elders by bowing low with one hand out, palm up, while she fisted her other hand on her chest.

"You are from the Tribunal."

"Yes." She bowed respectfully to show her assent.

"You told her why we are here?" one of them asked Artuk.

"She knows why we are here, and she is saddened by our loss."

"Now it is your turn to tell us why you are here."

Leona told them what had happened. She conveyed the

desperation of their decision to brave the pass and to do it without the Elders' consent.

Leona paused, but the Elders were silent and motioned for her to continue. She told them of what they'd encountered in the pass, how she'd been separated from the rest of her companions, and how she'd ended up in the well.

"It was brave and foolish of you to take the pass," one of the Elders told her.

"We paid for it."

"It might indeed have been your only choice."

"The one you call the Watcher is also here." An Elder pointed at something hidden in the darkness. There it was, the cloaked shadow. Unmoving, but she knew it was watching and listening.

"The Watcher appeared two nights ago. We all thought it was our sign we could venture out."

Another Elder turned to her. "Why does it wait for you?"

Leona was surprised by the question. "I don't think..."

"There are no coincidences in the Bruadar. Just as the Tribunal chose you, so did the Guardians."

"There is a game being played." The only woman in the council, Bel-Delilani, looked at her with intensity. "Bigger than you or I. You are a pawn. We all are. The Guardians have granted you the privilege of your life and the lives of those worthy in your companions. They want something from you. Think on it and have a care, for everything hangs on a delicate balance."

"What do you mean?" Leona asked.

"Just that the Tribunal do not choose their members lightly nor do the Guardians of who they spare. We know. I, and all my fellow Elders, have been tested. Time and again, we put ourselves through the test until death." Bel-Delilani pointed to the cloaked shadow. "Your actions are being judged. Now have a seat. Since you have been deemed worthy, then for now, so too shall we include you in the circle."

There was a warning in there. Though the Guardians apparently had chosen her and were willing to trust her, she was still not considered part of their tribe and should not speak out of turn or impose her will on them.

Artuk stood behind Leona. She was asked to repeat the specifics of her mission and not to omit anything.

"I was tasked to make sure the High King made it to the Gathering alive. I was told that it must not be revealed."

"But then you didn't have a choice but to reveal yourself to the High King," another Elder, Kal-Ranok, pointed out.

Leona nodded.

"Before you and Artuk came, we were speculating about the reasons the Rovers and off-landers suddenly turned on us. We've traded with them before. Why now? This king you were tasked to protect has a vision to unite all the kingdoms. This has never been done before. We've seen much in our lifetimes, and your kind has always conflicted with each other. If he is successful, a unified kingdom will be one of the most powerful alliances ever formed. Do you understand the fear that this brings to all? What is our place in this? Even the Guardians are quiet."

Kal-Ranok looked at the others. "The Rovers and off-landers were very convincing that our time of supremacy is coming again. That we, the Elders, are the only thing stopping them. This Gathering brings fear, and fear has taken the innocent lives of our children."

"You can't blame the High King for this slaughter."

"We are only trying to understand what happened. This king is forcing a change, and suddenly we are at war with our own people. We are broken. Even now, we are trapped, cowering. If we go outside, we will be slaughtered."

Artuk interjected. "We can't say with certainty how big of

an army awaits us. But we can't stay here forever. Our people crowd each other, and conflicts have arisen."

"You look troubled," Bel-Delilani observed.

Leona confessed that she was. "My mission is to protect the king, and if there's an army waiting outside the pass, then his life is in danger." She pressed on. "I need your help."

"You expect us to help this king before our people?" Kal-Ranok incredulously asked.

She raised both hands up in a gesture of surrender. "Please hear me out." After he nodded, she continued. "To ensure your people's safety, you'll need help. We can work together."

"What do you propose?"

"I need help to find the king."

"The Watcher is the only thing that can help you find him. That's not something we can help with."

"Can you reason with it?"

Kal-Ranok shook his head. "Reasoning with the mountain —it may give you what you want, but it will be twisted. No. You and the king are better off finding your own paths. If he passes the test of the Bruadar, then he and his companions are free to go. Your presence won't change a thing. Do you doubt he will succeed?"

"No." Leona's reply came quickly, and she realized that she believed it. "But I need to find them."

"The Bruadar is vast. This king's life and his four companions—they're worth more than our kin?" Bel-Delilani challenged.

"No, of course not. But my mission is to keep him safe."

"We've been in the Bruadar. More times than you have. You won't find him. Therefore, we do not allow you to go back. You will help us get out of here. The Tribunal, with every child taken, has promised us that they will help in our time of need. That is now."

"But there's only me," Leona countered. "I can't possibly protect your people by myself."

"You will have to find a way."

"The Tribunal has temples scattered across Bearnas. How far is the closest one?" Kal-Ranok asked.

"Normundir." Leona sat up straighter. "What if I can send a signal to Normundir's army? If we do get out here, I can do that. But I need your help. When the king reaches the other side of the Bruadar, he and the others will be vulnerable."

Bel-Delilani cocked her head. "How do you propose we summon the army from Normundir?"

"There's a watchtower west of Shemal Pass. I think there's a beacon there that I can deploy."

The Elders spoke in a cacophony of voices.

"It sounds perilous. We're taking a gamble with our people's lives."

"Will the army of Normundir really come?"

"Even the Tribunal isn't here!"

"Our alliances have failed us."

Leona leaned forward. "Normundir will come." She said it with conviction, but they were still unconvinced.

"Do you swear on your life?" Kal-Ranok asked.

"Yes."

"We will need to consider this," Bel-Delilani said. She must have seen the impatience in Leona's face, for she added, "Don't worry. In this matter, we will not tarry. Now, rest. Unless the Watcher wakes up, then the choice is taken out of our hands." She motioned for Artuk to take Leona.

Artuk led Leona to a group of tents by the lake. Artuk introduced her to Liha, who had lost her young son and husband in the recent attacks. Liha barely paid attention to Artuk when he told her that Leona would stay with her. Grief was etched deeply on her face, and yet her strength showed in the protective way she watched her young daughter. Leona wanted to tell Artuk that she would be fine on her own, that Liha probably needed privacy to deal with her grief, but it would be an insult to turn down the offer of shelter.

When Artuk left, Leona turned to Liha and thanked her for sharing her tent, but Liha only nodded at her. She stood up and took a pot from the makeshift table, stirred its contents. She took a cup, poured some of the watery porridge from the pot, and handed it to Leona.

"Thank you," Leona said gratefully, but Liha had already turned her back and sat at the tent's entrance. Leona ate the meager dish then slept the dreamless sleep of the tired.

She woke up to the sound of children running and laughing and a woman reprimanding them to be careful. Liha and her daughter were already gone, but there was bread on the table and a glass of water.

Leona got out of the makeshift tent. The cave was an explosion of activity. Livestock was being fed, and some Greyfolk were herding children and making sure they were out of trouble. There were women cleaning and cooking on small fires. She walked on the short path to the lake and washed the last dregs of sleep from her face.

An old woman approached Leona and tentatively asked, "Leona of the Tribunal?"

Leona looked up. "Suli, mother of Jaworek," she greeted the old woman.

"I am glad to see you. Artuk told me you were here."

"I arrived hours ago."

"What of Jaworek?"

"He isn't here. Last I heard, he was in Midroska. I'm sorry, Mother, but I didn't know what happened to your people until I came here."

Suli shook her head in sadness. "It was too late when we realized the evil that has taken over their bodies." She suddenly seemed so much older.

"I'm sorry. It's good you're safe, Mother."

"It's not your fault. Are you here to help us?"

"I'll try my best."

"Thank you. Be safe."

"You as well, Mother."

Leona watched her walk away. When she got back to Liha's tent, Artuk was waiting for her. "Come with me."

"We've considered your offer. We will help you, with the guarantee you will call the army of Normundir," Bel-Delilani told Leona, who closed her eyes in relief. "We didn't reach this decision lightly. As the Guardians of the Helligs are our witness, we are putting our people's lives in your hands."

"Thank you."

"You will go to Kal-Ranok to converse with the Watcher." Bel-Delilani gestured to the Elder who stood by the cloaked shadowy figure. "We found it here three days ago. We have been trying to communicate with it since it came here."

Leona walked the path alone to where Kal-Ranok stood with the Watcher. The black figure was still. Like a statue. And yet, its cloak moved, as if a soft breeze stirred it.

"Leona." He nodded to her.

"Kal-Ranok, I hope I didn't disturb you."

"You are just in time. I've asked the Watcher to act as our guide and lead our people out of the Bruadar and into safety. The Watcher is listening. Come."

Kal-Ranok held out his hand to her and reached the other toward the cloaked shadow, without quite touching it. She took his hand and copied his gesture. Tendrils of shadowy smoke met her hand and interlaced with her fingers, going up her palm, and twining around her arm.

She stilled her mind and quieted her heart. She felt Kal-Ranok's presence in her mind, probing. Leona kept her mind blank and her emotions at bay.

Suddenly, her vision expanded. The Watcher saw everything. She even saw herself with her hand in Kal-Ranok's.

A soft roar began in the back of her head. Like the sound of a raging river, it escalated until it was all she could hear. Leona sought to cover her ears, but she couldn't move. The ground sped away from beneath her feet. Disoriented, Leona found herself standing above the Bruadar's curving roofline.

Kal-Ranok was ahead of her, looking at what the Watcher showed them. Kal-Ranok walked farther ahead until he disappeared from view.

Leona heard a whisper within the vision. She turned around to a shadow watching her.

"I've seen into you, light wielder." The shadow hissed. It stretched itself until there were eight around her.

"The great war is coming."

Leona could barely make sense of the discordant voices that spoke all at once.

"Great war?" Leona asked.

"It will decide the fate of all," they hissed.

"Granter of life. Harbinger of death. The racht. The aellaium. Defeat him. Keep them safe. Use them wisely." They hissed and whispered all around her.

"The aellaium. What is it?" she asked.

"You were its keeper."

"Anva."

Leona winced as she realized what it was they were talking about. The pendant of Queen Anva's necklace that Leona had stolen two years ago. The Tribunal had sent her to the Borderlands to find Queen Anva and to see if she still had that necklace. But then, after a few days in the nomadic queen's kingdom, Leona had realized that Queen Anva was trying to bring back her feru'talent of grabbing. It had been a spontaneous decision when Leona had taken the necklace.

"What do the racht and aellaium do?"

"Granter of life. Harbinger of death," they repeated.

"I gave the aellaium to the Elders."

Some voices laughed. Others argued.

"Tribunal."

"You side with them."

"I am of the Tribunal. I lay my allegiance with them, and we don't take sides." Even as she said it, she knew that wasn't true.

"The Tribunal," they all hissed, "is at the heart of it." The shadows grew larger until they encompassed the whole mountain. Everything was plunged into darkness. Leona gasped as the surrounding air turned into smoke.

"What do you want from me?" she asked.

"To show you a taste." Red, hot anger lashed at her, and suddenly the landscape was blood red.

Legions of the dead clawed their way out of the mountain. Just when they were about to reach her, everything disappeared, and she was back just outside the Bruadar. The shadows retreated into the mountain where they stood like sentinels.

"Wait! You didn't answer me."

A light flashed from somewhere within the mountain itself. It should have been impossible, but Leona saw it. Its beat reverberated in her chest.

A whisper hissed in her ear. "Soon, everything will depend on the choices you make."

A shadow detached itself from the mountain and rushed at her. It looked at her for a moment, and Leona willed herself to stand still and not cower.

"Why are you telling me this?" Leona asked.

"You are the key to the undoing."

Before Leona could ask what it was talking about, it suddenly rushed away as fast as it had come. She was suddenly on the highest peak of the Hellig Mountains and could see all around her. There was a small army of Greyfolk in the trees, by the northern corridor just past the Bruadar. Beyond that was Arag'nilDarahoff, the ruined city of the Greyfolk. She turned to the east and saw a big army on the central and eastern regions of the Borderlands.

Kal-Ranok climbed up the mountain toward her and trembled at the vision.

"Please," he said while he looked around. "My only plea is to keep our people safe. We've served the Hellig Mountains and the Bruadar all our lives. We've never forsaken you. Please don't abandon us in our time of need." Ranok motioned with a hand raised in supplication to implore the Guardians of the Hellig Mountains.

"Granted." The growl came from deep below them. The whole mountain sighed after the word.

When Leona blinked, she and Kal-Ranok were back in the cave. He let go of her hand and stumbled to his knees. The link between them broken, it took Leona a few moments to collect herself.

"Are you all right, Kal-Ranok?"

"I need a moment," he coughed out. "Look." He pointed at the Watcher. It moved backward into the stone, and like pieces of a puzzle, the rocks folded over themselves until they revealed a wide doorway. The shadow moved within the doorway.

Leona helped Kal-Ranok up. She took the nearest torch and followed the Watcher.

The Watcher was fast, gliding up with a whisper. Leona waited a moment for Kal-Ramon to catch up, but he motioned for her to go ahead.

She followed the shadow up a dark and cold tunnel where the damp seeped into her skin. The air, heavy with moisture, was a thick wall she waded through.

The tunnel was an endless staircase—a pilgrimage that led

higher and higher. After a while, the air was lighter and less oppressive, but the cold remained. Leona sneaked a glance behind and found Kal-Ranok wasn't too far from her. His breath revealed his struggle, but his face betrayed no emotion, and he walked stoically like he could do so forever.

The Watcher stopped in front of a stone wall and vanished like smoke. Leona laid a hand against the stone where the shadow had vanished. She pushed and it give a little. Kal-Ranok gave her a hand, and with a mighty shove, the slab of stone gave way and fell over.

Leona was suddenly blinded by a light so bright she had to cover her eyes.

When her eyes adjusted to the sun, she saw they were in a bowl-shaped clearing. It was a rocky landscape interspersed with patches of snow and sparse, hardy trees, gnarly with age. Streams from the snowmelt carved out a meandering path along the trees.

Leona looked up at the clear blue sky. She held out her hand and felt the sun touch her fingertips.

"It feels good to be outside," Kal-Ranok mused. "But we're not free yet." He turned to Leona and regarded her for a moment. "I know that you saw something while we were conversing with them. That's between you and the Guardians of the Hellig. Against my better judgment, I will heed what they want—I won't say anything to the others, but I want to give you a warning. Whatever they wanted, you have to decide if it's the right choice. Their history has twisted them. You know that. You have been here twice now. I know your allegiance is with the Tribunal, but everyone has an agenda, and everything has a cost."

"Thank you, Kal-Ranok." Though she didn't say any more, she nodded, grateful for his promised silence.

Kal-Ranok took the lead, and Leona followed him back to the cave. There, he told them what the Guardians of the

Helligs had shown them. He told them of the clearing where their people could rest and wait for the Normundir army. He also told them of Arag'nilDarahoff and the Greyfolk rebels who had laid claim to it.

Leona and Kal-Ranok led the Greyfolk through the tunnel. They walked steadily in silence. Only the children spoke now and then, but their mothers would quickly shush them. Even the animals were quiet.

Their footsteps were the one thing they couldn't hide. They shook the ground they stood on and sounded like erratic drumbeats.

When they reached the sunlight, Leona and Kal-Ranok stepped out of the way and watched the Greyfolk make their way into the clearing.

Kal-Ranok turned to Leona. "My people give you our thanks."

"It isn't over yet."

"But we are closer to righting my people's wrongs. We've been punished long enough for our impudence."

"Kal-Ranok, I apologize for the intrusion, but I need to speak with Leona," Artuk said from behind them.

"It seems I need to stop taking your time and let you get to what needs to be done." Kal-Ranok walked off, and Leona turned to face Artuk and the warriors. She counted thirty strong.

Artuk didn't waste time with pleasantries. "Come. Kal-Ranok said the Guardians showed you what lies outside the pass."

Leona told them of the army that camped along the northern corridor of the pass and the small patrol that scouted the areas outside the army's scope. When she finished, Artuk talked to one of the Greyfolk warriors, who left with two others.

"Artuk, I need to send that beacon to Normundir. Can you...perhaps send a few of your men to look for the king?"

"The Bruadar is vast, Leona. Our Elders have told you that they must make their way through its challenges. I'm sorry. But we gave our word to you to look out for them should they make it out alive. We can handle it from here. Just keep your end of the bargain."

"I will." She reluctantly nodded. "They will make it out. Keep them safe."

✳ 10 ✳

eona hiked up to the highest point in the trail. She climbed until she saw the tops of the lower peaks.

It took a while, but she saw it now, a lone tower that blended with the mountaintop. Abandoned ages ago, it stood, a sentinel barely ravaged by time.

She climbed down and walked along the rocky path from where the trail ended. A Greyfolk warrior suddenly surprised her by appearing out of nowhere. He showed her a narrow trail that traversed the side of the mountain.

After a treacherous climb down, she slipped at the bottom of the trail and nearly ran into a patrol of Greyfolk riding nearby. She steered clear of their path and trekked through an old riverbed, following the path until she reached the foot of the neighboring mountain.

Leona looked up and steeled herself. It would be a steep climb in the freezing dark.

Hours into her climb, with only the moon as her guide, she finally reached the lookout tower.

It still looked the same.

She'd once been here. Years ago, with her father. He'd

shown her the watchtowers across the Borderlands. He'd had her memorize each one of them and where its flares were hidden—especially the abandoned watchtowers. He'd also taught her which color to use depending on what situation she was in.

Leona carefully made her way up the spiral staircase. Thin slits of light shone through the cracks in the stone. When Leona reached the circular room at the top, she counted six windows. Other than a table, chair, and chest, the room was sparsely decorated. Leona laid her sword and pack on the table. She walked to the third window and looked outside. She grabbed the ledge and stepped off to the right onto a small landing. Perched on it, she counted the rectangular stones on the wall, just above her head. When she reached the third, she felt for the notch hidden in the stone and pushed on it. The stone moved forward.

Leona pried it from the wall and placed it on the ledge. She then pulled out a black wooden box from the hidden shelf. As wide as her palm and longer than her forearm, it was heavier than she remembered.

She clambered into the room and sat in front of the table. She took her necklace off. Hanging in the middle dangled a silver tube. The tube was thin and as long as her thumb, and the workmanship made it shine as brightly as if it had crystals embedded in it.

Leona took the tube and laid the chain on the table. She pressed hard on the loop at the top until she heard a click. The necklace opened into four different sections with notches that poked out from all sides. She twisted the sections until she had the right configuration, and it looked like a key.

Leona inserted the key into the lock of the black wooden box. She turned left, then right twice before it clicked, and the lid opened to reveal four flares—two blue and two white. She picked one of each color and closed the box.

Strange lights were attributed to the pass, and Leona hoped that these would be treated as a couple more. She opened the chest and, ignoring the stack of red flares, took the flint and the long bow.

Leona climbed up to the roof, took the white flare, and propped it against the low wall, away from the wind. She took several tries with the flint before the flare lit up. She notched the flare into the bow, took aim, and released it.

The flare flew up in a swoosh, and as it started its descent, it flared into a bright white light. She shot the blue flare next. Leona stared at it and marveled at the sight. It looked like a star falling from the sky.

Leona held her breath and waited.

An answering blue flare shot up in the distance. Leona climbed down from the rooftop. She was sorely tempted to stay and rest, but she needed to get back.

A bright moonlight illuminated her path as she back-tracked to the Greyfolk. The explosion of stars and the rustling breeze kept her company. It was faster this time. She arrived at the Greyfolk camp just as the sun rose.

The warriors stationed at the trail greeted her with a curt nod when she entered the clearing. Leona found a small stream and splashed cold water on her face to wake herself up.

"You should rest," Artuk said from behind her. "We've seen no sign of the king. I have men stationed to watch the known doorway."

"I'll go—"

"You have to rest."

After a moment's pause, Leona conceded. "You're right. It's just...it's my responsibility that I'm handing over to you."

"We have a bargain. You've kept your end, I presume, and sent word to Normundir?"

"Yes. They've responded and will send an army."

"Then it's for us to keep our end of the bargain. Rest, Leona. We'll keep an eye out for your king."

Leona woke up to clear blue skies and the sun beating down on her. She'd only been gone for a night, but she felt like she'd been away for a week. She turned and found a young Greyfolk seated by her.

"Good morning." She looked at him in question.

"I'm supposed to watch you until you wake up and lead you to Artuk."

"Training?" Leona asked.

"I'm to make sure you're safe while you sleep."

"How long have you been watching me?"

"Long enough to do nothing."

Leona couldn't help it. She took her time and watched the boy struggle to stay still. Leona had to admire him. He tried his best to look disinterested but failed miserably. The boy stared glumly at everything around him.

Artuk finally tapped him on the shoulder. "You're supposed to watch her, not the sky, you idiot."

The boy suddenly stood at attention and firmly fixed his gaze on Leona.

"What's the use?" Artuk shook his head. "The Elders need help. Go."

Leona stood up. "Any sighting?"

"Nothing, but I can show you where we've been keeping the watch."

۞

DOYLE WALKED IN THE REAR THROUGH THE VAST MAZE OF the Bruadar. Carvings and faded murals filled the walls they passed. There was no conversation among them, just a grim determination to find their way out. He brooded as they made their way. Why didn't she call for help when she saw the creature? Why didn't he wake up before it was too late?

Something skittered behind him. He stopped and turned. Something leaped from the darkness and landed on top of him. It looked like one of the black-skinned creatures they'd encountered in the corridor. As small as a child, its thin limbs were leathery. It had no hair, its eyes were a pearly white, and its mouth was filled with sharp silver teeth.

Fast and feral, it tried to take a bite out of Doyle's neck. He kicked it away and rolled away from the creature. Colm stabbed it with his sword, and it shrieked in pain.

More shrieks answered from behind them. The sound echoed until it felt like it surrounded them.

Colm shone his torch toward the hallway. The creatures filled it. They ran on every surface.

Colm and Doyle shot arrows, but they didn't slow the creatures down.

Edward led them through the nearest doorway. Inside was a square-shaped stairwell. They ran up as the creatures jumped from balustrade to balustrade.

When they reached the top, they ran through the doorway and shut it to the shrieking creatures. The door banged against its hinges as the creatures slammed against it.

They were on a wide balcony overlooking a crumbling garden. It spread out before them, with broken statues and decrepit fountains overgrown with vegetation. The muted light of the sun shone from a sky full of clouds.

Pillars supported the curved ceiling above them. The balustrade was waist high and cold to the touch. To their right, a long balcony was carved into the mountain, sections of it in ruins.

"Where are we?" Alik asked.

"Outside...somewhere facing north," Gage replied.

Doyle followed Colm over to the balustrade. "How are you holding up?"

Colm rubbed his face with his hands. "I worry about Gawen. Whether we've lost him. And Leona—I can't believe she's gone."

Doyle patted Colm on the shoulder. "We'll give her a burial when we get back. Even without her body, it'll mean something."

Colm sat down, leaned against the balustrade, and closed his eyes. Doyle let him be. The boy was brooding but there was not much he could do about it.

Doyle unstrapped Leona's pack from his back and laid it on the ground. Taking her sword, he looked at it in the light. It had shallow symbols carved on both sides of the blade. The weight was evenly distributed and surprisingly light. The hilt was simple, nondescript. He lightly ran his fingers on the symbols.

"What do they mean?" Edward asked.

"They're prayers for the dead and for the bearer of the sword," Doyle replied. "The swords were a gift to her. When the blacksmith asked her to name them, she asked for a prayer instead. It's in the old language of the Greyfolk."

After a beat of silence, Doyle continued. "I've known Leona since she was adopted; even taught her for a while."

"I want the truth." Edward paused. "Why was Leona chosen for this mission?"

"Are you asking me if she was ordered to seduce you?"

"Yes."

"As far as she was concerned, she only had one mission."

"But you have your doubts."

Doyle didn't pretend to misunderstand. "She had no ulterior motives, but I'm not sure if my masters did," Doyle admitted.

Doyle waited until Edward had left before he sat down, the balustrade against his back. He took his sword and laid it on his lap, his hand on the hilt. Amidst the shrieking and the pounding on the door, he closed his eyes. Truth was, he blamed Edward, Gage, and himself. He blamed this whole mountain for taking her. She was the closest thing he had to a daughter.

❧

Edward drifted into a light state of sleeping. Tendrils of sand and stone rose behind him. They crept until they found his wrist. They snaked up his arm and tightened their grip.

He found himself dreaming of blood and death. Of a far away place that was a thousand shades of gold—of sand, sun, and gold-domed palaces. Countless men brutally murdered because of him. A woman, a nameless lover who'd comforted him but was killed before his eyes.

"Death follows you." Her mouth spilled blood as she said this. "It strikes all around you. You live because we died."

The darkness swallowed her. Edward stretched a hand out. The darkness was a solid figure in front of him. Death in its shadow cloak. "How many must shed blood before you wake up to the truth." Its cold formless hand gripped Edward's wrist. "You've always known the price. Your life and they shall live."

Jon, Niall, Simon, Corbin, and Leona. They flashed before his eyes. Death's face ever changing. "It's not too late for them. I can bring them back."

"This isn't real. Nothing can bring the dead back. You think me a fool?"

"How about them?" Death showed him Gage's, Alik's, Doyle's, and Colm's deaths. One by one, they succumbed to the forces that dwelled in the shadows of this cursed land. All for Edward to live. "It can stop right here. One death to save many."

Edward felt a clutch in his throat. His breath caught. The lessons he'd learned in Bahadur were etched in every scar on his body. As long as he lived for another day, the death and blood were worth it. But he'd never really believed that. If he had, then he'd be at peace with himself.

"Was she worth your life?" Death's face became Leona's.

Edward was standing in the courtyard as she was getting sucked into the ground. He lurched after her.

Edward was close. Close enough that their fingertips touched, and then her hand was in his grip. He tried to pull her back, but her hand slipped from his. She disappeared, and he tried digging through the sand.

A shadow passed behind him and spoke. "I'm all alone in the dark."

He turned, but nobody was there.

Another shadow passed on his other side. "I'm waiting for you."

Another shadow passed by. "I'm trapped. Find me."

They were all Leona's voice.

Edward lurched forward when the ground beneath him shifted. Something grabbed his feet and dragged him into the ground.

He couldn't breathe. He couldn't see. Rocks and dirt scraped against his face during his descent. Suddenly, he was free, and he landed hard on the ground.

Edward stood up and saw Leona. He called out to her, but she didn't hear him. They were in a tunnel, and though he could see her, it was clear that she was in total darkness. Her fear was palpable as she groped her way in the tunnel.

Edward woke up with a start. With his heartbeat thundering in his head, he glanced around. Everyone else was awake, but in their own spaces.

It was a deception. That's what this place was about, he reasoned with himself.

They were all dead. Even Leona.

Restless, he called out to Alik, who was closest to the door.

"Any sound?"

Alik shook his head. "All is silent."

Edward rubbed a hand on his face. His eyes were gritty from exhaustion.

Doyle laid a hand on Edward's shoulder. "Are you all right?"

"I saw Leona. Scared, but alive."

"A dream?" Doyle queried.

"What else could it have been?"

Everyone looked at each other. The realization hit them all. Doyle looked down and a humorless laugh escaped him. "Our dreams have fooled us. Alas, we didn't say anything because we didn't want to look the fool."

Edward turned around. He gripped the balustrade and looked out at the garden. Even he hadn't been honest about what he'd dreamt about.

Something moved below. Curious, Edward leaned forward. The tall grass slightly moved. He followed its progress as it approached ever closer.

A four-legged animal emerged, sniffing its way out of the grass. A long and frightful shadow on the ground, it was unlike any creature Edward had ever seen.

Edward put a finger in front of his lips and motioned for Doyle and the others to look below.

The creature's skin was mottled black and gray. Its long-limbed body moved unnaturally low on the ground. It was still looking down, sniffing. It looked left, then right.

Suddenly, it looked up. It had a grotesque version of a man's face. Its hands and feet ended in sharp claws that made marks on the ground below.

The creature crawled to the wall and reached. It stood on its legs as it investigated the wall with its hands.

Doyle stepped back and in a hushed tone, he said, "Leona told me she fought creatures that looked like men. She said they were very strong—nothing could harm them. Nor do they feel pain. She had to face them alone after she and Jaworek were separated."

"How do we fight them?" Gage asked. "My ferum's empty, and so is Alik's."

"We need to cut their heads off," Doyle explained. "Leona told me that once they're riled, they're fast. And very angry."

More of them emerged from the grass. A creature started to climb the wall, but it kept slipping down. Another one found a foothold, and it climbed higher than the last. It climbed and climbed, finding small cracks to hold on to. It was a long way up, but it climbed steadily.

Edward walked to the door and put his ear against it. Something rammed against it, startling him.

Alik and Colm shot arrows at the creature, but it kept climbing up, the arrows stuck on its body.

Just then, another creature climbed over the balcony and ran at them. Alik was the first on its path. He swung his sword and cut its arm off. It opened its mouth and screamed, its breath stale, its eyes bloodshot.

Alik swung his sword again and cut its head off, but it was too late. The silence had been broken.

Suddenly, the grass was alive. Hundreds of the creatures made a desperate run toward the balcony, climbing on top of one another.

The men shot arrows down at the creatures, but as soon as they landed on the ground, they got up and climbed again.

"This is futile," Gage said.

"Look, it's back." Colm pointed at the distance, past the horde of creatures. A cloaked shadow stood still. The Watcher.

"And still, it does nothing." Alik tried to light the arrows on fire, but he was drained of feru'talent.

Edward stared at the Watcher. He knew why it was here. To see if he'd fulfill the deal that Death had offered in his dream.

Edward pointed to the balcony on their right. "Go. I still have some fire left. I'll cover your backs."

Colm swung himself over the balustrade and stealthily made his way through the ruins. He tied one end of the rope on a pillar and threw the rest over to Alik, who also tied it to a pillar.

"Go!" Alik screamed.

Gage was the first. He took his cloak, swung it over the rope, and held on to each end with both hands. He leaped and slid to the other end. One by one, everyone followed, except for Edward.

He'd test this Watcher himself.

"Keep going. Don't follow me," Edward ordered before he jumped from the tower.

The fall seemed to last for an eternity. The creatures, seeing him, tumbled down. They cascaded in their hurry, like a waterfall. Edward focused on the nearing ground. With a blast of fire, he jarred himself upward and slowed his fall.

Edward looked up to where his men were. None of the creatures were trying to get at them. He spread his flames out, burning many of the creatures before he landed on the ground. Edward muted his flames until they were a thin barrier on his skin, his clothes, and his sword. A long time ago, before he had any control over his fire, he would have burned off all his clothes. But now, the trickle of feru'talent was second nature to him. He didn't have enough in him to burn every single one of the feral creatures that circled him. So he'd conserve until he had nothing left.

If there was something he'd learned well in Bahadur—it was to fight and kill mercilessly. When they surged toward him, he was ready. He fought without fear.

Time passed. Edward didn't know how long he'd been fighting. When his flames died out, he fought on, bodies piling around him.

A dagger whizzed past him and boomeranged through the monsters in front of him. He snapped his head back, surprised to find Gage and Alik just behind him, Doyle at their rear.

"Don't you ever follow orders?" Edward asked Gage.

"You wouldn't have hired me if I blindly did," Gage retorted. "It took a while, but they were focused on you. Barely paid attention to us."

As the feral horde thinned, Gage gestured toward the elevated balcony where Colm waited for them. As they ran for the ropes that Colm had prepared, something huge ran into the swathe of creatures that pursued them. A pack of wolves, bigger than the wild dogs they'd encountered in Shemal Pass, surged through and aimed for Colm and the others.

They barely made it up the rope before the wolves were biting at their heels. They made it up into the long balcony and ran down its seemingly endless length. Colm nearly fell at a drop-off, where a section of the balcony and the adjacent building lay in ruins below.

They clambered through the rubble and boulders, the other side of the balcony just ahead of them. The wolves growled and barked at them, trying to climb up to where they were.

Colm made it first. He was soon followed by Edward, Alik, and Gage.

The biggest wolf in the pack jumped up and narrowly missed Doyle as he made his way to the other side.

Another wolf landed behind Doyle. Colm shot it with an arrow to the neck, while Gage stabbed it with his sword and killed it. Suddenly, four wolves jumped into the balcony.

The biggest of the pack ran at them and swiped at Alik, who hit the wall and fell unconscious.

The wolf, sensing victory, pounced at Alik to finish him, but Edward lunged at the wolf. They grappled and rolled around on the ground.

The wolf pinned him to the ground. The pressure eased when an arrow found its way into its flank. The wolf howled in pain. Edward rolled away and jumped on his feet. The wolf chased Edward. It showed no signs of slowing down amidst the shower of arrows.

Edward swung out of the balcony, and using a pillar as a handhold, he swung back and lunged at the wolf as it jumped at him. The wolf bit him on his left shoulder and penetrated through the thick hard leather of Edward's armor.

Edward stabbed with a dagger at its mouth. The wolf howled, and Edward drove his sword into the wolf's exposed chest.

"Did it get you?" Doyle asked.

Edward's shoulder throbbed with the sharp pain from the wolf's bite, but they had to keep moving. He shook his head. "No, it only caught my armor."

"Its bite is poisonous." Doyle nudged the wolf's head. Its open mouth had rows and rows of teeth. Dark-green venom oozed from its gums.

The other three wolves, seeing the biggest of them killed, ran away, and leaped off the balcony.

"Look." Colm pointed at the man-like creatures gaining ground just behind the wolves.

They ran to the end and reached a doorway that led to a stairwell. Down in a spiral, they went until they arrived at a big hall. It was so large it astounded them. Pillars high as far as the eye could see were aplenty. Light came in through skylights carved into the ceiling. Ahead, in the far distance, were grand double doors.

Steps led up to the biggest and grandest doors they had ever seen. Made of gold, they rose before them. On each side stood a silver sentinel, giant statues so high their faces could barely be seen.

They tried to open the door, but they couldn't budge it. Edward, Gage, and Alik stood guard, just in case the creatures followed them inside. Doyle stepped back and, after some searching, found pulleys cleverly hidden in the sentinels' legs. Doyle and Colm turned the pulley. The door slid and opened to the blinding sun.

They walked out into blue skies and pine trees. The air smelled fresh and sweet. The sunlight and the cold breeze were like a drink of water after being parched.

The door slid shut behind them with a loud boom.

A moment later, the loud blast of a horn resounded, and a thunder of hooves came rolling in. Before they could retreat into the Bruadar, they were surrounded by Greyfolk on horses. Stripes of red were painted on their rough skins.

Edward and the others backed toward each other, swords drawn.

A large Greyfolk urged his horse forward. "Who are you?" he asked menacingly.

"We are travelers on a journey to Arag'nilDarahoff," Doyle answered.

"Nobody travels through the Bruadar. The truth."

"We heard there's treasure in the Bruadar. We came to seek it."

"And did you find any?"

Doyle shook his head. "My comrades remind me we have our lives, and those alone, we can consider as treasure."

"Do you know it's punishable by death to trespass into our lands without my people's permission?"

"And that is why, with your permission, we plan to make our way into Arag'nilDarahoff to offer our apologies, make peace with the Elders, and hopefully have a taste of the famous Greyfolk beer."

"Do you think this is funny?"

"Well...somewhat. It's funny there're only five of us and, what, fifty of you? Don't you think that's overkill?"

Some soldiers in the enemy ranks snickered in laughter. The Greyfolk looked around, and the snickers immediately stopped.

"I am sentencing you and your companions to death."

"Wait." Doyle held a hand up. "Don't we at least deserve to be heard by the Elders in Arag'nilDarahoff? It's only a short ride from here."

"Silence! Arag'nilDarahoff is no more. I have vowed to rid this land of all traces of those weak traitors. However, I can be merciful and grant you a swift and painless death. If you tell me who helped you in the Bruadar and if you tell me what you saw. No man can survive here without a Greyfolk's help," he arrogantly said.

"The Guardians of the Helligs took pity on us—" Doyle started.

"I told you not to test me," the Greyfolk interrupted. "I know you're lying. You're lying about why you're all here, and now you're also lying about not having any help."

"If you will kill us anyway, does it matter?" Doyle raised an eyebrow.

Edward signaled to Doyle. He wanted to talk to this Greyfolk.

"To me, yes," Edward said.

"Quiet, man," Doyle reprimanded.

"No. Let him talk," the Greyfolk ordered. "I can be merciful and grant you all a quick death, but to live...that might be an option I'm willing to think about."

Edward stepped forward. "Give me a guarantee."

"Do I look like I negotiate with weakling scum like you?"

"All right then." Edward reared back and shot his dagger at the Greyfolk's horse's eye. The horse went crazy and kicked at everything as the Greyfolk tried to gain control of his steed.

"Run back," Doyle warned Edward and their other companions before he used his feru'talent of whispering into minds to strike at the horses. His particular talent was more geared for people's minds, but he didn't need to be refined. He just needed to confuse the closest horses to them.

The horses bucked and roared—a shrill sound of anger. They went crazy, trying to throw their riders off of them.

"What the...?" Before the Greyfolk leader could react, his horse had already thrown him off. The horse reared on its hind legs, kicking at the Greyfolk.

As Edward, Doyle, and the others ran back for the Bruadar, suddenly a rain of arrows fell from the sky and shot at the Greyfolk.

Amidst the horses in the front lines bucking and screaming, more arrows rained down. Edward looked up at the direction of the flying arrows and saw a whole line of Greyfolk up on the mountain charging down on them.

"We're fucked," Colm yelled.

"Wait!" Doyle pointed up. "Look!"

Leona, along with Artuk and the other Greyfolk warriors, ran down the side of the mountain shooting arrows at the army, while those who were on the top of the cliff shot at the middle and rear of the Greyfolk contingent.

"Let's turn back and fight, then," Edward said. Without waiting for Leona, he and the others turned back to the fray.

It was a bloody battle. Greyfolk against Greyfolk. It was chaos. Dust and horses swirled around the battlefield.

❧ 11 ❧

When the fighting was done and in the silence that followed the clash of weapons, Leona stood where she was with her weapons still in hand. She looked at the dust-filled mist, eerie in the redness of the sunset.

Shadows of men formed in the haze. Edward was the first to step forward. Bloodied, but alive.

Edward stopped a step away from her. "You're still alive."

"You made it." Leona couldn't help her wide smile of relief.

Edward looked her over. "Did you ever doubt it?"

"Still arrogant and full of yourself, I see."

He quirked a brow. "Thank you for the rescue."

"My, my, how we've come so far."

Artuk stepped forward and bowed. "You must be King Edward?"

"And you are one of our saviors. My thanks."

"I am Artuk, leader of the Sukn'arag tribe."

Leona turned to see Doyle looking at her in disbelief. "You're alive! But how?"

Colm grabbed Leona in a hug. "It's really you! How did you survive?"

"It's a long story. Did they mention another army?" She gestured at the slain bodies on the field.

Doyle scowled. "Their leader said nothing. He was more concerned about the survivors of Arag'nilDarahoff, who I assume, were the ones who helped us?"

Leona nodded. "They're up in the mountain. The Guardians of the Helligs showed me a vision. There's another army, bigger than this one, and they're just a day's ride away. I sent a signal to Normundir. But they'll encounter the Grey-folk army before they get here."

"I say we ride there," Colm said.

Leona nodded. "We'll ask Artuk if they have spare horses for us."

She turned and watched Edward and Artuk. The Greyfolk was gesturing up the mountain when Edward grimaced, clutched his shoulder, and pitched forward. Artuk caught him as Leona rushed to their side.

Edward's shoulder bled profusely, and his face was ashen pale. Leona, with Gage's help, took Edward's leather armor off. The tip of a broken spear was embedded in his shoulder, but it was the color of the skin around the wound that worried her. It was dark gray and veins of dark green had spread from the wound.

"Venom." Artuk looked at one of his warriors, who shook his head. "Murthu got stabbed in the leg, and he's walking just fine."

"There were wolves in the pass. One of them bit him, but he didn't seem hurt." Doyle knelt down beside Leona.

Leona investigated the wound. "It could have been a broken tooth, and the spear could have pushed it in. We need to do something. Artuk, do you have anything for this?"

"My apologies, Leona, but this requires a skilled healer. Ours were killed while we were trying to escape."

Leona nodded and then turned to Doyle. "I need to take him to Storwood." It was a small village in the far north, small enough and poor enough that nobody ever bothered its residents.

Gage and Alik wanted to accompany Edward, but Leona was adamant she take him alone. Leona reminded them they would attract more attention.

"They won't be suspicious with a man and wife traveling to their home," she told them. "The longer we argue about this, the longer we prolong his agony."

"I'll go with her. Alone." It was the first time he'd spoken since they'd seen his wound. Every word seemed to drain him of his strength.

Gage and Alik reluctantly agreed after Colm volunteered to follow them at a distance.

"The Elder gods watch you, Leona," Doyle said as they watched Leona ride away with Edward.

She rode hard under the darkening sky. Once they reached the boundary of the Greyfolk lands, they separated from her friends. She sped on as fast as her horse could take them. Through the night, they raced. Forests and fields hurried by. Eventually, light broke through, and the sun rose. Still, they rode. Edward's breath was labored, and he leaned heavily against her.

"Hold on," she told him.

They broke through the trees and arrived at a small clearing. In the middle stood a small stone house with a thatched roofed. Smoke trailed out of the chimney. Sheep looked up at them with disinterest as Leona brought the horse to a stop in front of the stone fence.

Leona helped Edward from the horse. She struggled

under his weight as she dragged him through the small wooden gate.

"Where...?" he asked with bleary eyes.

"This is Margret's house. She is a healer who used to work in the temple in Normundir. When I was a child she looked after me."

Leona pounded on the door. "Nam! It's me, Leona."

An old woman opened the door. She had a stout figure she covered with a brown wool shawl. Her gray hair was pulled in a hurried bun that left wavy tendrils around her face. She looked at the man who leaned against Leona.

"Please help him."

She helped Leona support Edward. They took him to a small room with a fireplace and laid him on the bed. "Show me."

Leona peeled off his coat, leather armor, and tunic. "I didn't take the shaft out. It might increase the bleeding."

Margret looked at the dark veins and bruising around the wound. The dark veins had spread to his wrist and were creeping to his chest.

"Wolves from Arag'nilDarahoff?" Margret said.

"From the Bruadar. He didn't seem seriously hurt."

Margret touched the skin around the spearhead on Edward's shoulder. At the base of it were small white shards—tooth fragments that stuck out from the wound. "I need to gather a few things. Put a thin blanket under his shoulder. Start a fire, too."

Margret left the room as Leona took the rest of Edward's tunic off. Leona went to the fireplace and started a fire. She took a while since her hands were shaking.

Margret came back with a pot full of water and put it on the fire. She also brought with her a jar of leeches and pieces of long cloth she put in the water.

"Hold him down. This will be very painful."

Leona scooted to the other side of the bed and sat beside Edward.

Margret took the leeches from the jar and put them on the vein on his wrist and on his chest around the wound. She then took the broken spear from his wound. Dark blood gushed out, so dark it was almost black. The pain must have been unbearable because his body buckled and his arms thrashed.

"The venom makes the pain worse. I'd try to take the pain away and make the blood flow faster without the leeches, but that would use my ferum up. Keep him still."

Leona took his face in her hands. "Edward. Look at me."

He tried to focus his eyes on her. "Leona? You're alive?"

"Stay still. You injured your shoulder, and Nam is trying her best to help you."

"I saw you in the tunnels, and I left you to die there."

"I was, but now I'm here. We're not at the Bruadar anymore." Leona pushed his hair out of his eyes and took his hand in hers. She put her other hand on his chest and held him down. "This will be painful. I'm sorry."

He closed his eyes, then nodded. Leona looked at Margret. "He's ready."

Margret laid her hands lightly above the wound. He barely moved, but he struggled. Oh, how he struggled. His muscles bunched under her hand, and his hand clenched hers. "I'm working on destroying the venom. You'll see it breaking down by the lightening of the veins," Margret explained. There was barely any effort in her stance, but sweat broke across her forehead.

After a long, long time, Margret finally stopped. She smiled with satisfaction before she began her work of meticulously plucking the shards of wolf tooth until there was nothing left. The bleeding had lessened, and the blood trickling was a dark red, instead of black. Margret took a long strip of cloth from the pot of boiling water and stuffed it in the open wound. She prodded the leeches she had attached to him, and they fell off, dead. She threw them in a bucket, then took more leeches and put them around the wound and on his wrist. They died, just like the first batch. She kept doing it again and again until the leeches didn't die and detached themselves engorged and full, but alive.

Edward's skin was still pale, but his breathing was less labored. By this time, he was exhausted from fighting the pain and from the loss of blood; he succumbed to a troubled sleep.

Margret took the saturated strip of cloth and replaced it with a new one. "We must keep this in his wound to ensure all the venom is drained out. When his blood is clean, it will be a true red. The wound will heal fast since that is what the venom does. It seals the skin to keep the venom inside the body. It was a good thing the spearhead was left there. It kept the wound open."

Margret laid a hand on Leona's shoulder. "You have to rest."

"Not yet."

"Leona, he'll be fine. The worst is over. I'll keep an eye on him. You are of no use to him exhausted as you are."

Leona stood up and hugged Margret. "Thank you."

"You're welcome, child."

◈

LEONA GOT UP FROM THE FLOOR AND STRETCHED OUT THE kinks in her body. For the past three nights, since she and Edward had gotten there, she'd been sleeping on the floor. Her days were filled with errands for Margret, some of them backbreaking labor.

The crackling fire and the bright sun that shone through

the small window made the room hot. She folded the blankets she'd layered on the floor before turning her gaze to Edward. He was still asleep. His breathing was deeper and steadier than in the past few days.

Leona sat down on the bed and put a hand on his forehead. He was warm, but not burning anymore. She ran her fingers down his cheek.

He'd lost weight, making his face gaunt. She took her hand away and turned, only to have her wrist trapped in his hand.

"Don't stop on my account." Edward's deep voice was raspy.

She looked up and met his eyes.

"Had your fill?" His eyes were amused.

"You're still an ass."

"Ah, there's the Leona I know. Can you help me sit up?" Edward let her wrist go, and she helped him up. She would have pulled the blanket up, but he stopped her. She fluffed the pillow behind him and made sure he was comfortable. His chest had a lot of faint scars that she hadn't really noticed until now.

Edward looked under the sheet and raised an eyebrow.

She caught the look and rolled her eyes. "Get your mind out of the gutter."

"How long have I been here?"

"Three days. How do you feel?"

"Like I've been pummeled over and over again."

There was a knock on the door before it opened. Margret stepped into the room and frowned when she saw the two of them. Leona smiled at her and stood up. "He's all yours."

Margret pulled aside the blanket on his shoulder, looked at his wound, nodded, then put the blanket back. "How are you?"

"Tired. Hungry. Thirsty."

"Of course you are. I'll get you something to eat and drink."

Edward reached up to touch his shoulder.

Margret stern voice turned soft. "It'll heal soon. Once I remove the strips of cloth, it will close immediately."

Edward didn't look all too sure, but he nodded. "Thank you for your help. One other question. Who are you?"

Leona grimaced. "My manners are lacking. This is Margret, she's a healer who used to work in the temple in Normundir."

Once Edward was done eating, Margret came back in the room. "How are you after eating? Are you dizzy?"

"No, I'm better than I thought I would be."

"That's a good sign." Margret took the blanket off his shoulder. Dried blood caked the cloth under it. "I'll take the strip of cloth out of your wound. It won't hurt at all, but it will feel strange."

Blood gushed out when Margret was done. She inspected the flow and told Leona to press on the wound with a clean piece of cloth. When the bleeding eased, she took another clean piece of cloth and put that on the wound. She then covered the whole thing by wrapping another set of long strips of cloth around Edward's chest.

"There. All done. It should close soon. Try not to exert too much effort in the next few days. Rest, food, and water is what you need."

"Can I take him for a walk?" Leona asked.

"I suppose fresh air will also help. Listen to your body," she told Edward. "Make sure he doesn't get tired. He lost a lot of blood, and his body needs to make up for that loss," she reminded Leona.

Edward was winded, even with just the short walk around Margret's land. He'd asked Leona what had happened, and she told him everything, even her battle with the boy she'd once killed.

"I don't know if I can still grab people's feru'talent, and I haven't tried since then."

"I'll have to keep working on you," he said after a moment.

"You're stingy with your approval."

"Is that what you want from me?" Edward asked.

"No, but I do want to know what the Bruadar tested you with?"

Edward was silent for such a long time that Leona thought he wasn't going to answer. When he finally did, it wasn't what she thought he would say.

"My men dying for me." He gave a small chuckle. "I jumped in the middle of those half-human, half-beast creatures. I thought I'd give Gage and the others time to escape."

"But they followed you instead?"

"They never listen."

Leona smiled at that. "Let's take you back home. I don't want to have to carry you."

By the time they got back, Edward was so tired, he immediately fell asleep. Leona stayed out with Nam until sundown. Edward was still asleep when went in the room.

She quickly changed and laid the blankets down on the floor before she, too, fell asleep. She must have only dozed for a short time before she was jerked awake by Edward's voice.

"Leona, wake up."

She rubbed her gritty eyes. "Do you need anything?"

"What are you doing on the floor?"

"What does it look like?"

"Must not be comfortable."

"It will be, once you stop talking and let me sleep." Leona

burrowed into her blanket and turned. She groaned, forgetting that she wasn't on a bed.

"Get up and get in the bed."

"Absolutely not," Leona replied. She heard a rustling in the bed that she could only assume was Edward moving to make room for her.

"If you're going to be my mother hen, you might as well be comfortable doing it."

"I can sleep in the kitchen."

"Come to the damn bed. I won't touch you."

As if she'd want him to. She rolled her eyes. "Go back to sleep, Edward."

He continued nagging her. "I won't be able to sleep if you stay there. You're making me uncomfortable. Even my servants don't sleep on the floor."

Leona huffed a breath and stood up. She got into the bed, but it wasn't that big, and they were shoulder to shoulder.

"Now, that wasn't bad, was it?"

"Just strange," Leona muttered. But Edward was already asleep.

❦

THE NEXT DAY, EDWARD INSISTED ON GOING FOR ANOTHER walk. This time, Leona took him through a nearby trail that led to a small village.

"I've been meaning to give this back." She handed Simon's ferum beads to Edward. "I don't need them anymore. Thank you."

"Are you sure?"

"There isn't anything left. You should give it to someone who could use it."

He nodded and took the ferum from her. "When you wield someone else's feru'talent, can you feel them?"

Leona looked up at Edward, but all she saw was sincerity in his question. "Yes. Just the essence. I can tell if it's man or a woman. Even a little bit about who they are. How it feels to be around them—like a scent."

He pocketed the beads, but then he took his ring off and handed it to her. "Practice with this."

"I can't." She pushed his hand away. "It might run out. You don't have enough strength to…"

"It won't run out," he assured her and forced the ring on her. Without it in his hand, he summoned fire. It stayed longer than it should have, especially with him not regaining his strength yet.

Leona experimented—not with his fire, but with her own feru'talent. She summoned ice, but only a snowflake appeared.

Edward laughed. "That was admittedly pathetic. Why don't you work with the fire?"

Leona clenched the ring on her hand and opened her other hand, palm up. Nothing happened.

"It's the fear," Edward said. "It will always be there. You have to deal with it."

"Easy for you to say," Leona muttered.

"Keep practicing," he ordered her.

But still nothing came out of her.

"How did you summon metalforce in the Bruadar?" Edward asked.

"I wasn't ready to die. And the other time, I was pissed off at you."

"Since your life's not at stake at this moment, that's not going to work."

"Don't worry, you're starting to annoy me," Leona reassured him. "Here, why don't you take it back?"

"No."

Without saying a word, Leona took off her necklace and

summoned what was left of her ice She let frost form on the ground she stood on. When she'd emptied her ferum, she handed it to Edward. "I'd feel better if you replenish this with fire."

He nodded with reluctance and looked at the necklace. He fingered the pendant with curiosity. "Is this a key of some sort?"

"Yes, but not for anything special."

They walked on in silence. Leona weaved her fingers through the golden grass that bordered the path. It was nearly as high as her waist and danced with the wind. She turned her gaze up to the clear blue sky. "Isn't this amazing? I love this place. No dangers or expectations. The world is mine, and it's perfect just the way it is."

At Edward's silence, she turned to look at him. He was looking at her with a perplexed expression on his face. He cleared his throat. "I saw you in the village in the Borderlands."

"If I recall, you were demanding an answer from me."

"I saw everything," he explained.

"Why did you interrogate me, then?" she teased.

"Because I wanted to know why you did it." A smile hovered on the side of his mouth. "Because you were beautiful, remarkable, and pissy."

Leona never thought of herself as beautiful. Maybe more than passable. But never beautiful. Hearing him say that made her uncomfortable. "Not so much anymore?" she asked to diffuse the feeling.

"Still remarkable. More pissy."

Leona barked in laughter. "You have the ability to bring it out of me. I'm surprised you haven't challenged me to a sparring match yet."

"I'd lose in a heartbeat. Give me another day." As if to

demonstrate, Edward rotated his arm and winced in pain. "I haven't properly thanked you—for saving my life."

Leona shook her head. "You don't need to."

"Only fulfilling your duty?" he challenged.

"Don't be an ass, Edward." Leona stopped walking and waited until he looked at her. She wanted the clear the air between them. "I didn't bring you here because it was my mission. I'd like to think that we're friends."

He nodded and chucked her chin. "Then, as your friend, I'd like to tell you that you're infinitely more beautiful now than when I first saw you."

Leona opened her mouth. Closed it. Then opened it again, but no sound came out.

"Cat got your tongue?" Edward crossed his arms, amused.

"You're doing it on purpose." She grabbed a fistful of stalks and threw them at him.

He swatted them away. "You've a violent streak, you know that?"

Leona laughed. "That's why you love sparring with me." She took him by the arm. "Shall we? The village is just up ahead."

"Do you know if there's a blacksmith there?"

"Do you want something made?"

"In a manner of speaking."

Leone handed Margret the satchel of herbs from the basket she carried. She'd been accompanying Margret around the village for the past week as Margret did her rounds as the village healer.

"Do you mind if I go ahead?" Leona asked.

Margret waved her away in assent.

Leona made her way to the blacksmith. Every day, Edward had been going there after breakfast and going home before sundown. They'd spar before supper, then after eating, Leona would join Edward in bed. She'd tried to put a pillow between them, but she'd ended up falling off the bed and gave up.

She didn't know what Edward did at the blacksmith and whenever she'd ask him, all he would tell her was to come by so she could see for herself. When she arrived at the village smithy, she was surprised to find the blacksmith sitting outside. He waved her in as soon as he saw her.

Leona nudged the open door wider and found the place as hot as an inferno.

Edward was pounding on the anvil with a hammer. He had his shirt off. His skin was dripping with sweat. She looked for the fire but found none. The heat was coming from Edward and whatever it was he was making.

He acknowledged her with a nod without breaking his rhythm.

Leona watched as he pounded on the long strip of metal that looked like a sword. With fierce concentration, he controlled the heat of the metal. It glowed red as he turned it over and pounded. Again and again, he did the same motions. She'd seen him without his shirt at Margret's as he was healing, but this was different. Every movement was control and strength. There was a beauty in the way he moved.

She watched him. She couldn't help it.

Even when he fought, there was a grace in the way he never wasted a movement.

Leona found him looking at her intensely. She must look like a fool staring at him. She shook herself out of her stupor and walked around the workshop. Farming tools, horseshoes, hammers, knives, and a few swords lined the wall. She turned, planning on going out and waiting for Edward when she saw his back. Whiplash marks crisscrossed his skin. Some were thick jagged scars that looked as if they'd torn through to the bone.

Leona went up behind him and reach out to follow the most jagged of them with her finger. He stilled, his muscles flexing beneath her touch. Leona traced the next scar, wondering how this could have happened.

"Stop," Edward said in a hoarse voice as he put the hammer down. "Stop touching me."

Leona jumped back. "I'm sorry. I shouldn't have."

He didn't answer. Nor did he turn to face her.

"I wanted to see how you were doing. I'd better go," she stammered.

"Stay. I'm nearly done. I told Sam I was going to finish this sword for him. This I know how to do." Without waiting for her reply, he picked up the hammer and started working again.

Leona scurried to the door and leaned against the frame, letting the cool air ease her embarrassment. She wrung her hands and closed her eyes. She'd acted like a veritable fool. First, he'd caught her staring at him, then she'd gone and touched him. Mortified, she wanted to run outside and back to Margret's place. It was the thread of pride that made her stay.

True to his word, after a short while, he took the sword and dipped it in oil. Smoke sizzled at the contact. When Edward took the sword out, he checked the quality. Satisfied, he laid it back on the anvil. He wiped the sweat off his back and chest before shrugging into his shirt. Edward grabbed something from one of the tables and tucked it in the pocket of his pants. He then took the coat that hung beside the door and swung it on his arm.

Leona let herself out, with Edward following her. "How's your shoulder?"

Edward rotated it. "Feels like nothing happened. Margret's a good healer."

As they walked back to the house, they were both silent. Colorful flags waved from the houses they passed and even the trees, marking the celebration of the changing seasons.

In bed that night, Leona looked up at the shadows on the ceiling. An image of him at the blacksmith's flashed in her mind. The way he'd looked as he worked. The way he'd flinched when she'd touched him. She hated that it bothered her. Beneath the mortification was hurt that he would react that way.

She turned to her side, at the farthest edge of the bed, trying to get comfortable. It was futile. After a long time, she gave up. There was no way she'd be able to sleep like this. She took the covers off and was about to slip out of bed when Edward covered her hand with his.

"Don't leave."

Leona went still, not sure if she should stay.

"I got them in Bahadur," Edward explained. "Two years I was there. A slave in a fighting ring. I escaped, and it took me months to get back. By the time I got home—to Mandubrath —my father was dead. That was more painful than the whippings."

Leona turned to him and leaned up on her elbow. "The rumor that you were there as a guest wasn't true?"

He turned his head and looked at her. "No. The part where I was drunk and all the parties after. Those rumors are all true. It took me a long time to wake up."

"How did you end up there?"

Edward sighed. "I was brash, looking for a fight every-where. My father thought it would do me good to work on our trading ship. We went to Breven and on our way back home, we got caught in a storm. A Bahadurian ship captured us. We all got sold to the fighting pits. The crew got killed one by one. The only other one who survived was my shipmaster."

"Was that where you learned to blacksmith?"

"When we weren't fighting, we worked."

There was more to his story, that she was sure of. But he'd tell her when he was ready. "Thank you. For telling me."

Edward tightened his hold on her hand. "Stay, Leona. I like having you here. My nightmares aren't so bad when you're around."

The next morning, Leona looked out the window and watched Edward. He was chopping firewood to take to the bonfire in the village tonight. He'd decided not to go to the blacksmith today since the celebration would go on for the whole day in the village.

Even after their intense sparring session this morning, he looked like he could keep chopping wood forever.

The past week had been a strange reprieve. It felt so normal being here with him. Living the life of a villager. She couldn't help but think of how life would be if they never had to go back. She wondered if Edward felt restless. He seemed at ease with his surroundings, never once making her feel like he was lacking in comfort.

"Who is he, Leona?" Margret asked from behind her.

She knew what Margret was asking her, and she wasn't sure either. "Does it matter?"

Margret walked up to stand beside Leona. "When you look at him like so, it does."

"He's the High King. The ruler of Mandubrath."

"And you have feelings for him?"

"He's just a friend. After all, how many people can say that they're friends with a king?"

Margret shook her head, letting Leona know that she didn't fool her.

"I don't know what else to say, Nam. Maybe if things were different." Leona smiled at Margret before going back to the kitchen table to finish packing the sachets of herbs.

WHEN THE SUN WAS HIGH IN THE SKY, THE THREE OF THEM walked to the village. When they arrived, the celebration was in full swing. It was small, but makeshift tents and flags made it a colorful affair.

Children ran around while the men and women took part in games and dances. Music and gaiety rang out in the air. They were offered food from a long table and were invited to join the games. Leona, particularly, had fun watching the tree-tossing contest.

Edward sat back and contented himself watching the goings-on. Leona tried to get him to join in on some of the games, but he good-naturedly refused, stating that he needed to regain his strength. Leona rolled her eyes and left him on his own. She'd always loved a good celebration, especially in Margret's village.

People here knew she was from the Tribunal and because of that, she'd had to do a lot of judging—from archery to the best baked breads. As the sun began to set and the music and dancing began in earnest, she walked back to Edward and found him with five giggling girls. They looked to be between seven and ten. Edward was holding some threads as one of the girls braided it in knots.

"Are you learning a new skill?" Leona asked.

"They tried to teach me, but my big fingers got in the way." He held up a wrist and showed her a threaded bracelet in blues and greens. "We're making one for you."

"Ah, I'm flattered."

The girls giggled some more. The one who was braiding the threads smiled up at Leona. "He was so clumsy. Since he's helping, it's not cheating."

"It makes a lot of sense." Leona leaned down and watched the girl tie the bracelet.

Edward crooked a finger at Leona. "Let's see how yours fits."

The girl tied it around Leona's wrist.

"I like it." Leona curtsied to the girl. "This is a fine piece of jewelry. Thank you."

"We all have bracelets," the girl boasted. "One for each our best friends."

The girls behind her whispered, and one of them spoke up tentatively. "Are you a princess?"

"We were wondering," another girl interjected. "You're so graceful, just like in the stories our mamas tell us."

Leona pretended to look left and right, and she raised a finger to her lips. "Perhaps in a past life I was a princess."

"Oh." The girls' eyes went big. "What happened? How can you be a princess again? What's another life? Are you under a spell? Where's your prince?"

"Girls!" a woman called out. "Stop bothering them and come over here. I need your help to serve the sweet cakes." With that, the girls ran as one toward the woman while waving goodbye to Leona and Edward.

"I guess sweet cakes trump royalty any day," he mused.

"Of course." Leona stretched out a hand to him. "I was going to see if you wanted to do something other than sit and sulk."

"Like what?" He raised an eyebrow.

Leona gestured behind her. "Can't you hear the music? Let's dance."

Edward shook his head. "I'll sulk for a little while longer."

"Come on, just for a little bit."

"Absolutely not. Why don't you go, and I'll watch from here?"

Leona sighed. "Fine. You're no fun." She left him and joined the villagers as they danced to the music. It was less structured than the dances in court, so Leona had fun dancing with everyone, even the children.

When it turned dark and the games and dancing were over, bonfires were lit, and the storytelling began. Tales of ghosts, romance, war, magic, princes, and princesses were told, interspersed with music.

"Shall we walk back?" he asked her.

They found Margret standing by a very pregnant woman who was walking back and forth in pain. "I must stay behind."

Leona laid a hand on Margret's arm. "Do you want me to help you?"

"No, go home," Margret said kindly. "I have more than enough help here."

As they walked back through the meadow, the music was muted and the moon bright above them.

Leona spied a spark that flickered ahead of her. She walked ahead and followed the spark. "I think that's a firefly. But I've never seen one here."

Edward crossed his arms and watched Leona.

More sparks appeared and flitted around her. Like stars, they twinkled to existence, and then disappeared. They danced with the breeze, flickering.

Leona, her face aglow with joy, turned to Edward. "You're doing this, aren't you?"

More sparks appeared until the meadow glowed golden.

"How?"

"The sparks are looking for something to burn. There's nothing but the wind and whatever is caught in it."

She waved her hand, displacing the sparks.

"Care for a dance?" Edward bowed.

"Not shy anymore?" Leona countered.

"I didn't care for an audience. Would you do me the honor?"

"Why, yes, Your Majesty." Leona curtsied.

And with the music playing in the background, he took her in his arms and danced with the sparks flickering all around them. And there and then, amidst the laughter and the music, her heart fell into place.

❧

LEONA WOKE UP THE NEXT MORNING, HER BACK PRESSED against Edward's body, his face burrowed in her hair, and his arm heavy around her waist. She tried to remember if she'd woken up when he'd shifted in his sleep. Strange, because she was such a light sleeper.

She stayed longer than she should have in his arms. Savoring his scent, his warmth.

She was in so much trouble.

She shouldn't have, but she'd fallen for him. Last night, she'd thought he would kiss her, but he'd just tucked her hand in his and walked her home.

Leona extricated herself carefully so as not to wake him. Margret was already in the kitchen, crushing herbs with a pestle and mortar. Leona hurriedly tried to fix her hair.

Margret looked at her shrewdly. "Good morning."

Leona kissed Margret on the forehead before she took the kettle and poured herself some tea.

"So," Margret began, "you stay in his bed, but he hasn't taken you."

Leona almost choked on her tea. "Nam!"

"Either that man is strange, or he's got an amazing reserve of self-control."

"We're just friends."

"And pigs can fly." Nam scooped the herbs from the pestle and added them into a small sachet.

Leona sniffed at the smell of pungent herbs. "What are you making?"

"A tonic to prevent pregnancy."

Leona set her cup down. "For someone in the village, right?"

"You're a grown woman, Leona. I won't tell you how to lead your life. Just put a pinch in a cup of boiling water the morning after the deed is done. Do it for three days."

"Nam, you're overreacting."

"Am I?" Margret pursed her lips. "It's better to be prepared. I'd hate for you to be trapped in a situation you don't want to be in."

The bedroom door opened, and Edward came out. His hair was gleaming wet.

"Good morning," Margret called out. "And how was the water this morning?"

"Freezing," Edward replied.

"Exactly what you needed?"

"Almost," he said with amusement.

Margret turned to back to Leona and raised an eyebrow.

Leona looked at the two of them and rolled her eyes. She finished her tea in one gulp and stood up. "I'm going to get more water."

Margret chuckled.

Edward followed her outside with a steaming cup of tea. He watched Leona as she unlatched the well's wooden cover and laid it on the ground. She lowered the pail into the well as Edward sat down on a tree stump.

He looked out at the meadow and trees beyond it. "Makes you want to stay here forever, doesn't it?"

Leona stilled, then kept lowering the pail. She weighed her words before speaking them. "It certainly is a simpler life."

"I've forgotten how it felt to just be."

"You're doing a good job of it." Leona inclined her head at him. "I was worried that you'd be bored."

He smiled at that, the corners of his eyes crinkling. She watched the smile make deep creases on his cheeks. "How can I be? There's always something that needs to be done. I like working with my hands."

Leona hefted the rope up and noticed his tea was still steaming hot—as if fresh out of the kettle. "Are you heating that up?"

"Of course. You want some?" His smile deepened.

"Cheat. I always have to drink mine as fast as I can if I don't want it to turn cold."

"I can give you some ferum and teach you how to do it."

She shook her head. "I'll just get spoiled. Then what do I do when I run out?"

"I'll just have to make sure you never do."

Leona laughed. "Thank you. That's a very generous offer."

"It's the least I can do. Make sure you have warm tea in the mornings." Edward stood up and laid the cup down. He went behind her. "Here, let me help you."

"I don't need help," she protested.

But Edward already had the rope in his hands, his arms on either side of her. He hefted the rope up, took the full pail, and laid it on the ground. Edward put both hands on the edge of the well and leaned against Leona. His nose was grazing her neck, not quite touching her. "You smell like lavender and pine." Edward's breath was warm against her neck.

She couldn't move. Her breath strangled in her throat.

The sound of hoofbeats thundering on the ground made Leona look up. Edward straightened up as well and turned his gaze toward the sound.

"It's them." Dread curled in Leona's gut. She and Edward had gained something here. She wasn't quite ready to part with it yet.

But as the horses came nearer, she shrugged his arm away and took that step. Away from him. Away from whatever they had.

Margret was waiting by the door, watching the riders when they joined her. It wasn't long until the riders came to a halt in front of Margret's house. Colm raised a hand in greeting as he slid off his horse. He stepped aside as both Gage and Alik dismounted to greet Edward.

Leona left them to their reunion and turned to Colm. "How was your journey?"

"We would have sent a message sooner, but we needed to secure the borders."

"Edward needed the rest, anyway."

"He looks good."

"Margret can work miracles."

"She's definitely better than Matheu," Colm said, mentioning the healer in Normundir's temple. "He irritable and passes all his work to others."

"Tell me what we've missed."

"The army was there as you said. Jamie's troops got there nearly a day after you and Edward left. They secured the lands between Normundir and the Greyfolk's."

"That's good news." Leona gestured at the horses. "They probably need to eat and rest before we leave."

Colm nodded in assent and was about to take the reins of the horses when Edward stopped him. "Why don't you go in? I'll take the horses out back."

Leona accompanied Edward to where their horses were also staying. "We should leave this afternoon."

He nodded as he took a bale of hay from the shed. "Let them know, will you? I need to finish a few things for Margret before we leave."

Leona watched him for a while, itching to help, but he clearly wanted her to go. "I'll let her know." She spent the rest of the morning packing her things and food for the journey.

That afternoon, as Leona secured her pack on the horse, Margret came out with a satchel filled with her medicinal concoctions.

"Thank you so much, Nam. I'll miss you." Leona hugged Margret tight.

"Don't wait too long before you visit again."

"I won't. Take care of yourself."

Edward came forward and took Margret's hand in his. "Thank you, Margret, for healing me and for your hospitality."

She gave him a stern look. "Thank you for the ferum.

Goodbye, my lord. Take care not to overdo it. Remember to rest to replenish your strength."

They rode toward the borders of Greyfolk land. At sundown, they arrived at a small army outpost. Soldiers carrying the crest of Normundir mingled with the few Greyfolk warriors from the Bruadar. There was an underlying feeling of urgency in the camp. Their arrival must have been watched from a distance, because soldiers stood at attention along the perimeter of the camp. Among them was Doyle.

Leona got off her horse and made her way to Doyle's side. "It's so good to see you."

"Edward looks well. Margret did well. He had us worried there," Doyle commented.

"Me, too. More than you know."

"Did Colm fill you in?"

"Briefly. I didn't want Margret to needlessly worry."

"Part of the army will stay here while the rest of us will escort Edward to Normundir." Doyle inclined his head behind Leona, where Normundir's general stood.

"Leona." Brannon gave her a slight bow in greeting.

"General." Leona nodded in greeting.

"I've a message from Prince Jamie of Normundir." Brannon gestured at Leona to follow him. They walked through the camp, and Leona took note that the Greyfolk stayed in their own groups. She also saw where Edward's tent was and where the wounded were being treated.

"All is well?" she asked him.

"Yes. I must coordinate with Edward if he wishes to join the rest of his army in the Borderlands or whether he would like to be escorted to Normundir. Rikard would rather that Edward go to Normundir where they can both coordinate a plan of attack."

"I thought he was in the Borderlands."

"Correct, but he plans to head back to Normundir once

Jamie arrives and takes over for him. They've almost stabilized that area, but there is news of ships on the eastern coast and people from that area seeking shelter in the North." He handed her a letter from Jamie.

She opened and read it. "It also looks like I have my pick of men from your soldiers to escort Edward." There was also another message. Edward needed to go to Normundir to assuage the rumors that he had disappeared.

Leona folded the letter and put it in her pocket. "Tell me what's happened."

"There was trouble brewing in the Borderlands. We've seen snatches, especially after news of the impending Gathering spread. Rikard increased security and scouts by the Borderlands. Not enough to antagonize the Rovers. We've had some of our scouting parties attacked. Nothing big, but we did not understand the scope. The next thing we knew, there was an attack on Edward's camp.

"Jamie was sent to see what he could do to help, but Rovers arrived with an official message that Edward had made his way to Central Valley while the rest of his court had gone back to Kentigern. Lance confirmed what he said and made it known to us that there was a concealed army in the Borderlands. The Tribunal sent their people to help the army see the concealed.

"From what I was told, Rikard sent no soldiers to guard the Borderlands by the Hellig Mountains and Arag'nilDarahoff because in the past, this has angered the Greyfolk. We were all surprised when flares went off from this location. Jamie was supposed to head to the eastern coast, but instead, led the attack here. And good timing it was, because the enemy's scouts had already alerted their larger army. The Greyfolk did well holding their ground, but that army would have overwhelmed them."

Leona cocked her head and thought of the concealed

army in Central Valley. "Any word on whether we're close to defeating the army in the Borderlands and the coast?"

"From what I've been told, we're fighting an army of which we only see parts. One moment they're there, the next they're not."

"The source of concealment isn't known yet, then?" Leona asked.

"That is correct."

"Will the Gathering still take place?"

Brannon nodded. "As far as I know, it still stands."

After Brannon left, Leona stood at the edge of camp and watched the comings and goings. In the distance, she could barely make out the lights of Normundir.

Home.

She couldn't wait to get back. She should have been home over a month ago. Edward flitted into her thoughts. Yesterday, there had been no titles or duties or expectations.

Yesterday felt like a long time ago.

❦

THEY RODE WITH THE SUNRISE. WHEN THE FIRST TOPS OF Normundir's watchtowers appeared, Leona felt a sense of relief wash over her. She closed her eyes to breathe in the familiar air.

She was finally home.

Stark and gray, the walls of Normundir and its castle weren't known for their beauty. The castle had four stout and circular watchtowers, one for each corner of the castle. The castle itself was a squarish structure. Two stories tall, it had none of the embellishments that the other castles in the lands had. The thick walls, made of unpolished stone, were supposed to have been part of the first castle that wasn't built by the Greyfolk. She'd heard it said the castle looked unwelcoming.

Word of their arrival spread, and people crowded the streets to watch the arrival of the High King. They arrived at the castle gates, where Rikard and Leticia waited to welcome Edward.

Leona stopped and gestured for Edward and his guards to move ahead while she waited in the back with Doyle and Colm.

Rikard looked at them briefly and nodded in greeting. They took that as their signal of dismissal and quietly rode away.

PRINCE LORIS LOOKED OUT FROM THE SOUTHERN COAST IN the kingdom of Varannis. He waited for the ships that his master had promised him. The God of Midir was his ally. Loris was the trusted one to pave the path for his master's return. When all was said and done, Loris would become High King of Bearnas.

His father and all his brothers had underestimated him. Just because he didn't have the physical strength they all had didn't mean he was weak.

And now, he also had feru'talent his father had always said he would never have. He couldn't help but smile smugly when he thought of how far he had come since he'd left his home for what was just a whim. He'd gone to Midir with what some would say was a foolish mission to wake the sleeping god, the Asshai. His men had died, but he'd survived and had even been favored by the dark lord.

Now, his father's kingdom was his and soon...all of Bearnas.

Soon, they'd cower under his name.

Soon, no one would ever think to laugh when they talked about him. People would fear him and rightly so.

"When are they supposed to arrive?"

Loris turned to see Cain slightly behind him. "Any day now."

"Do you think he'll arrive with them?"

"He didn't say. One of the masters is supposed to arrive first, and after that"—Loris shrugged his shoulders delicately —"is anybody's guess. Any problems with the Rovers?"

"They're subdued." Cain looked back at the big and bulky cloaked figures who stood at quite a distance from them. They stood unmoving, looking at the water. "Do you suppose they know something we don't?"

"Patience, Cain." Loris put a hand on his arm. "Things will all fall into place."

Loris looked at Cain, his lover, his Rover. Cain's long black hair was pulled in a braid behind his back. His eyes had a slant to them that Loris thought interesting. It was what had drawn him to Cain the first time he'd seen him. Cain was slightly taller than him, but his muscular body made him so much bigger. He thought of last night, and his skin still tingled with the memory of Cain's touch. The big man seemed to read Loris's thoughts because he put a hand on Loris's and gave him a small smile.

Loris shook off the distraction that Cain presented and turned back to watch the cloaked beings. Behind them, the Greyfolk worked tirelessly, making weapons and building forts and catapults to prepare for the army coming from Bahadur.

"I received a missive, and you won't be too pleased about this." Cain handed the parchment to Loris. "Edward made it to Normundir."

Loris read through the message. He crumpled the parchment and threw it on the ground. "How could he have escaped? I thought Shemal Pass killed all those who passed? Did they have help from the Tribunal?"

"They may have." When Loris just glared at him, Cain raised both hands up. "Loris, it has been a long time since I defected from the Tribunal. I have no knowledge of what they're doing."

"Don't you have spies within the Tribunal?"

"Even they don't know everything. I told you we weren't always privy to what the others were doing or ordered to do."

"Damn it. I thought we had a Greyfolk contingency to take care of the rebels? What happened to them?"

"They were overrun by the rebels hiding within the Bruadar."

"After all this work."

Cain made Loris face him. "It will work out. Once the army from Bahadur is here, we'll conquer all of Bearnas. Don't forget that you have most of the Greyfolk behind you. Who convinced them to join this fight if not you? Have faith. It will work out. When the master comes here, everything you've done will be worth it."

"Will you face him this time?"

"Still upset at me for not accompanying you?"

"Not anymore. I understand that the mark of the Tribunal would have spelled your death, but surely you've more than proven your loyalty to the master. He won't harm you." He laid a hand on Cain's shoulder. "You are the reason the Asshai is awake."

"Don't give me too much credit. I told you about the writings in the Great Library. You did everything else."

"If you hadn't told me that the Elders feared him, I might not have been intrigued. We both hate the Elders for our own reasons. Mine is purely selfish, but yours...you have valid reasons for hating them. After they killed your birth parents, nobody deserves to let them get away with that crime."

"You are destined for greatness. I don't understand how your father can't see it, but it's clear as day even from the first moment I saw you." Something caught Cain's attention, and he pointed toward the water. "Look, here they come."

The horizon was filled with the shadows of ships.

❧ 13 ❧

Leona waited in the temple for the priest, Orin. His study was ruthlessly white, just like the temple inside and outside. Even his table and chair were of the lightest color of wood. She paced the room, hungry and impatient to get out of her dirty clothes.

Priest Orin raised an eyebrow when he came into the room. Leona immediately stopped the pacing and gave him a curt bow. He inclined his head and made his way to his chair. The ixmus beads in his necklace clinked against each other, the black beads a sharp contrast to the whiteness of his robes.

Once he sat down, he rested his elbows on the armrest and touched his fingertips together. "The journey didn't go as expected?"

She told him everything that had happened from the time she'd left Midroska up to their arrival in Normundir. His eyes grew grim when she told him of the vision she'd had with the Greyfolk Elder. And when she told him about Edward getting injured and having to stay at Margret's, her voice wavered enough that Leona had to clear her throat before continuing. She didn't mention sleeping in the same bed as Edward or the field of sparks he'd created, but the way Priest Orin looked at her made her conscious that she was omitting this information.

When she was finished, Priest Orin nodded. "It's more serious than we thought."

Leona opened her mouth to say something, but he waved her off. "Is there anything else?"

"No, that's all."

"What's your impression of Edward?"

"He's arrogant and a tough man who doesn't trust easily. But his guards are loyal to him, not out of fear, but something else. Love, maybe? They trust that he also serves them. His feru'talent was strong. Stronger than I've seen even within the Tribunal."

"Fire, isn't it?"

Leona nodded in assent.

"Did you earn his trust?"

"I think I did. It's hard to tell with Edward." Leona wondered at the line of questioning but remained silent.

"He would be a good ally for the Tribunal to have."

Leona felt uncomfortable all of a sudden. A favor for a life saved—she wondered if that's what her superiors were after.

Priest Orin kept his steepled hands in front of him. "High Historian Trevelyn and High Healer Irena are going to the Gathering. You and Doyle will be their official guards in the castle during the day. Jaworek and a few others will take shifts afterward."

"We don't need to split it. I'm sure Doyle and I can manage for the whole day."

"I'd rather their guards are well rested than tired and careless. It's an honor for them to be here. I don't want them to feel unwelcome or that we're lacking in any way."

A knock at the door interrupted their conversation.

"What is it?" Priest Orin demanded.

"A message for you." The servant bowed low before handing him the folded piece of paper.

"It seems Doyle and High Healer Irena will be in the village for a while. You are to go the castle." Priest Orin pocketed the message. "High Historian Trevelyn has just arrived."

Leona winced as soon as she was outside of his study. Resigned to another long day, she made her way to the castle. The temple was in the unkempt part of town. It stood out like a beacon among the narrow streets and narrow houses stacked one on top of the other.

She had always wondered why people crowded amongst themselves, but she supposed the cold in the North drove people to crowd together to conserve heat. It always smelled of peat, fire, and sweat. The cold ground crunched under her feet as she walked. As she neared the castle, the path got wider and the houses bigger.

She looked around at the familiar sights. She knew the merchants and their routines. Nothing much changed in their lives except for the passing seasons. Sometimes she was part of the whole flow of the town, but other times, she felt so different, so far removed from everything.

The castle lay in front, unassuming in its grayness against the cold and darkened sky. It was a huge fortress designed to defend more than inspire a sense of peace. There was nothing graceful about the structure, nor was there anything to soften the hardness it portrayed.

There was nothing decorative to convey the Gathering was occurring. Instead, the atmosphere was one of war. Everyone walked with a purpose. The talk that accompanied them was one of urgency and hushed voices. A constant pounding came from the makeshift structures, where the blacksmiths worked to make and repair weapons.

The only strips of color in an otherwise bleak place were the flags from the different kingdoms.

Leona entered the main doors and walked into the receiving area. She was then ushered into the great hall. It looked different from how Leona had last seen it. Instead of the dais holding two thrones, there were a row of chairs. The spacious room was crowded with war boards set on one side and a table with a big map of the Borderlands.

Leona saw Edward for the first time since they'd reached Normundir. He was quiet amidst the noise and the surrounding people. He had changed clothes. Gone were the bloodstained shirt and the beard he'd grown during the long journey. He looked different. She met his eyes and found him with an eyebrow raised—as if mocking her.

She stopped herself from rolling her eyes and waited until Rikard signaled for her to come closer. Trevelyn, who stood beside Rikard, clasped his hands together. A stocky man with a flaccid and average face, his manner was always pleasant, always neutral. He had a quality that made people miss him in the crowds. However, it was folly to underestimate him. There was a cunning in him that rarely missed anything. Even the way he gestured with his hands was calculated.

Without waiting for any formalities, Rikard looked at Leona. "Tell me your side of this."

Leona stole a glance at Trevelyn, who, with a single look, conveyed that she should stick to the basics and nothing else.

She spoke of their journey through the Borderlands, the decisions that led to Shemal Pass, the discovery of the Grey-folk and then of summoning Normundir's help. As she spoke, Rikard's frown deepened until the frown became etched in anger. When she finished, Rikard clenched his jaw.

"You mean to tell us you consciously decided to go through Shemal Pass, thinking my army was at the Tribunal's disposal? That you decided to endanger the lives of your men, Edward, and those of his guards?"

"It was a well-thought-out decision, born of necessity." Leona clenched both hands, trying not to say more.

Edward spoke for the first time. "That decision saved my life. I accepted the risk when we journeyed to Shemal Pass. I am grateful for Leona's help and for her role in getting us safely here." He regarded Leona as he spoke. He then turned to Rikard. "I am also grateful that your army came just in time."

The two men eyed each other, Edward unwavering while Rikard coiled in anger.

Rikard turned to Leona once more. "And what is this business of your disappearing when the army got there? We have healers, too. Skilled at that."

"Your Majesty has excellent healers. However, we were pressed for time. I apologize we weren't there, but we are grateful that you sent your army to our aid."

He nodded curtly at her and shifted his questioning to Trevelyn. "You have men in Bahadur. Why have we not heard of their masters planning this attack?"

"Because we haven't heard from any of our agents. Even the pirates are silent." Trevelyn looked at Edward. "Except yours. From what I've heard, he's extremely talkative."

Edward shrugged. "He does the job. He and his people are mine now."

"And you've done nothing but wait this whole time? One would think you'd be sending for word through different channels." Rikard challenged Trevelyn.

"Oh, we have, Your Majesty. But as you know, it's not that easy getting word to and from Bahadur."

"You didn't think to tell us?"

"It's happened in the past where we have lost contact. It's the nature of the assignment there. Edward has seen it with his own eyes, have you not?"

Edward nodded as Rikard and the others looked at him in

question. "Yes, I've seen it," he acknowledged and shrugged it off. "It was a long time ago. Do you know how to free those used to power the source of concealment?"

"Yes," Trevelyn nodded. "We need to eliminate the source."

"There is no other way?"

"I'm afraid not. They cannot be set free, or else they go mad. They're lost already." Trevelyn gestured for Leona to stand down. She made her way back toward the doorway and stood there until they were done.

Edward nodded at her before she walked out of the great hall. They walked through the castle in silence, and as soon as she and Trevelyn were in the courtyard, Jaworek came forward and relieved Leona.

She made her way back into the castle and asked for an audience with the queen.

When Queen Leticia saw Leona, she dismissed everybody. Leona stood by the door and waited as everyone filed past her. Leticia smiled and held out her arms.

Leona moved into the queen's arms and embraced her. "Mother."

Her usually reserved mother held on for a long time before letting go. "I was so worried. All this fighting. Jamie's off somewhere, and then it turns out, so were you. When you signaled for help, your father couldn't get that army out there quick enough. I thought you would be safe once Jamie got there, but then he sent word you weren't there."

"I'm sorry for worrying you, but I can handle myself. We didn't have time to wait."

"Edward praised you and not so much the Tribunal. He said your quick thinking and actions saved his life. All the same, your father was upset you were caught in the middle of all this trouble."

Leona shrugged. Even though she understood where the anger came from, it still stung.

"Don't mind him." Leticia gestured to a chair for Leona to sit down. "Is something the matter?" Leticia asked with concern.

"I'm tired, and I haven't had time to rest." Leona knew her mother well enough to know she struggled, wanting to push Leona to confide in her. Instead, Leticia smiled serenely and invited Leona to stay for supper with her. Leona preferred to go to the chapterhouse. But with the busy times ahead, a quiet dinner with her mother would be a rarity.

Shortly afterward, the doors opened, and Rikard entered. He regarded Leona with a scowl. "So, you're still here."

Leona just shook her head and smiled. "Father."

"Come here." He gave her a great big hug. "You had me worried there, my girl."

"I apologize for that."

"It's Trevelyn who should do the apologizing. He shouldn't be sending you on a mission like that."

"And I'm glad he doesn't treat me differently," Leona interjected.

"He should know better," Rikard spat out. "Your place is in the temple. Here in Normundir."

"Warriors get sent to different temples. I refuse to be treated any differently."

"You're not just any Tribunal warrior. You're my daughter. A princess."

"I am not a princess of anything. Very few know of my ties to Normundir. Or have you forgotten?"

"Doyle was with you. He knows who you are. He should have done better."

"Enough." Leticia stood up and looked from Rikard to Leona, and back to Rikard. "Leona's joining me for supper. Would you like to join us?" Leticia said.

"Not today. Edward and I are riding out."

"Can't it wait until tomorrow morning?"

"We've stayed here long enough," he said gruffly and with a tinge of impatience.

Leona followed Rikard and Leticia as they walked out to the balcony overlooking the courtyard. It was an organized mess with soldiers getting ready and mounting their horses.

Leona stayed above while she watched her mother accompany her father to his horse. She saw Edward issuing orders to his men and, to her surprise, Finbar. It was the first time she'd seen him since the Borderlands.

As if sensing her gaze, Edward turned and looked up at her. He inclined his head and gave her a small smile. Leona wanted to be down there with him, to wish him luck. She held his glance for a moment longer, then she stepped back into the shadows.

Edward and Rikard left with a contingent of soldiers from Normundir. The only companions that Edward had were his guards, Finbar, and a band of Rovers.

They reached the Trading Route and veered eastward toward the coast. From their vantage point up on the hill, far from the battle, they could see the landscape of war. It was a sight to behold. The rebel Greyfolk and Rovers who fought against Rikard and Edward's army would disappear and reappear in the battlefield. When they disappeared, an eerie quiet settled in the field, and when they reappeared, the loud clash of weapons and screams drowned everything out. Catapults boomed and arrows shot across the field. The sky was gray with smoke, and the ground was dark with blood.

"By the Elder gods," Finbar exclaimed. "I didn't expect this."

"Nobody ever truly does," Edward said. He urged his horse forward, and they rode to the edge of the battlefield where their men held their ground.

An old watchtower lay ahead of them. Behind it, a long wall followed the curve of the land. Rumored to have been built by a king who wanted the Borderlands, it had been torn down when the Rovers had rebelled against Normundir and minor kingdoms of the North. But a good portion of it still stood along the edges of the borders.

Edward and Rikard's army had extended it on both sides with timber and stones. A river bordered part of the wall, and they'd used that to their advantage. Edward could see the sigil of his much bigger army standing along Normundir's, fighting past the wall.

"You could have held out for your army," Rikard said without looking at Edward.

"I expected an army, but not an army of invisible forces. I couldn't risk more lives when it was just mine they wanted at the time. To divide my army would have been folly."

"Your Majesty," Brannon called out to Rikard. "We've a tent ahead prepared for you and Edward."

He looked at Edward with annoyance before getting off his horse and stalking off to the tent.

"It's been like this since we discovered them," Brannon said, frustrated. "We can't predict where they'll show, and we have limited people from the Tribunal who can tell us where they are."

"Has the Tribunal come any closer to finding the source of concealment?" Rikard asked.

Lance spoke up. "We've looked everywhere, and we still haven't found it."

"We can't fight like this," Edward's general said. "Every day, the army seems to find our most vulnerable spots."

"I agree," Edward said. "We have to do the unexpected. We can't expect to win this war with old tactics."

"What do you propose we do, milord?"

"We need to direct their appearance and use their own tactics of ambush against them."

The generals looked at him in confusion, but Rikard nodded in agreement.

"That drumbeat marks their appearance and disappearance in the battlefield. We have to look for the drummers. Whoever's directing it will be close by. The source may be there," Edward said.

"The one who controls the source is there, but the source itself can be anywhere," Lance informed them.

"Keep looking for the source," Edward told Lance. "We'll take care of the one who controls it."

"Now, let's go fight these bastards," Rikard said.

Edward looked around the field. He and his contingent had fought in the middle of the chaos of the battle. Pushed from behind, he'd landed on the ground, barely missing an axe to the head when he'd rolled to his right. The axe glanced on a rock, and the Greyfolk had disappeared.

"Retreat!" Rikard screamed. White flags came up all along the walls and all the soldiers in the field ran toward their camp. Greyfolk and Rovers, sensing victory, chased after them. For every boom of that distant drum, they appeared and reappeared in the field. But now, there was no strategy, except to kill and chase after the retreating soldiers.

As the soldiers retreated, Brannon and his cavalry added to the chaos by splitting from the retreating soldiers and riding into the enemy's army. Another cavalry, led by Edward's soldiers, rode into the enemy going toward a different direction.

Within the chaos, Edward got closer and closer to the drumbeat. With every enemy attack, he and his soldiers made their way toward the drummers. Among them were cloaked figures. Larger than the Greyfolk and Rovers around them, they seemed content to watch the battle from a distance. Edward snagged a horse from one of his attackers.

Edward picked up a spear impaled in the ground and struck a drummer. His soldiers threw spears at the cloaked figures, but they shimmered out of existence and disappeared.

The enemy's army disappeared, and the soldiers who fought in the field looked around, waiting for them to reappear. When long moments passed and there was still nothing, they all trudged back to the camp to wait for the enemy's next appearance.

With the respite, Edward wasted no time and rode toward the coast. There, Jamie had taken control of the small port village of Ludfar. He and his men had prevented the other ships from docking by shooting at them with catapults and flame-tipped arrows.

As Edward and his soldiers waited for Jamie, they watched the battle from the safety of the rocky shore. A turtle washed ashore, and the surrounding birds tried to peck at it.

The turtle kept on retreating in its shell, and it would wait for when the birds would give it a moment alone, then it would venture out and take a few steps. Edward picked the turtle up and gave it a considering look before putting it back in the water.

"If we show any weakness in our defense and those ships make it to shore, we are done for," Jamie told Edward as they made their way to the lookout point.

Jamie looked just like his mother. His golden hair was on the longer side and curled against his nape. His blue eyes and good nature made it easy for people to trust him.

"A ship! A ship has crashed by the shore," a man shouted.

"You know what to do," Jamie yelled. He and Edward ran toward the ship that had crashed, ready to fight, when they saw that the people getting off were innocent.

"Peace! Don't attack us," the shipmaster yelled as he waved a white shirt that he'd taken off.

"We're from Varannis," a woman just behind him added. The woman who said this had long sable hair that fell in lustrous waves and framed a face that was heartbreakingly beautiful. Though she was as tall as Jamie, she looked delicate, willowy.

"Who are you?" Jamie asked her, but before she could speak up, another woman suddenly appeared and interjected.

"Jamie." She had his own mother's features—the golden hair and complexion warmed by the sun, though she looked peaked, and her mouth was pursed in a thin annoyed line.

"Aunt Ailene?"

The woman nodded, though she still didn't smile. "This is my stepdaughter, Adrina. And Tobin is our shipmaster," she said, referring to the man who waved at them with his shift. "My king and husband, Jannik, is still out there. He sent a message to Varannis to send more ships to help us."

"How many ships does he have here?" Edward asked.

"Aunt, this is—"

"I know. Edward." She looked Edward over before she continued. "Just three. We were on our way to the Gathering when those ships ambushed us. We didn't expect to be attacked here, so far north. There's a group of ships, close to where Jannik was fighting. That's where we got rammed."

"Where is your husband now?" Edward asked.

"Jannik was going to come with us, but he saw a slaver's ship. He wanted to take a look to see who they've captured. I told him if it was those nasty Rovers, to leave them be."

"It's on the water," Edward exclaimed. "We've been wasting our time looking for the source of concealment when it's on the water. Alik, get Lance and Finbar."

"What do you mean it's on the water?" Jamie asked curiously.

"The source of concealment. The people who disappeared from the Borderlands."

"You want me to do what?" Finbar said incredulously.

"You heard me." Edward waited for Finbar assimilate the information.

"You want me and my men to go steal an enemy's ship and ride in the middle of everything and find the source of this concealment you talk about. Great. It sounds so easy to do," Finbar said with a heavy dose of sarcasm.

Edward crossed his arms. "Finbar, don't tell me you've never done this before. I'll be sorely disappointed."

"Fine," Finbar admitted. "And we were good at it, too."

"I thought so."

"And then what? We shoot a flare and then get attacked. All martyrs for the great cause."

Edward just looked at Finbar until he stopped with his theatrics. "You won't be alone out there. We'll be going with you."

"We?"

"Jamie and I," Edward said.

Finbar opened his mouth, but nothing came out. After a moment, he nodded to himself. He held out a hand to Edward. "From what I've seen and heard of royalty and noblemen, they give the orders and their soldiers risk their lives. You're crazy for going out there. If we get out of this alive, I will be your servant for the rest of my natural life."

Edward took Finbar's hand in a firm grip. "I'll hold you to that."

That night, Finbar and his men stole one of the enemy's scouting ships by luring it into a cove. They hurriedly outfitted it with a catapult. "It's not pretty," Finbar told Jamie, "but it will do."

"Edward mentioned that you used to be a pirate?" Jamie asked, as Finbar maneuvered the ship away from the cove.

Finbar flashed him a smile. "A reformed one. We can't have it be going around that a pirate works for the High King, now, can we? Although this brings back memories, doesn't it?" He elbowed the man beside him, who grinned. "The tales we could tell you."

Tobin, the man from Queen Ailene's ship, frowned. "Aye. Good tales for you, but not for your victims."

"Now, now. You can't blame a man for trying to make a living, can you? My men and I are reformed, and that's the truth."

Tobin just shook his head.

"Where to, my good man?" Finbar raised an eyebrow and looked expectantly at Tobin.

"Would be better if I steered us myself," Tobin said.

"Well, who's the expert in secret sailings here?"

They sailed through the moonlit sea, weaving toward the battle being waged between King Jannik's small forces and those of the enemy ships. They watched the shower of flame-tipped arrows between ships.

"We have to help them," Tobin exclaimed.

"No," Edward said. "They're a good distraction."

They reached the battling ships and weaved from ship to ship, staying within the enemy lines. Edward recognized the ships right away. "Bahadur."

"Aye," Finbar replied. "You've seen them before?"

"Yes."

"Been to Breven, then?"

"Yes. I'd recognize the make of those ships anywhere."

"I'm impressed. Didn't think you royalty types would be keen to go anywhere but here." He continued to navigate the ship and ordered silence when they neared what looked like their target.

"That's it. Those are the ships I told you about," Tobin

whispered and pointed toward the three ships that surrounded the one anchored in the middle.

One of the ships called out to them as they neared it, and Finbar called back in a guttural language, similar to that of the Greyfolk.

"What did they say?" Jamie asked him.

"I told them we are Rovers, and we have something of interest for their masters." He turned to his men. "Are you ready for this? We're out of practice, but I'm sure it will come right back to you how to take a ship this big."

"We need them distracted, Finbar," Edward reminded him.

"Don't you worry about a thing. We're good at distraction."

Tobin took the wheel over as Finbar and a few of his men waited for the bigger ship to lower a rope ladder to them. Edward tightened his cloak around him as Finbar and the others climbed up.

Tobin took the helm and veered the ship away from the bigger ship. They watched until they saw the flames and the sounds of fighting reached them.

"That's the signal." Jamie gestured with a hand. "Now, go."

Two other ships sprang into action and went toward the ship on fire. Using the distraction and the darkness, Tobin steered the scouting ship toward the one in the center.

Jamie pointed at the helm of the ship. There were Greyfolk coming up aboard, dragging hostages with them. Women and children who stared blindly at them, calm as could be. They didn't scream or move. They just stood there as the Greyfolk put knives against their throats. One of the Greyfolk motioned for them to go away or they would kill the hostages.

Edward looked behind him, at the ships that had finally noticed them. "Shoot it down."

"What?" Jamie exclaimed. "We can't do that. There are innocents on board."

"We'll all die and the rest of Bearnas will too if we don't do this."

"We have to find a way."

"No, Jamie. The time of action is now. If we fail to act, all else will be lost." Edward turned to those manning the catapult. "Shoot it down."

Edward clenched his jaw as he watched the first of the big rocks fly into the sky. He saw the shocked look of those manning the ship, the blank looks of the hostages who stood swaying on the bow of the ship.

They were lost anyway, Edward reminded himself. All the same, he felt the heavy weight of his crown. Edward forced himself to watch the sinking ship. They had shot all the stones they could get on the scouting ship. It teetered on one edge and started to sink on one side.

The other ships now tried to salvage what they could of the hostages, but they weren't very successful, especially since Finbar and his men took control of one the bigger ships.

They rammed themselves against the other ship, damaging the hull and forcing water into it. They clambered up and fought the Greyfolk and off-landers there.

Edward and Jamie looked toward the ship that contained the source of concealment. It was fast disappearing from view. Bodies floated on the water along with the debris of the sinking ship.

"So many," Jamie said in despair.

"There was nothing we could have done." Edward glanced at Jamie. Although Jamie wasn't that much younger than him, he felt decades older than the prince. "The death of innocents should never be regarded as commonplace. One day, when you are king, you'll make decisions like the one I just did, and just as you'll accept that decision as the right one, the responsibility, the weight, will always be with you."

Edward put a hand on the younger man's shoulder. "It wasn't a weakness that you wanted to spare their lives. Consider it a lesson you can look back to when you are a king. It wasn't cowardice that stayed your hand, but sympathy for the innocents. What you take as weakness is strength."

Jamie looked away, still unconvinced, when he saw ships in the horizon. "Looks like they're finally here."

Varannis's fleet gleamed white and shone on the water as it surrounded the enemy ships.

Off in the distance, on land, Rikard's army fought the Greyfolk and Rovers who were no longer under concealment.

"Milord," a squire called to Edward when he arrived at the camp. "King Jannik has captured their leader."

Edward followed the squire to a tent. Jannik stood over a prisoner seated with two guards on both sides. The man had the tough skin of the Greyfolk, but his was a warm mix of orange and red. On his forehead was a line of small protrusions that looked like white horns. His black-on-black uniform's only embellishment was a six-pointed star embroidered in gold thread on his belt.

"Jannik." Edward held out a hand.

"Edward." Jannik took his hand and shook it. "Where's Rikard?"

"He's dealing with the last of the Greyfolk rebels and Rovers."

"This piece of scum was on a ship retreating from the battle."

The man sneered. "Imbecile. You don't know who I am and what I'm capable of."

"You're from Arshavir," Edward said.

The man looked up in surprise. "How?"

"You carry its symbol."

"Then you know the power the Shahans wield. They've come as one to take these lands from you fleshers." He spat when he said the word.

Edward crossed his arms and cocked his head. "Tell me now, who are you?"

"I am Maru'ath Al Dun, the thirteenth leader of the army of the Shahan of Arshavir. This was only a sample of the force you'll encounter if you don't surrender to us."

"Fancy you saying that, when you are our prisoner," Jannik said.

"I am but one of a legion. By now, somebody else will have taken my place. I have fulfilled my duties."

"Where is the rest of this legion?" Jannik countered.

"You'll find out, for if you live long enough, you'll see it with your very own eyes," Maru'ath answered.

"How did you conceal the army?" Edward asked.

"The Asshai has granted us the gift of his Weavers for our loyalty and worship."

Jannik chuckled. "Weavers? Like sewing fabric? Making a dress?"

Maru'ath shook his head. "You are disrespectful. The Weavers are powerful beings. The Asshai's own soldiers protect them, and they are where the Asshai has willed them to be."

They tried to ask him for more information, but he just repeated the same line, "the Asshai has willed it."

"We have our ways to get you talking," Jannik threatened him.

"I understand." Maru'ath leaned forward. "Do your worst, for nothing can match the wrath of the Asshai."

"The Asshai?" Jannik asked Edward once they were outside the tent.

"The god they worship. Arshavir's people, that is. Not all of Bahadur believe in the same thing. I think the Asshai is the equivalent of the black snake that the Tribunal has spoken of as the one that started the Great War from a thousand years ago. The antithesis to the Tribunal's Protectors. The Asshai is the shadow snake that they supposedly will destroy in the end."

"That's all nonsense they spew."

Edward shrugged. "I've seen stranger things in Bahadur." Edward turned to a soldier. "Have someone guard the tent at all times."

"Shall we bring him food and drink, sire?"

"He'll be questioned on the morrow after a night of hunger and thirst."

That night, supper was served in the largest tent. Since they'd been there, Edward had always chosen to eat by himself in his own tent, but Jannik insisted that he had extra provisions for everyone. Soldiers rotated in and out of the tent as soon as they were done eating, and the next were ushered in.

Edward, seated in the front with Rikard and Jannik, watched the soldiers who trudged in and out of the tent. The next day would bring the misery of burning the bodies.

❧

ADRINA WATCHED EDWARD FURTIVELY FROM A NEARBY table. He looked displeased about something. She wondered if it could be the food. It was tasteless gruel she could barely stomach. Instead, she took a drink from her goblet.

"Are you done eating?"

Adrina turned to her mother and shook her head. "I was going to ask if I can get a piece of bread..."

"Yes, yes, this is horrible." Ailene agreed. "Edward's

almost done eating. We don't want to miss our chance. Go there before he leaves."

"But I don't know what to say."

"Ask him how the battle was or the food. It doesn't matter. Let him do the looking. Here, fix your hair. Your pins are askew." After some tugging and repositioning, Ailene gave a nod of approval. "Now, go."

Adrina made her way to Edward, conscious of the glances she attracted from those around her. Rikard, who sat beside Edward, was the first to notice her.

"Adrina. It has been a long time since I last laid eyes on you. I remember you were but a child."

"Your Majesty has a long memory, for I don't remember it anymore. My father still talks of your visit as if it were yesterday." She gestured at Jannik, who nodded in approval and invited her to sit beside him.

Adrina gracefully sat down, the picture of beauty. She turned her gaze to Edward. "How are you? I know the battle was tough on everyone."

Edward gave her a small nod and answered, "Tired, but glad we were victorious."

"I'm sure you can't wait to get back to Mandubrath. I heard it's beautiful over there."

"Yes, it's beautiful. Though home sounds tempting, we need to go to Normundir for the Gathering."

"The Gathering still holds? Even after all this?"

"Yes, especially after the battles we've fought," Edward said with conviction.

Adrina smiled at Edward, waiting for more, but he remained silent. After a few more tries to engage him in a conversation, she soon gave up and left, her pride in tatters. She returned to her table and found her mother gone. Adrina sighed. Her mother was most certainly not pleased if she'd gone without waiting for her.

"Princess Adrina." She took a deep calming breath before she turned to see Jamie. She didn't know why, but he annoyed her. More so because he had probably seen Edward's dismissal of her and found it amusing. A lifetime of manners made her acknowledge him, albeit in forced politeness.

"Jamie." She gave him a regal nod. "What can I do for you?"

He inclined his head, "Just the pleasure of your company," he said good-naturedly.

"I'm tired. I was heading back to my quarters to sleep."

"In that case, permit me to walk with you."

She shook her head. "Thank you, but I don't need an escort."

He gestured in front of him as if he didn't hear her. She hurriedly walked away, but he pleasantly matched her step for step.

"Pleasant evening, isn't it?"

She wasn't in the mood to talk, and so she stayed silent, hoping that he would get the message.

"Did I do something to offend you, Your Highness? I'm sure my aunt had good things to say about me?"

"No, I mean, yes...she has a good opinion of you. It's just that I'm not—"

"Interested. I can see that."

She pretended not to understand. "Whatever does that mean?"

"Did it ever occur to you that I just want to be your friend?"

That stopped her, and she looked at him suspiciously.

"It's that way, is it? You're beautiful, and you look like you're floating on stars when you move about."

She looked at him in surprise at the compliment, but he kept on going, "You've also probably been drilled right from the beginning to aim for the highest title, so in this field everybody's outranked by Edward. I don't wish my father ill, so I'm perfectly content where I am. I've accepted my status in life and that's why I think we should just be friends."

"Are you mocking me? I don't think I've ever been insulted like this before." She still smarted from Edward's dismissal of her, but now all that was thrown away because this...this person in front of her assumed that she was shallow, stupid, and had no opinion of her own. Gone was the polite reserve and in its place was haughty anger, but what he said next just flabbergasted her.

Jamie put his hands out as if in surrender and smiled brilliantly at her. "I know exactly how you feel. People can't seem to get past my looks and charm. They don't see the real me."

She looked at him in complete astonishment, not knowing what to say.

"Ah," he smiled as if proud of himself when they arrived in front of her tent, "here we are. Safe and sound. Good night and sleep well, Your Highness." He bowed to her and walked away whistling.

THE NEXT FEW DAYS, ADRINA STAYED IN THE TENT THE majority of the time with her stepmother. She'd go for short walks, but everyone seemed so busy that she felt guilty not doing anything. She wanted to help with the wounded but felt that she'd just get in the healer's way.

She learned a lot during her walks. People talked, and they didn't seem to care who could hear them. Adrina heard that a prisoner from Bahadur, the one that her father, Rikard, and Edward had interrogated, had died by his own hands. That fascinated her because he supposedly had hidden a small dagger in the sole of his boot and cut his own neck.

Adrina also learned that whatever it was that was

concealing their enemy was gone. She'd heard someone say that it was easier pickings—whatever that meant. But something else that she'd heard worried her.

She didn't mean to spy on Jamie, but she was doing her usual walk around camp when she saw Jamie. She tried to call for him, but he went into one of the tents. Adrina found the tent and since there was no guard, she was going to call for Jamie when she heard him talking to his father about some men they'd captured. She knew she should leave, but she leaned in and listened.

"Well?" Rikard asked Jamie.

"We found one of the Greyfolk lieutenants," Jamie replied. "He knew more than the other prisoners." Jamie sounded displeased, but he continued. "He said they were planning to flaunt Edward's body before all the kings at the Gathering. He also said there are more forces arriving from Bahadur."

"Jannik said the south has been secured. He also sent ships to inspect the waters. Did you learn anything else?"

"They serve the Shahan of Arshavir and some god, the Asshai."

"Why didn't the Tribunal tell us of this danger?" Rikard demanded.

"They said they were also caught by surprise. Their last reports of Bahadur said that the leaders have shown no inclination to invade Bearnas. They also reminded me that they've been warning us it was a possibility."

Rikard huffed a breath that sounded like a roar to Adrina's ears. "Yes, they've been warning us. But the Tribunal has been saying the same story for hundreds of years. Edward was the first one who was gullible enough to believe them." Rikard paused and after a moment said, "Stay here and make sure it's secure. I don't know how much time we have, but I'd rather get the Gathering done and over with."

"I won't be too far behind."

Adrina immediately walked away from the tent, not wanting Jamie to find out that she'd eavesdropped on their conversation. She felt overwhelmed by the things that she'd just learned. She needed to talk to her stepmother—she would understand and be pleased that Adrina had news for her.

⚜

ADRINA RELAXED HER HOLD ON HER HORSE'S REINS. HER hands were starting to ache from holding on too tightly. Actually, her whole body was starting to ache. She wished they were in a carriage where she didn't worry whether her horse would throw her off or suddenly run wild. Her stepmother, Ailene, who rode beside her, looked worse.

"Mother, do you need to rest?"

"I'm fine."

And that was all Ailene would say every time Adrina would ask her if she needed anything. She took her gaze off of her mother and looked ahead. They'd been traveling for a few hours now. The war on the coast had been won, and the evening before, her father, along with Rikard and Edward, declared that it was time for them to go to Normundir.

She wondered at the gigantic trees and the open spaces of the Borderlands. She could no longer smell the saltwater in the air and instead something else permeated the air. Hours later, she was grateful when they finally stopped to rest. She and her stepmother had just come back from relieving themselves when they spotted Edward. They made their way to him and curtsied. Adrina felt her stepmother's elbow dig into her ribs.

"What is that?" she asked Edward, sniffing the air.

"The trees?"

"Is that what it is?"

"You've never been away from the coast, have you?"

"No," she said, chagrined.

"The sap of the trees is thicker the further you travel north," he explained.

"Do you travel north often?"

"I've only traveled once to the Normundir. It's a fascinating place. Different from the lands south of the Borderlands."

"You've been to Varannis then?"

"My kingdom has interests in Breven. I've been to Varannis a few times when my father was still alive." He gestured for her to get up. "It'll get cold soon. I suggest you put on more layers."

He intrigued her. Always, men flattered her with compliments about her looks.

Edward did none of that. He was always polite and answered all her questions, but she sensed absolutely no interest on his part, which made her try harder to get him to notice her. She did as her mother had taught her—be there, but don't be overt. Always let him take the lead. She was only there to support him and to inflate his ego. But none of it seemed to work.

For the first time, Adrina wondered if she was lacking. All her life she'd been trained to be a queen and a proper wife to the person who her parents would consider their equal or more. Her stepmother, with just one look, reminded her that this was the coup of a lifetime. But now, it was more than that. She wanted him to actually like her.

❊ 14 ❊

Leona was tending to an old man, wounded while escaping the Borderlands with his family, when she saw children running and screaming excited exclamations of "They're back!"

Anticipation hit her quick and hard. She fought to tamp it down, telling herself that it was Jamie and her father she wanted to see. But the truth was, Edward was back and she needed to see him. Just to make sure he was safe and whole.

Leona wiped her hands on her skirt and made her way through the crowded ward in the temple. She took her time before walking outside. She looked toward the city gates and saw riders had already entered Normundir. People rushed around her to the gates like a river.

She was far away enough not to make out any of the riders' faces, but she recognized Jamie. More riders came in, and then there was Edward. She could tell him by the way he held himself—relaxed but in the sense that a wild animal can seem still and attack in the next moment.

Pleased that he was uninjured, she walked back to the

wounded. When night came and the streets of Normundir cleared, Leona was called into the temple's library.

There, Trevelyn was waiting for her. He sat in front of a desk piled high with books. He nodded amiably to her and gestured to the seat in front of him.

Leona sat down and waited.

Trevelyn aimed his gaze at her and kept it there. She tried her best not to flinch.

"The Gathering begins." He had a slowed speech, and it took some patience to listen to him. "Pay attention to any communication happening in the background and report it to me. Any nuances during a particular issue are important. Every detail. You understand? Hmm?"

"Yes, sir."

"Good, good. There's a banquet tonight. I'd prefer for you and Doyle to go with me and Irena. Jaworek will stay here. He tends to make people uncomfortable."

Leona stifled a sigh. It was going to be a long night.

⚜

LORIS PAUSED AT THE SLIGHTLY OPENED DOOR, HIS HAND on the handle. His father and brother stood by the fireplace, oblivious that he could hear everything.

"What the hell is Loris doing here?" Jannik, the king of the southern lands of Varannis, exclaimed to Joran.

"This is a surprise to me as well," Joran replied.

There were marked similarities between father and son, including their tanned skin and brown hair bleached by the sun. Jannik's hair had turned half gray, and his skin was more rubbery. Both wiry and average in stature, there was a strength born out of facing the sea.

Where Jannik was rough in his dealings with others, Joran

was smooth and had an uncanny ability to say the right thing in every situation. Where Jannik was quick in his decisions, Joran would take his time. He smoothed his father's rough edges. It was no wonder that Jannik wanted Joran at the Gathering.

Jannik, Loris knew well, was not a patient man. He didn't like it when his orders were not followed.

Loris tamped the smile of anticipation and entered the room. Unlike his father and his brother, his hair was a light gold that went past his ears and framed a thin and sallow face. No good on a horse nor on a ship, he spent a lot of time in the library, pouring over books, as evidenced by his pale skin. Thin and slight, he had been sickly as a child. A veritable weakling compared to his four older brothers, he disgusted his father when he would throw up on the prow of the ship whenever they sailed out to sea. Now, his father gave him the same look when he entered the door.

"What are you doing here?" barked Jannik.

"Why, hello to you too, Father." Loris bowed low.

"Didn't I tell you to stay with your brothers?"

"I'm in charge of our libraries and our records. This is a momentous occasion. I can be of help to you."

"And how can you help me?"

"Why, I can be your precept."

"I have one already."

"Father, I'm smarter than he is."

"Don't get in the way, Loris. I don't want you playing with our chances here."

"I'm not stupid, father. Give me some credit."

"You may stay here in Normundir, but not to attend the Gathering."

There was no moving Jannik. "As you wish," he said petulantly.

"Father," Joran interjected. "Why not let Loris sit in? He has traveled a long way."

Jannik took a deep breath. "You are not allowed to talk, do you understand?"

"Thank you, Father." Loris smiled at Joran in thanks but seethed with rage inside. He didn't need his help. Now Joran thought he had done him a favor.

"Does Jaken have any messages for me?" Jannik asked.

Loris answered with his practiced replies. "He has everything handled and wishes you and Joran a successful bout of negotiations."

"What about the enemy ships? Have they retreated?"

"Those that weren't captured sailed off when it became clear that the spell of concealment was broken. The Lord of Breven made good on his promise and sent more ships to our aid. Even now, we're taking steps to rebuild the destroyed sections of the port."

Jannik gestured toward the door. "That's all. You may go."

Loris was about to say something, but Joran grabbed his arm and pulled him outside.

"Stop aggravating him."

"I didn't say anything."

"You were about to. I can tell."

Loris shrugged. "I can't help it. He's easily riled."

"Since when did this all become a game to you?"

"When I finally realized that he'll never approve of me. Now, if you'll excuse me, I have to visit Mother."

Ailene stood in the middle of the room when Loris came in. She was a stately woman, and he always found comfort in her gracefulness. He went into her arms and embraced her. Loris knew that his mother suffered. All his brothers were just like his father—brusque and uneducated. There was no culture in them or interest in things other than fighting and drinking.

Adrina was seated by the window. She'd risen when he came in. "Loris."

Loris gave her an exaggerated bow. "My lovely sister."

"Adrina, why don't you ask Joran if he can take you for a walk. I'd like a word with Loris." Ailene ushered Adrina out of the room and shut the door. "Come, have a seat. You must be famished and tired." She led Loris to the table she had prepared for his arrival.

"Did you convince your brothers?" she asked without preamble.

"Yes, Mother."

"And they agreed?"

"They had no choice. Our forces were bigger."

She smiled and nodded. "We are only doing what's best for the kingdom and for your father."

"Even though he treats you like a second-rate citizen."

"Loris, you will not speak ill of your father. He is our king and sovereign."

"Well, he never gave a fig about me."

She took his hand. "It's because you're different from your brothers. They're all just like your father. You are more like me. Who do you think guides your father's rash thinking? Who ensured the alliance with Breven and the lesser kingdoms?" She squeezed his hand gently. "We are running the kingdom, you and I."

"I wish it didn't matter."

"It will always matter my dear, for you are his son. But always think of the bigger picture. Isn't that what I have always taught you?"

He smiled a little then. "Yes, Mother, you taught me well."

She looked at him, suspicious. "Did you veer away from our plan?"

"I improvised, but don't worry yourself. I was able to wake the God of Midir. Now, we have control of our kingdom. Breven and the island kingdoms have cooperated."

"Are you sure about your stepbrothers? Jaken?" Her voice trailed off.

"We've reached an understanding. Don't worry, mother."

"It's a necessity we have had to do," she said bitterly. "Or we would have lost everything. Even now, Edward's forces are getting stronger. We have to stand our ground and hold our own."

"Varannis will never bow to Mandubrath."

"Your father still seems to think a compromise needs to happen for peace."

"He doesn't strike me as the type to compromise."

"Your father's getting old and has talked about being tired of war. He doesn't want to bow down to Edward, but he wants a deal that will ensure peace and a place on the throne. Are you able to attend the Gathering?"

"Yes, Joran convinced father," he sneered.

"Joran's a good man. Try to get him on your side."

"Yes, Mother."

"Remember, everything hinges on you now."

"I won't fail you, Mother. Now, if you'll excuse me?" He stood up.

She nodded and kissed his cheek. "Well, off you go. You should introduce yourself to your aunt."

Loris kissed her cheek and promptly left. He walked away from her rooms and to the window facing the village. He saw the royals, and the nobles seated at the dais, watching the games. Rikard and his aunt, Leticia, sat beside none other than the high and mighty Edward. You'd think they'd take the Gathering more seriously. Joran had said they had these games to raise morale, build camaraderie. What a bunch of idiots.

Look at all those fawning women trying to get Edward's attention. He probably fucked all of them. He turned his attention back to the joust and scowled. Stupid games. All brawn and no thinking. He'd never been good at fighting, but he was smart. Smarter than everyone in this godforsaken place.

He remembered when he was young, how he'd wished that one day the Tribunal would take him away and make him their own. But it had never happened. All he had was loneliness and ridicule.

All that had changed now. He had Cain and the God of Midir. His beautiful Cain, who looked like a Rover with his long braided black hair and eyes that slanted upward. He was in the Borderlands, awaiting Loris's signal to attack Normundir with the army they had put together. With the God of Midir, these lands would be theirs to rule.

He clenched his fist and felt the strength there. Yes, things were different now, and soon, everyone would learn of his greatness.

৩৯৩

THE CASTLE WAS ABLAZE WITH LIGHTS. PENNANTS FOR EACH kingdom and tribe hung outside by the great doors as a reminder to everyone who passed by that the Gathering was taking place.

Drinks and food were given out freely to all. Leona watched those who stayed back. There was a grimness to them, the ones who had lost loved ones. They'd won the battle but had lost everything. Once inside the castle court-yard, people's clothes became more refined, their actions more stilted.

Doyle looked at her sideways. "Wish you were somewhere else?"

She wrinkled her nose. "I suppose you will say you're glad to be invited to this banquet."

"Of course." He was practically rubbing his hands together.

"Tanya can take my place. She'd be a good substitute."

"Hmmm, not quite. She'd distract all the men. That changes how they talk and act. You can help corroborate what I see and hear. Tanya has her uses, in the right moments."

"You're saying I'm a wallflower?"

"You're a good wallflower, Leona. Pretty as the most vibrant heather I've ever seen," Doyle added.

She laughed. "I'm not sure if I should be flattered."

"Definitely flattered."

"In that case, thank you for the compliment. I wanted to ask you if you've heard if Belinda is here? I haven't seen her."

Doyle nodded. "She's back in Kentigern. I heard her father sent soldiers as soon as the message came out that we were attacked."

"That's too bad. She would have enjoyed this," Leona said wistfully.

The doors to the main hall opened with rows of guards on either side. An explosion of sounds and colors greeted them. The hall had always been big, but Leona had never seen it this full. Lords and ladies in full regalia milled around. Up on the dais, the kings of the land sat alongside each other, talking with whoever was closest to them.

A small group of minstrels played music along the far corner of the room. Tables filled the hall, except for a large area in the center where a few people danced and conversed.

Leona and Doyle went to the back of the hall and found a table there. Leona's attention strayed to the dais. It was the first time she'd seen Edward since he'd left with her father. Edward sat with the careless ease of one used to sitting on the throne. Though his eyes betrayed nothing and he seemed amiable, there was a wall that nobody could penetrate. The perceptive ones were more careful and kept the conversation short, but many others were oblivious or didn't seem to care.

Helen was in the latter group. She stood with the other women and as per usual, they fawned all over him. Leona couldn't help but roll her eyes. She was about to turn away when she realized Edward was watching her, a brow raised in question. Leona just smiled and shrugged. He inclined his head slightly, his eyes going past her right side. She turned her gaze to where he was gesturing when she spotted Gage walking toward her.

"Gage," she beamed. "It feels like a long time."

"It does, doesn't it?" He extended a hand to shake hers. Curious at the action, she took his hand and felt a small folded piece of paper. She took it and retracted her hand, keeping the note in her palm.

A bard sounded a horn to signify the beginning of the banquet.

Gage inclined his head. "It seems we're about to begin. It was good seeing you, Leona."

"Likewise."

Another horn sounded, and the room hushed as the first group of nobility came forward. It was a dizzying array of people.

From the Borderland Rovers, Raygar of the Horse Whisperers and Enori of the Midori Gypsies. Raygar was a big burly man with tattoos all across his arms. His beard had taken over his face, and it was impossible to tell what he looked like.

Enori was a dark-skinned woman whose forehead had small black thorn-like protrusions. The expression in her almond-shaped eyes and the way she held herself made her fierce. Her hair was in braids and bangles circled her arms all the way to the elbows.

Anva, the undisputed queen of the Borderlands, was

absent from the Gathering. But nobody truly expected her to be there. She disregarded the customs of those who lived beyond the Borderlands, just as all the Rovers did.

Leona watched the lords and ladies as they walked forward and introduced themselves. She looked at all the ladies in their fineries and glanced at herself. She wore a long, fitted tan jacket and a white shirt. Her dark green pants and black boots were a contrast. She had no jewelry and the fanciest part of her outfit was an intricately carved belt. The simplicity of her outfit emphasized her natural beauty. She wore her twin swords like a woman would wear her jewelry.

"Entertained?" a voice said from behind her.

"Highly," she answered with a smile as she turned around and stood up. "Jamie! I thought you didn't get back until tomorrow?"

"Couldn't miss all this now, could I?" He gestured to the seat beside Leona, "May I?"

She raised an eyebrow. "Aren't you supposed to be there?" She gestured to the center of the hall where much laughter circled around a group of men and women who danced to a lively tune.

"Charm the women and find a wife?" Doyle chimed in with a grin.

"Oh, please. Not you, too." He grimaced as he sat down. "Believe me, old man, I've had the talk. I'm counting myself lucky that Edward's here. All the women here seem to think he's here to find himself a wife. Takes the pressure off of me."

Leona just shook her head in amusement. Jamie had inherited their mother's fair hair, blue eyes, and sunny complexion, while Leona had the dark hair, dark eyes, and pale complexion that was more in line with their father's side of the family; although Rikard's hair and beard had gone gray with age.

"Well, how are you, Doyle, old man?" Jamie slapped him on the back.

"Same as always. Trying to keep up with you youngsters, making sure there's no trouble to be had."

Leona gave a hoot of laughter. "Thank you, Doyle. You're doing a mighty fine job, if our last mission was any sign."

At a gesture, a servant laid a plate of food in front of Jamie. "I heard you had an adventure trying to get here."

"That's an understatement," Leona said.

"I also heard you got reamed."

Leona shrugged. "In front of everybody."

"Father said you went through Shemal Pass. What did you see?"

"Things we probably shouldn't talk about here," Doyle said. "I suppose people could call it an adventure since we got out of it alive. It's a long story; Leona could enlighten you at another time."

"I'm surprised you didn't get it out of Father or Edward," Leona remarked.

Jamie shook his head wryly. "First, Father was furious. I'm not stupid enough to bring it up until he's calmed down. Second, we were not idle the whole time out in the field; we were in a battle, just in case you forgot."

Leona just smiled sweetly at him. He looked almost offended, but he continued, "And third, Edward isn't the most talkative person. You should know since you've spent enough time with him. Even the lovely Adrina couldn't get past his shell. She spent most of the journey trying to get him to talk."

"Did she travel with you the whole time?"

"Father tried to get Adrina and our aunt to come here sooner, but they wanted to stay."

"Were you pleased that they waited? Since she was lovely?" Leona teased through the stab of jealousy over the mention of this woman who apparently had been with Edward during the journey back to Normundir.

"Yes," Jamie said after a moment.

Leona smiled consolingly at Jamie. "I'm glad you're being the obedient son and on the search for a bride."

He grimaced. "Don't start on me. I've had enough of the 'find a bride before your father takes things in his own hands' talk from Mother. Not everyone can be as lucky as you, dear Leona."

"What a nightmare," she said with a teasing smile. "Why don't you tell us of the battle on the coast? Everyone's talking about how you and Edward defeated the enemy. You are quite the hero."

Something dimmed in Jamie's eyes. "I suppose, in the scheme of things."

She pretended gaiety, but in a soft undertone asked him, "Do you want to talk about it?"

"I—" Jamie saw their mother signaling to him and winced.

Leona followed his gaze. "Go," she urged him. "You'll pay later if you don't."

Leona watched her brother resume the pleasant smile and charm as he conversed with their noble guests. Edward sat by her father, content to be apart from the rest of the party. Turning back to Doyle, she said, "Something's wrong."

Doyle nodded slowly. "He's never been exposed to the gruesome reality of war. Might do him some good if you talk to him."

At the tail end of the banquet, Leona excused herself. She walked to one of the smaller gates along the courtyard walls. The guard recognized her and moved aside. She walked up a set of stairs that led to the top of the courtyard walls. From there, she made her way to the tallest part of the wall and walked to the watchtower's roof.

She sat down on the rafters and hugged her knees to

herself. The angle hid her from the castle and offered a magnificent view of the mountains. The cold air on her face felt like freedom as she watched the moonlight dance on the peaks.

Leona took the note from her pocket. She was expecting something soulful—maybe Edward had thought of her while he was gone, but all it contained was a location in the castle in the western wing. He wanted to see her. The typical arrogance made her smile.

It was quite some time before footsteps alerted her to an incoming presence. Without turning, she greeted Jamie.

"You scared me!" he exclaimed.

"I knew you'd come here." She gestured to the space beside her. He plopped down and looked out at the mountains and the star-studded night sky.

"It does get tiring," he admitted.

"Want to talk about it?"

"Am I that obvious?"

"Only to me."

He was silent for a time. After a while, he spoke up, "What have you learned of our so-called exploits?"

"That you and Edward led the attack that saved the day. Everyone's talking about it. Some say you won the battle at sea; others say you drove the enemy out to sea. Which is it?"

"There's truth to what you've heard. We were out in the sea..." He told her everything that had happened. At the end of it all, he fumbled, his eyes haunted. "That ship was full of innocent people. Just like that, they died. I tried to reason with Edward to save them all, but he'd already decided and called out the order."

Leona had an image of the ship appear in her head. People crowding the ship and begging for their lives. Anger bubbled up inside her. She wanted to do what Jamie had done, but more. She had this need—no, a demand for answers. Edward should have thought of those people. They had been far removed from him, but that was the least he could have done.

The anger gave way to an image of Edward in Storwood, pounding and shaping that sword in the blacksmith's workshop. She recalled the scars across his back. And she recalled the vehemence in his voice—his call for better lives for the people in all the lands.

Leona forced for her voice to be calm. "Are you upset because he made the call that killed everyone on board?"

"I'm upset at myself for not being man enough. I knew the consequences if we let them live, but I faltered. How can I be king one day if I fail in making those types of decisions?" He paused and looked at his hands. She wanted to comfort him, but he needed somebody to listen.

He looked up and at her. "You know what Edward told me?"

"What's that?"

"He told me it was right to feel that way. That I should always make the right decision, regardless of my emotions. I saw those people. They did nothing wrong. I thought every life is precious. Then war happens. When we came back on land, Edward said nothing about me faltering. He let everyone believe I made the right decision. Father's proud of me for all the wrong reasons."

"Jamie, don't do this. You didn't fail. Your first instinct was to protect the innocents. That speaks highly of your character. Making that decision to sacrifice those people for the greater good comes with experience. Edward has had more years as king, and I bet you he's faltered, too."

"Edward said I should consider it a lesson learned. That one day, when I'm king, I'll look back to that moment in my time of crisis. Because of that, I'll make the right call when it's needed."

"He's right, you know. When the days comes, I know you'll be a good king."

"He carries a lot on his shoulders."

"Yes, he does."

Jamie looked at her with narrowed eyes. "You're not one of his admirers, are you? There are legions of women fawning over him. Please tell me you're not one of them."

Leona rolled her eyes. "Do you see me fawning?"

"That'll be the day. Good! Somebody has resisted his charms," Jamie mocked. "I'll tell him he's losing his touch."

"You are ridiculous. Is it because the lovely Adrina isn't immune to his charms?" She raised an eyebrow.

"She's charmed by his title," Jamie muttered. "So how was it? The journey with him?"

"Plenty of annoying moments, especially with the women."

He laughed again. "You know you're also a woman, right?"

"I nearly pulled my hair out."

Jamie immediately sobered up. "Will you tell me about Shemal Pass and the Bruadar?"

She grew pensive. "It was like being in a dream, except every time you think you'll wake up, you don't. I'm not even sure how we made it out alive. I've been through it before. This time was different." She told him about her encounter with the boy she'd once killed. How her grabbing had started to come back.

Jamie raised a hand and stopped Leona. "I wish you wouldn't call it grabbing. You're wielding power, not stealing it."

"It feels the same," she muttered.

"Well, I'm glad you're home."

"Me, too," Leona sincerely said.

Jamie left shortly, leaving Leona with her thoughts. She looked at mountains and remembered Shemal Pass.

Leona made her way down and back to the castle through the servant's entrance. This was her playground. She had grown up exploring every nook and cranny. She and Jamie used to play games where they would hide and one would try to find the other.

Her mother had mentioned where she planned on putting her guests, and Leona used that knowledge as she quietly made her way through the halls. She reached up for her necklace as she entered one of the hidden doors. The same key she'd used to deploy the flare, she also used to open locked doors and entryways within the castle's tunnels. She and Jamie had been given identical keys when they each turned fifteen.

She groped her way along the narrow tunnel and ignored the claustrophobia that crept up her throat. She squeezed through a narrow section toward another door. She took her necklace off and transformed it into a key.

Leona wound the chain around her wrist before inserting it to the small notch on the door. She pushed at it and quickly closed it as she saw a servant walking nearby. She waited before she opened the door again. Straightening up and making sure she had no cobwebs clinging to her hair, she proceeded into the deserted hallway.

It was quiet in this section of the castle and conspicuously empty. She walked toward the double doors guarded by Gage and Alik. They both looked surprised when they saw her, but before she could say anything, they opened the doors.

Now, it was her turn to be surprised.

She walked inside, and the doors closed behind her. At the far end of the room, Edward sat by the fireplace with a goblet of wine in one hand. He made no move to acknowledge her.

Leona wasn't sure what he was thinking, and she almost regretted coming here. He sensed her hesitation and held out a hand. She took the remaining steps to him but didn't take his hand.

"You look different," she said with hesitation.

"I'm still the same, Leona."

"I didn't plan on coming here."

"What made you change your mind?"

"I suppose..." she paused and shook her head. "I couldn't stay away."

"I was wishing for you, and here you are." He smiled a little.

"You look younger, but you still look like a wolf in a herd of lambs."

"Yes, that's what I am." His eyes clouded with grief.

Instead of disagreeing with him, she said, "That you are. But I know you. You would never use your power with disregard for the consequences, so you grieve for the innocents and the lives lost on the battlefield."

He closed his eyes. "Even though there was a chance for those innocents to live, I didn't think to save them. They were mothers, fathers, daughters, and sons."

"They were gone already." Her voice broke. "Heed what you said to Jamie. Be content knowing they are no longer in pain. You did the right thing."

He opened his eyes and looked squarely into hers. "Jamie told you what happened?"

She nodded.

"I saw you talking with him at the banquet."

"I wasn't aware you were watching me."

"What is he to you, Leona?"

His question caught her by surprise. She wished she could tell him that Jamie was her brother. "I grew up knowing him. I told you I was a loner when I was in training. He's one of the few I got along with when I was young."

"I imagine he was lonely growing up."

"Curse of royalty as an only child," she stated as a matter of fact.

He chuckled, but there was no humor in his eyes. Wanting to cheer him up, Leona sat down on the adjacent chair and rested her chin on her hand. "So, Your Majesty, why don't you tell me about tomorrow? What do you hope to accomplish in the Gathering?" she asked in as grand a voice she could conjure.

"You want the truth?"

"Always."

"I don't want any more wars. These idiotic skirmishes between the seven kingdoms. It does nothing but hurt our people. Not the nobles. Everyone else—just like the villagers in Storwood. They just want to deal with their lives. To raise their children and feed themselves. But because of the power of the few, they live and they die by our words." Edward paused and shook his head. "Have you seen how the people who work in the mines are treated? They're slaves for a pittance. We want to call ourselves more civilized than the Bahadurians because we don't have slaves. But that's what they are. They're given food and lodging. Nothing else. They need to be paid better so they can provide properly for their families and not live miserable lives that don't mean anything."

Leona wanted to reach out to him. The anguish in his voice was palpable. "Was that how it was in Bahadur?"

"I felt like nothing there. Sometimes, as punishment, I'd be sent to the mines. One week there was torture. But that's nothing to be compared to when Rhys suffered a blight on their crops. All the kings and nobles just debated how much they should ask in exchange. People were starving, and nothing was happening. I sent as much as Mandubrath could offer, but that wasn't enough. We have all have a duty to each other."

"And when you unite the kingdoms? Will Mandubrath always be the seat of power?"

"It should be a vote," Edward said with a faraway look in his eyes.

"Will you let people vote now?"

"We're not ready for that."

"So you think you're the only one capable of doing this?"

"Yes."

"That's arrogant of you."

"Everything I've seen doesn't lead me to believe that anyone can do better. I need to start this. Show everyone that it's possible to create and maintain wealth without having to put ordinary people at your mercy."

"Did your father think this way?"

"Somewhat. He wanted to unite the lands. But he never thought about the lives of the normal people. He was a good man, but it never crossed his mind. Just like it never crosses the minds of any of the kings and nobles."

"You've really thought about this, haven't you?"

"What else do you think about when you're forced in a cage or work in a mine as punishment?"

"I think you're a dreamer, but I like your dream. I still think you're an arrogant ass, but if you pull this off, maybe you'll show them what's possible."

Edward gazed at her, as if trying to gauge her words. He eventually nodded. "Will you stay with me tonight?"

She thought back to Margret's and couldn't help but say yes.

Early morning, before the sun rose and dawn was still but a whisper, Leona woke up. Edward still lay asleep on his side, a shoulder's width away. She eased away, careful not to wake him. Her clothes were rumpled from sleep, and she wondered how she could get back to the temple and change without anyone noticing her.

Leona braided her hair before she shrugged into her boots.

"Are you going to leave without saying goodbye?" He leaned up on his arm.

"I didn't want to wake you."

"Come here." He crooked a finger at her.

"Why?" She crossed her arms.

Edward sat up and combed a hand through his hair.

Leona shook her head in disgust. "How can your hair be perfect and mine's all tangled up?"

"I have something for you."

"It's not ferum to heat my tea, is it?" Leona teased.

He held up a small ring between his thumb and forefinger. "It's a trinket. To match your bracelet and necklace," he added.

"Where'd you get it from?" Leona still had her arms crossed.

"So suspicious. Come here. Let's see if it fits."

"Fine." Leona sat down beside him. "Let me see it."

He handed it to her. Leona looked at the ring closely. The white silver metal was slim but heavy. Three green round stones adorned the ring.

"Is it praevadium?" Leona put it on her ring finger. It was too loose, but it fit her middle finger perfectly. Curious, she tapped into the metal and yelped at the fire that bloomed out of her hands.

Edward frowned. "You need to practice."

"People stopped giving me their ferum years ago. And yours...it's different." She narrowed her eyes. "You didn't make this at Margret's, did you?"

"No." He chuckled. "I'm not that skilled. I can make you a sword, a shield, or a hammer."

"I really like it, Edward. But this is rare. You should keep it for your future wife." Leona was about to take it off when he closed a hand on her fist.

"Keep it. Just in case your necklace runs out of fire. This will keep your tea warm. You can make your own campfire. Maybe even do the sparks as a magic trick."

"I really can't take this."

"Leona, I've enough rings and jewelry in Mandubrath. Keep this one. You took Margret's gift of ferum, why not this?"

She twisted the ring between her thumb and forefinger. Why she hesitated at the gift made her feel silly. "Thank you. I will always treasure it."

Leona left Edward's room and made her way out of the castle without anyone noticing her. She looked to the brightening sky and felt unsettled, still wondering at the symbol the ring stood for. Or why she'd accepted it, knowing that she'd always think of him.

❦ 15 ❦

Leona entered the great hall just behind Trevelyn, his assistant bobbling about with paper and writing implements. Leona ignored the two of them and looked around with wonder. The cavernous hall had flags from every kingdom and even the Borderlands. A large map hung on one wall. Long tables formed a big square in the center of the hall. Around the perimeter of the square were long-backed chairs. Benches lined the walls behind the chairs.

Leona took her seat in the back and watched as more people came into the hall. The hum of voices became a roar

A bell clanged proclaiming order in the room. Those outside the Great Hall were ushered inside. The kings, nobles, tribes leaders, and Greyfolk Elders sat down on the chairs along the tables. Precepts sat on the benches by the walls. Most of them were holding onto maps and books.

"Silence, please. Silence." The deep voice boomed over the dim roar of voices in the great hall. "Now I have your attention, for those who aren't seated, please find a seat." He was a tall man, made even bigger by his girth and his large presence. He looked at everyone in the room with the serious demeanor of someone who had a big job ahead of him. Leona leaned forward. Esra was the one who manned the Great Library in Midroska. Esra spent his days greeting visitors and telling stories to all who would like to hear them. Leona thought of Belinda and how she would have loved to hear him talk.

His official role at the Gathering was to welcome all and to facilitate the games as the Master of Ceremonies.

When everyone was seated, Esra began by weaving a tale of times past, of peace and then of war. He talked of heroes, warriors, and kings. He talked of past glories and a hope for a future that would outshine all else in the past. When he reached the present—the battle waged on the coast, and the threat that came from a force that was sight unseen, everyone was enthralled.

Esra spoke of the Gathering and what it represented for everyone in the lands. He expounded poetry and played on the mood of the room. Everyone was captivated with his tales of courage and what it meant for the future.

Leona looked around the room and noticed that Edward listened, but betrayed no expression. She thought again of the ring he had given her. What it might mean. He said it was just a gift, but still, she couldn't help but feel that there was more.

Her father couldn't hide his impatience to start. Rikard was never one for stories. He used to tell her not to dillydally with anything—say it like it is and do whatever needed to get done. Then he would add, "It's cold up here, and it can kill you if you wait too long." Most of the northerners shared that thinking.

Leona returned her focus to Esra. He ended his message with one of hope for a golden future that would begin with the first annual Gathering.

People couldn't help it, they all clapped. He was fantastic, a master storyteller. He bowed, and he turned the stage over to Trevelyn.

"Rules and courtesy. Yes. Hmmm. Shall we talk about how we are to comport ourselves during the Gathering?" Trevelyn looked for input from the leaders in front of him, but all of them were impatient to start. He talked about common courtesies and expectations and succeeded in almost putting the whole room to sleep. "And since none of our Elders can make the journey, Irena and I are the Tribunal's representatives."

Robert, the King of Menoa, rolled his eyes at that. Leona could take a guess at what he was thinking. To everybody, the Elders were a figment of the Tribunal's imagination. A ruse. A myth they used to propagate the mystery of the Tribunal. Leona thought the same but had never voiced it. Some of her brothers and sisters in the Tribunal had said the same thing and had always been punished for it.

Robert asked the question on everybody's minds. "Are the Borderlands secure?"

"For now," Trevelyn replied. "From what knowledge we've gotten, Normundir and Midroska were the ultimate targets of this attack."

Bel-Delilani raised a hand. "Not all the Greyfolk agreed with this. I speak for those who fought those who lost their way."

"As do we." Raygar gestured to Enori and the other Rovers. "We have lost steads and tribes. Most were victims. I won't apologize for those who joined the enemy's forces. I don't speak for them."

"The prisoners we've interrogated have said more are coming," Edward said as Rikard and Jannik nodded in assent. "We have to prepare."

Trevelyn spoke up. "Bahadur is a large land. We've mostly left each other alone because of the vast expanse of the Gowad Sea. Bahadur is also divided. They have their alliances just like everyone here does. The attack mounted on the eastern Borderlands was by the Shahan of Arshavir, one of the more powerful leaders in Bahadur."

"You never even gave us warning. I've heard rumors you have people over there," Jannik pointed out.

"We have less than a handful. They are there to observe, and what we learn is available in the Great Library. Truth be told, we have received no messages." Trevelyn raised a hand when the other leaders sputtered. "Which is not unusual. It's far away, after all. They have to be careful for our kind are, more often than not, commodities in a land that thinks of us as inconsequential and barbaric. I believe the term they use is 'flesher'."

"Inconsequential and barbaric? They're the ones who look barbaric," Robert said.

The Greyfolk and Rovers looked at him in derision.

"Guard your tongue, else you see barbaric actions against you." Raygar, the rough-looking tribe leader from the Borderlands, stood up with fists clenched.

"Are you threatening me? You can't even protect the Borderlands. We had to intercede."

"My people are grateful for the help; however, we do not wish to bow down to anyone."

"We know what you want as repayment," Enori, the leader of the Midori tribe in the Borderlands, spat out. "You want our lands."

"I don't understand why it should be so hard. We could help you live better lives and not live off the scraps of the land," Jannik explained.

"We are not stupid. Spare me and Raygar the filth of your lies."

It was Robert, now, who sputtered and got to his feet. "You dare call me a liar?"

"In our tribe, I would have called you out for your disrespect. For the sake of this occasion, I will hold my tongue. I can't guarantee that for the next time," Enori warned him.

Robert sneered. "Well, then, call me out now. I have no problem defending my honor."

Raygar looked him up and down, smiled, and shook his head. "She is more than you can handle, impudent king. The Midori tribe, peaceful as they are, are also savage warriors, more so the women than the men. Another thing you have to consider is the White Queen. She will let no one touch the Borderlands. She protects what's hers."

"What kind of protection is it when half your people are dead because she did nothing to stop the invaders from going into the Borderlands? She isn't even here. Do you speak for Queen Anva?" Jannik asked.

Enori pierced him with her eyes. "We speak only for our people. We carry the risk for our own existence. Why, the Greyfolk have their spirits, and even they were not protected against their own."

Now it was the Greyfolk Elders' turn to be angry. "The Guardians of the Helligs harbored us in our time of need and gave us what we needed. That is how they protected us," Bel-Delilani replied in a placid tone.

"You hid in the mountains while the courts of men traipsed along." Enori sneered.

Those who had traveled with Edward northward were angered and joined in the fray. Throughout the conflicted and heated exchange, Leona marked the tension in the room, save for one person. She glimpsed the momentary glee and amusement before it was masked. Strange, she thought. Whoever he was, he was enjoying the conflict.

"Who's that?" she asked Doyle and inclined her head at the pale-faced young man seated behind Jannik.

"I believe it's one of Jannik's many sons."

"He looks nothing like his brother," she mused.

"He takes more after his mother's side of the family."

Leona saw it now. The golden hair, the blue eyes, and the shape of his face—just like her own mother's.

There was something about him—the gleeful smile and the sly look in his eyes—it made the hair on her arms stand up. He turned his head and captured her eyes. He gave her a slight smile as if he knew she was watching him and then turned back to the heated exchange.

"His father doesn't think much of him," Doyle continued. "Jannik had a ship built for each of his sons, except for this one. Loris. That's his name. Makes you wonder what he's doing here."

Half the room quieted when Edward raised a hand. "I'm not asking for repayment. Our victory is everyone's."

"And yet we lost more than you. We fight for our existence and in that fight, we also defended the other kingdoms when this threat came into our lands," Raygar pointed out.

"Such arrogance. You're not the only ones that suffered," reminded Bel-Delilani.

"Weren't most of your people responsible for this war? Traitors can't be trusted," Robert added.

Kal-Ranok, a Greyfolk elder, narrowed his eyes and stood up. "Who did you call traitors?"

"Enough," Edward said in a soft voice. "Protecting our lands is a shared responsibility. Didn't we all fight together and emerge victorious? There is much to resolve amongst ourselves." He looked at everybody in the room. "We saw what they are capable of."

"What do you propose?" Raygar asked with a tinge of sarcasm.

"I'm saying we have to show a unified front to protect Bearnas." Edward was much in control of the room, and he continued. "Bahadur's leaders have strong alliances amongst themselves. They may have already joined forces to attack our lands, and Arshavir was just the beginning. There are tribes among the Greyfolk and Rovers that have joined with them, and that is as much our fault as theirs. Our disunity and prejudice has blinded us to the fact of our shared destinies. We'll face them again—that much is certain. My proposal is that we use this respite to figure out how we can create this unity we need to defend our lands. This bickering will be our downfall."

Rikard gave a signal to Esra, who then nudged the squire beside him. The squire received an annoyed scowl from Rikard, and he promptly rang the bell for luncheon.

The Gathering went on for several more hours. When it finally adjourned for the day, the games began. The courtyard was transformed into a joyful place of celebration.

Royalty, nobles, and commoners all crowded together in the main area where the master storyteller, Esra, once again took the stage and introduced the games and the main contenders. He swept everyone up in the majesty of his wondrous prose. Thunderous applause and cheers met him when he finished.

There were sword fights, archery, horse riding, jousts, and even pig races. There was singing, dancing, and acrobatics.

"This is amazing," Leona exclaimed to herself. She walked around, content to watch, until she saw a familiar face.

"Tanya!" She waved and called to the woman with the long red cloak. Tanya, one of Leona's sisters from the Tribunal, was a warrior whose main post was in Midroska. She was tall and beautiful, with long brown hair filled with gold and red flecks. Her laughing eyes were a deep rich blue and framed with long and thick eyelashes. Her skin was a perfect bronze and her bone structure was sharp, and she had a veritable group of men who openly stared at her.

"Leona!" Tanya gave her a hug. "It's so good to see you."

"When did you get here?"

"Just this morning, but I'm to leave soon," Tanya said with regret. "This is wonderful! It's like a festival. I thought things would be stuffy for the whole Gathering."

"I did, too. Not that it would be bad, but this makes it fun for everybody."

"Anything exciting in the Gathering?"

"Trevelyn got blamed by the kings for not warning everyone about the concealed army in the Borderlands."

Tanya shrugged. "What else is new? Why don't you tell me about your last mission?"

"Where do I start?"

She hooked an arm through Leona's and walked through the booths. "You can start with Edward. Tell me about him."

"He's a good fighter and a good leader," Leona said warily.

"Come on, Leona. Help me out here. There has to be more. You make him sound like a bore when he looks absolutely delicious. When I heard you were assigned to provide safe passage for him, I was so jealous. What's he like? Did he talk to you?"

Leona rolled her eyes. "He had to at some point."

"Why are you playing coy?" Tanya narrowed her eyes and tilted her head.

"I'm not playing coy. He wasn't stuffy or arrogant like I thought he would be. He's a decent person. More than decent, actually."

"That's not bad. It almost sounds like he made an impression."

"He did." Leona looked at Edward then, seated on the dais, watching the joust. He was listening to the beautiful woman seated beside him. Jamie's Princess Adrina. They looked good together. Leona couldn't help but feel that quick stab of jealousy again.

Leona turned back to Tanya. "What did you want to know?"

Now, it was Tanya who rolled her eyes. "Heaven help me," she exclaimed. "How does he look naked?"

Leona nearly choked. "Excuse me? Was I supposed to see him naked? I didn't know it was expected of me to inspect him."

"Never doubt the power of inspection. You'll be amazed at what you might find out. Lord Carbry. I needed to get information from him. He looked built. All big and beefy arms. Strong face and big hands. Narrow waist and straight back. Well, let me tell you, when he took his clothes off..." Tanya trailed off.

"What?"

"A corset!"

"No, he did not."

"Yes, he did. I was so shocked I was speechless."

They both doubled in laughter.

"You have exciting assignments, Tanya. You never fail to astonish me."

"So do you. You just don't always tell." Tanya pointed to the dais. "Who's that with him right now? She's a looker."

Leona looked at the dais again. "Her name is Adrina. According to Jamie, she's my uncle's daughter with his first wife."

At that exact moment, Edward locked eyes with Leona and looked at her until somebody walked to his side and asked him a question. Tanya saw the exchange and looked mischievously at Leona.

"He's got it bad, and it's for you." Tanya gave him an appraising look. "He doesn't look like the type who would just twiddle his thumbs. Edward seems like someone who would take action. Am I right?"

"I won't even justify that with an answer."

"Hmm. All right."

"What?"

"Nothing. Bitch ahead," Tanya said under her breath as she pasted a bright smile.

Leona looked over to where Tanya angled her head and groaned when she saw Helen and her retinue headed in their direction.

"Why, little Leona," Helen greeted.

"Your Highness."

Helen looked at Tanya and arched an eyebrow. Leona took the cue and introduced Tanya. Helen nodded in response. "We keep running into each other. I hear you're in the Gathering."

"Yes, I am." Leona nodded.

"Goodness! You are desperate for Edward's attention, aren't you?" The other women around her snickered. "I'm surprised you're not with Edward right now. He might need your protection or to write something for him."

Tanya spoke up through a sweet smile. "Your Highness, it looks like somebody else is looking after His Majesty's needs right now." With that, she inclined her head at the dais.

Helen scowled. "Don't overstep your boundaries, Leona. Just a reminder." With an imperial nod of her head, she hurriedly made her way to the dais.

"Well, then, that was pleasant," Tanya said.

"She's been at it right from the beginning."

"I feel sorry for you. Although, since it looks like you hooked the big fish, dear Helen has something to be snippy about."

"Tanya, there's nothing between the two of us," Leona said, exasperated.

"If you say so."

THE NEXT DAY, AT THE GATHERING IN THE GREAT HALL, things were starting to get contentious.

"Absolutely not!" Raygar pounded a fist on the table. "We are not to be herded like animals."

It was the third day of the Gathering, and Leona had heard this argument in several variations already. She stifled a sigh and wished she were outside.

"A census of tribes and steads differs from herding the Rovers," Trevelyn patiently explained.

"Don't you think we know that you document our whereabouts? We only tolerate your meddling."

"Meddling is a far cry from the aid we provide."

"We pay you for your services. Even your taking some of our children, we accept. A formal census will never happen."

Edward interjected. "It's not just for the Tribunal, Raygar. It might help the Rovers in the future."

Raygar shook his head. "If we want your help, we will go to you ourselves. Otherwise, we like to be left alone."

"Understood," Edward said. "However, the Borderlands are vulnerable to attacks, and your people may not survive another one. I'm proposing to add my own troops to Rikard's in strategic places along your borders."

"Next thing, those troops are taking over."

"My men will bring their own supplies and will only set up camp in places designated by you."

"If we agree to this, it will be so, unless Queen Anva decides to bring her kingdom to those places. Then you'll have to uproot your camp, and we'll help you find another place. If you don't, you willingly sacrifice your troops with no retaliation to us," Raygar warned them.

Enori added, "The supplies that your men bring, make sure they are plentiful enough for our people."

"I will assure that."

Rikard raised a hand. "I can give refuge to anyone who

needs it from your people. Beyond this kingdom and into the mountains where the cold is its own threat, I have a place of sanctuary and enough supplies that would ensure survival should anybody need it."

Enori and Raygar exchanged a glance. "We speak for the Rovers, and we agree to your stipulations."

Edward nodded to them in assent. Rikard seethed as he turned to Edward. "It's impressive that in one fell swoop you expanded your alliances. Is this your plan for inviting all of us to this Gathering? To reel all of us in one by one?"

"An alliance where both parties benefit. Is that not a good thing?"

"Not when it's unequal. Is your goal to assimilate the Borderlands into this thing you call Greater Bearnas?" Rikard challenged.

"Not without Queen Anva's consent or the Rovers."

Edward's calm reply seemed to enrage Rikard. "And if they refuse? Will you wage war on them like you did with the other kingdoms? Will you wage war on me? Jannik? The Greyfolk?"

"Only if you threaten the existence of us all by fighting against Greater Bearnas instead of our common enemy across the sea."

"It's nothing more than a heap of lesser kings bowing down to you waiting for scraps," Rikard huffed.

At this, the nobles that fell within the bounds of Greater Bearnas stood up, angry at the insult that Rikard had just given them. An argument ensued after that, splitting the great hall into chaos.

At a signal from Trevelyn, Esra stood up and called order to the room. When those in the great hall resumed order, Edward spoke up. "Well done, Rikard. Not only have you insulted these men who rule their kingdoms as they see fit, you also insult me and the ideals of our partnership."

Rikard waved a hand across the room. "You control their army. What's more insulting than that?"

"Brother, let's give him a chance," Jannik said calmly.

"Fine." Rikard crossed his arms. "Tell me about this arrangement you've reached with the other kingdoms."

"Peace and a united front. Our best men die on long wars waged against each other. This has made us vulnerable to outside forces that seek to destroy us. The Treaty of Greater Bearnas means that all leaders shall rule their lands as they see fit, but there are laws and rules we hold one another accountable for. As High King, I am the arbiter of justice, to uphold the vision of a prosperous and safe land. To strengthen every kingdom and tribe, instead of weakening them. Yes, I control the armies, but wouldn't you call it a necessity, especially after the battles we've just faced?"

"What's in it for Normundir to ally ourselves with lands that we are separated from by the Borderlands?" Rikard sputtered.

"You need our help to ensure that no enemy reaches your borders, and we need your help should that happen. The mountains beyond the walls of Normundir may provide refuge to those in need," Edward explained.

"We don't have enough supplies to last everyone."

"Then we'll fill your coffers enough to provide insurance, should our people need a place to go to."

Rikard was still unconvinced. "The Haig is a great distance away."

"Just give me your assurance," Edward said.

"It's the only thing I can guarantee."

Jannik leaned forward. "Refuge is all good, but you all forget that my kingdom is at the edge of these lands, the closest to Bahadur. Your proposal to ensure refuge is commendable, but if my kingdom fights, it's also to protect everyone's interests. You control the army of Greater Bearnas. How am I to know you won't attack us with your force to gain control of Varannis? Even now, that's a threat looming over my head."

Edward met Jannik's blazing eyes from across the table. "I'm the least of your worries if the masters of Bahadur attack."

"I'm aware of that. Give me a guarantee that if I need help to defend our lands, I'll have your support, that I won't be caught in between two opposing forces wanting my kingdom."

"What are you proposing?"

Jannik looked around the table before he turned to Edward. "I will join your Treaty and all it implies, given we become allies through marriage. I have a daughter of age. Your marriage to her will give me all the assurance I need. All else means nothing."

Edward was silent, seemingly nonplussed. But he cocked his head as he regarded Jannik. Leona wondered what was going through his head. Her father looked shocked and Jannik was his usual angry self. But Edward...she couldn't tell.

Something tight wound itself in her chest. This was the moment she'd been dreading when he'd asked her to go with him to Mandubrath.

"Even the threat of war?" Robert sputtered out.

"Are you threatening me?" Jannik challenged.

"Don't you think it's presumptuous that the only option is marriage to your daughter when there is a war looming over our heads?"

Jannik slammed his fist on the table. "I want a guarantee that is set in stone."

"Ambition will be the downfall of man," Kal-Ranok said. "Edward is offering a truce to end all wars and fight together, but you will not commit and risk peril to your lands if there is no marriage." Kal-Ranok then turned to Edward. "Our home is ravaged and our own tribes are divided, but we will fight alongside your army with what we still have. You've been through Shemal Pass and the Bruadar and lived to tell the tale. The Guardians have given their blessing, and so I shall."

"I stand by my word," Jannik growled.

Edward raised an eyebrow as he leaned back in his chair. He looked relaxed, but Leona could tell he was expecting this. That was why his reply surprised her. "And if I choose not to marry your daughter?"

"Then should the off-landers come, we still fight the enemy, but under my terms. Your army can do what they will beyond my lands. But know this, I will do whatever it takes for the betterment of my kingdom."

"Frankly, I don't like ultimatums," Edward said. No one breathed for a moment.

Leona waited, like everybody else in the room. Ulterior motives, she thought. Edward's was to unify the kingdoms and Jannik's, for power. Her father, she knew, didn't want to bow down to anybody.

Edward seemed so different from how he had been in Margret's village, Storwood. He wielded power and influence. Gone was the man who seemed content with the simple things in life.

Even though Edward could overpower their armies with his and force their alliance, there was still the hope that one of their daughters would ensnare his attention and therefore ensure theirs was the kingdom that controlled most of the lands.

The room was pregnant with tension when Trevelyn stood up. He looked from Edward to Jannik. "I am only a servant of the Tribunal, but I speak on behalf of the Elders. Discord will be the undoing of our lands. Therefore, we stand by the unity of Greater Bearnas."

Edward nodded at Trevelyn in thanks.

Jannik scowled. "An answer, Edward. This would all be laid to rest. Marriage is all about alliances."

"Is that your way of saying that, should you need our help in defending the seas, you'll turn us down if there is no alliance by marriage?"

"If my army goes down, every kingdom goes down."

"Not necessarily."

"Look upon it as assurance you won't abandon my people in our time of need."

"I have abandoned none of the kingdoms that signed my treaty. The alliance is strong."

"I need a stronger agreement than a signed piece of paper. My daughter or there's no alliance."

Edward seemed tired of the exchange. "I'll consider your proposal."

"I can't believe it," Doyle muttered.

"What part?" Leona asked. She was drained. She'd known this was coming. Edward hadn't said anything while they were in Storwood, but it was only a matter of time. She shouldn't let it get to her, but she had to admit, Edward sort of fascinated her. Leona cringed and quickly covered it up. Doyle was perceptive and nosy. He'd just try to get it out of her if he suspected something.

Leona was so deep in her thoughts that she had to ask Doyle to repeat what he was saying, which earned her a strange look.

"That Edward would turn down that alliance. With Varannis in his hands, Normundir would soon follow," he repeated.

"He didn't say no."

Doyle shrugged. "It's the same thing."

Leona turned her attention back to the table and noticed that Raygar seemed amused. "I always wondered how unions were handled by royalty."

When none found humor, Raygar continued. "There was another matter that was brought to our attention. Your request on neutral territory where none of the travelers will be in danger. Enori and I discussed this and agreed that the Trading Route will be neutral territory."

Robert spoke up. "Ha! I've yet to see a Rover that won't be tempted by coin."

"Now you're insulting us, once again." Enori and Raygar stood up, glaring at Robert and the other nobles who were nodding their heads at what Robert had said.

Robert raised his voice. "Here's my question. How much did the Tribunal pay the Rovers and Queen Anva? Why have you let the Tribunal claim two plots of land in the Borderlands? One of them right on top of my kingdom, from Midroska to the coast. Why wasn't I part of this decision?"

Trevelyn took a while to answer. "We have an arrangement with the Rovers."

"It wasn't ours to keep." Raygar shrugged. "The Tribunal has owned them for far longer than we've been tending to the land."

Rikard furrowed his brow and looked at his precept in question. The precept shook his head. "I can find out, milord."

The other precepts said the same thing. At this, Jannik scowled. He turned around and motioned for Loris. "You know something. Say it then."

"Yes, Father." He smiled smugly, to the disgust of Jannik. "The Borderlands, in its entirety, were in fact the Tribunal's. It wasn't until after the great war when the Tribunal was weakened greatly, and their Elders retreated into their sanctuary, which is now Midroska. Queen Anva claimed the land and gave permission to the Rovers to roam free as gratitude for their help in the war."

"Arrogant," Doyle said under his breath.

A thick silence descended on the hall as everyone looked at Trevelyn. Nobody had known the Tribunal had owned the lands in the past. That would give them the most right to reclaim the lands.

Trevelyn took his time before answering. "We don't wish to claim the Borderlands except for the lands we already have. We don't have the manpower, and frankly, it's a pain to try and tame the Rovers."

At that, the two representatives from the Borderlands almost smiled, for they would make life hell for anybody who would try to claim their lands. "And there's also Queen Anva's nomadic kingdom. We choose not to antagonize her."

"How sure are you that Queen Anva even cares at this point?" one of the nobles asked. "There has been no sighting of her during the battle. She hasn't communicated with any of us. There's absolutely no proof she'll do anything. Is she still alive?"

"She is there. That we are certain of," Enori said.

Trevelyn nodded his head in assent. "We are certain as well."

Leona knew Queen Anva's kingdom was intact and well. She knew with certainty that there was a patch of lush trees, green and silver, somewhere in the Borderlands, for the trees always followed Queen Anva. Her kingdom was sometimes aboveground, sometimes belowground, but always with the trees of green and silver.

LEONA JOINED IN ON THE FESTIVITIES AFTER THE Gathering. This time, it was Tanya and Colm who accompanied her.

"Don't you wonder why the High Healer is here?" Tanya

asked as she watched an archery contest. "If she barely says anything during the Gathering, why bother?"

Leone replied without turning her eyes away from the current archer. "Maybe her presence will remind everyone that she's the best healer across all the kingdoms and lands."

"True... just seems like a waste." Tanya turned to Colm. "What do you think?"

"What I'm wondering is what Edward and High Historian Trevelyn are talking about." Colm nudged his head toward the shaded platform.

Curious, Leona turned her gaze toward Edward and saw that he and Trevelyn were deep in conversation. "I'm sure it's about the Gathering."

"So, Leona, where have you been spending your nights?" Tanya wickedly raised an eyebrow.

Leona rolled her eyes. "The queen offered one of their rooms. Who am I to turn her down?"

"Must be nice to be friends with the queen."

"Being friends with Jamie has its perks. After all, he got me into a lot of trouble when we were kids."

When night fell, Leona went back into the castle and into Edward's rooms. He wasn't there yet, and so she went out into the balcony. From a distance, the snow-capped Hellig Mountains shone under the bright moon. Majestic and mysterious.

The moon itself was full, and in the clear sky, it looked as if she could touch it.

"It's beautiful, isn't it?" Edward's deep voice interrupted her thoughts.

He walked up beside her and gazed at the view. "I'm glad you're here."

"You say that every night," Leona reminded him.

"It's because I'm never sure if you'll show up."

Leona didn't know what to say to that. She wasn't sure

either. Every night she had a debate with herself whether she should or shouldn't be here. She looked up at the sky, at the brightest star that shone. "I remember my father would tell me to look up, to look for the North Star. He said I'd always find home."

"Mine used to tell me to keep my head out of the stars." Edward cocked his head and leaned against the balcony, facing her. "Have you seen your father since the Tribunal?"

"Every now and then."

"Does he know who you are?"

"Why all the questions?" Leona feinted.

"I'm just interested. Why aren't you answering me"

Leona followed the lines of the moon with her eyes, trying to search for an explanation that would appease him. "It's because it's difficult to explain how it is to belong and not truly belong."

"If you're going to lie to me, I'd rather you didn't say anything." Those perceptive eyes bored right through her.

"Fair enough. I should probably leave."

His hand snaked out and caught her arm. "We're not done yet."

"You're leaving soon, Edward. Back to Mandubrath, while I stay here."

"Come with me."

Startled, she looked up at him. "What did you say?"

"Come with me to Mandubrath."

"You know I can't just decide to leave whenever I want. Is that what you and Trevelyn were talking about?"

"Among other things." Edward still hadn't let go of her arm. "He said you could be transferred. If you wanted."

She pushed his hand away. "I can't believe you talked to him."

"He offered it."

She shook her head and took a step back. "And what did you say?"

"I told him it was up to you."

"You know my opinion doesn't matter," she retorted back, her hands fisting at her sides to fight the shaking.

"Don't you want to explore whatever it is that we have?"

"I don't know what you're talking about."

He took her chin and forced her to look at him. "Don't do that. Don't diminish what we have."

"And if I were forced to go with you, what then? I'll be your mistress? Your harlot?"

"Don't put words in my mouth." Edward bit out, then softened his tone. "I'm not asking you to give anything up. Even your freedom. If you have to travel, I won't stop it. I just want you to come home to me."

"No." Leona fought against the rising panic. Edward made it seem like she had a choice, but however good the Tribunal had been to her, once a course had been decided for her, that was it.

"What are you so afraid of? Storwood showed us how it could be with us."

"We weren't anybody there. If I go to Mandubrath with you, people would watch us."

"Who cares about what other people think?"

"I do. I don't like people looking at me as if I'm strange."

"Nobody's going to do that. Just because you're a wielder doesn't mean that everyone is against you."

"You don't know what it's like." Leona looked down at her hands, the panic paving way to clarity. "It doesn't matter, I still won't go with you. I'm sorry if I gave you the wrong impression."

"Look at me when you say that," Edward snapped.

Leona met his eyes. "I didn't mean to give you the impression that there was something more between us."

"We've slept in the same bed almost every night. I look for you when you're not around. Tell me you don't feel the same way."

"We're just friends. That's the way I see us."

"Is it because of Jamie?" Edward bit out. "I've seen how close the two of you are. Have you slept in his bed too?"

"Yes." The lie came out easy. "I've known him for far longer than you. Who do you think I would choose if I had to?"

Edward's eyes shuttered, and he clenched his jaw. Fire shimmered against the edges of his skin. The blaze of heat that came from him nearly made Leona stagger back. It was only pride that held her in place.

"Get out of my sight," Edward finally said.

Leona bristled at the order but left without another word.

She walked blindly to the temple. The image of Edward angry and defeated flashed in her mind. She'd never consciously hurt someone like that before. He'd eventually see that he was better off without her.

She'd been grilled since childhood that every action should be for the greater good. He needed to marry somebody who could further the alliances and strengthen the unity between the lands. He needed someone who could give him an heir to continue his vision, someone who wasn't from the Tribunal, or a grabber like her.

The quiet of the temple was a welcome salve. She looked up at the carved paintings of the Elders. Their golden faces flickered with the thick candles lit all around the circular space.

Not for the first time, she whispered a prayer to them. The same one she'd wished for years—that they'd take her feru'talent away.

But now, she added a wish that they'd also take this crushing feeling off her chest.

"Leona?" Tanya called out from behind her. "I heard you come in and called your name, but you seemed preoccupied."

Leona turned and tried to muster a smile. "I just came back from the castle."

"Are you all right?"

Leona shook her head. Tanya put an arm around Leona's shoulder. That gesture did it. All the tears she'd been keeping inside spilled over.

❧ 16 ❧

Adrina followed Jamie through the hallway of Normundir's castle. She stole a glance at Edward, who walked beside her. She was surprised he'd agreed to go with them. She'd heard from her brother that the Gathering hadn't gone so well.

Edward was particularly morose today, and his attention seemed focused on Jamie, though he was mostly silent. Used to her father's moods and her mother's admonitions, she kept a lively stream of conversation going. Jamie was easy. She was almost grateful he was here because then, she wasn't just talking to herself.

Jamie pushed open a big heavy door and waved them inside. "And this...is my mother's pride and joy."

Moist, warm air hit Adrina's face. Steam drifted from a hot spring in one corner. Two chairs and a small round table stood by the pool of water. Potted wild mountain flowers and Greyfolk sculptures, delicate versions of forest animals, were artfully placed around the room.

Adrina smiled in delight. "This is lovely." She walked

around and noticed a painting on the wall. "Is that a family portrait?"

Jamie nodded. "From a long time ago."

"You look quite displeased in it."

"I had to stay still for hours."

"You had a sister?" Adrina pointed at the little girl that Leticia held.

"I was thirteen, and she was two. It's a story that didn't have a happy ending for my mother and father."

"I'm sorry." She laid a hand on his arm.

He smiled with mischief. "I'll tell you plenty of sad stories, so long as you give me your undue sympathy."

She snatched her hand away, but not before Jamie had captured it and kissed the back. She rolled her eyes in irritation and tried to engage Edward in conversation, but he was still distant and silent.

Once they were back in the hallway, Jamie kept up a constant flow of conversation.

"Why do you suppose the Tribunal enlists so many children, when there's so few of them?" Adrina asked.

"I can answer that for you." She gave Jamie a look that plainly said she wasn't asking him, but he continued. "It's because the members have shorter lifespans."

"Why is that?" Edward showed interest for the first time.

"The nature of some of their missions and the way they fight. They have immense skills, but it ages them quicker than all of us."

"Your friend in the Tribunal?" Adrina shook her head, not understanding.

"Leona? Yes, she's aged."

"How long have you known her?" Edward asked.

"Well, now, I don't even remember. I've known her since we were children."

Adrina held her breath. For a while there, she thought Edward looked angry at Jamie.

Jamie turned to Adrina. "Do you have any childhood friends, Princess?"

She tamped down the flash of annoyance that came quickly. "I have four brothers."

"And a very strict mother." Jamie added.

"She just cares for me."

A servant approached them. "Prince Jamie."

"Yes?"

"Queen Leticia requests your presence at the dining hall."

"Shall we return?" Jamie motioned to them.

Edward shook his head. "It's been a long day. I'll be dining in my rooms."

Jamie and Adrina watched him walk away.

"He's in a bad mood," Jamie commented.

"I'm sure whatever is bothering him is none of our business." Adrina couldn't help but roll her eyes at Jamie.

As soon as they entered the dining hall, Adrina went to her stepmother's side. "Mother."

"Where's Edward?"

"He decided he wanted to have supper in his rooms."

Ailene took her arm and led her out of the dining hall. "Follow him." Ailene snapped a finger and a servant immediately appeared at her side. "Edward wants supper to be served in his rooms. Take it up to him."

The servant bowed and left.

"Go to Edward. You know what to do, don't you? We've talked about this countless times, and you know where his rooms are, right?"

"Yes, Mother." Adrina nodded meekly. She clutched at her dress as she made her way through the castle. She was so nervous, she felt faint. Only the thought of her stepmother's ire kept her walking.

Once she was close to Edward's rooms, she waited until servants appeared with trays of food. With a regal nod, Adrina had the servants follow her.

She approached his guards and, taking a deep breath, she raised her chin. "I have Edward's dinner and would like to join him."

"Wait here," one of his guards said. He entered the room and shortly came back out. He held out the door and gestured her in.

Adrina entered with trepidation. She could swear her hands were sweating, and they never did.

Edward was seated at the head of the table, the fireplace behind him. He didn't get up. Instead, he regarded her silently.

"May I join you for supper?" Adrina waited for his nod of assent before she took over placing the platters of food on the table. As the servants filed out of the room, Adrina poured the wine. Relieved to see one of his guards staying inside by the door, Adrina sat down on Edward's right.

She did everything her mother had taught her—she showed off her best side and tried to engage Edward in small talk. The dinner was full of awkward silences, though. Adrina drank more wine and found it loosened her tongue, giving her courage. "I hear the Gathering is going well."

"The unending wars between the kingdoms have taken their toll on all of us. With the last threat, it was just a matter of time before we pulled together or apart."

"I'm certain there's much more that goes into those decisions." She moved closer to him. "I have yet to thank you for rescuing me and my mother."

"You're welcome."

A breath away from Edward, she brushed a hand on his thigh. "If there's anything I can do to repay you..."

Edward cupped the back of Adrina's neck. He pulled her closer as her hand drifted higher. "Tell me something."

"Yes?"

"Are you always so obedient to your mother and father?"

Adrina swallowed convulsively in fear. "I—yes."

He yanked her hair back and grabbed the hand on his leg. "Tell him I don't like being manipulated. Now go." He stood up and gestured at his guard. "Alik, escort the princess back to her room."

As soon as Adrina was outside Edward's room, she wiped at the tears that started to stream down her face. "You may stay," she said with as much dignity as she could to Alik before she fled back to her room.

❧

THE NEXT DAY, THE GREAT HALL WAS FRAUGHT WITH tension. It was in the middle of the day and still, Edward and Jannik were at a standstill.

Leona watched as Edward tapped the side of his chair. She tried not to think of him trying to convince her to go with him to Mandubrath, but that was all she could see and hear in her head as she looked at him.

She was a grabber. Once Edward's people found out, they wouldn't respect her. Or him for being with her. Even her own mother and father didn't know what to do with that part of her.

And there was no future for them. What would she do once Edward got married? Leona didn't think she would be able to stand being there after that.

Edward leaned forward and addressed Jannik. "I'll make you an offer. Do as you choose to guard the borders of Varannis, but if your army weakens and gives the enemy a window of opportunity, I will step in, and my army will take over."

Jannik glared at Edward. "You can't do that."

"I can and I will. It's a generous offer, don't you agree?"

"We talk of peace, and now you're proposing war."

"I'm offering to protect your people."

"At what cost? That I may give you authority over my lands? Equal partnership is what I ask for."

"You should have thought of that before you tried to play games with me," Edward reminded him. With one look, Edward silenced the murmurs in the room. "What is it to be?"

"A compromise. I stand by my offer of alliance through marriage, but I will take your offer of help only until Varannis is secured and nothing more."

"If that time comes, I'll have full autonomy over your army and over your people."

"I trust that the Tribunal will be fair and give their judgment on this matter?"

"Of course," Trevelyn said. "You have my word."

❧

ADRINA LOOKED AT HERSELF IN THE MIRROR AS HER stepmother fussed over her. The dress she wore showed off the colors of Varannis. Shades of blue and silver were woven together as if she were the water and sunlight was glinting off of it. There was to be a celebration later—food and dancing that she was too mortified to attend.

"Stop making that expression." Ailene pulled at the strings that held the back of Adrina's dress. "You'll have lines on your face before your firstborn."

"I don't know if I should go..."

"Nonsense. Once Edward sees you, he'll regret that he didn't take his chance with you. Mark my words."

The door slammed in the adjacent room, startling Adrina.

Ailene finished tying the last of the strings and patted Adrina on the back. "Let's see what your father accomplished today."

Adrina followed her stepmother, hoping her father wouldn't see her right away.

"This is all your fault," Jannik barked at Adrina.

She shrunk back. "I'm sorry, Father. I tried…"

"You should have taught her better," Jannik accused Ailene.

"What do you think I have been doing all these years?" Ailene stood with her back stiff and straight. She didn't back down even as Jannik raged a long tirade about how useless they were.

"Stop this!" Loris was suddenly there in the room with them, Joran just behind him. "It's not their fault, Father. Don't blame your weakness on theirs."

"What did you just say?" Jannik growled.

"You just gave up our kingdom to Edward. You. Not them," Loris sneered as he made his way beside Ailene.

"How dare you question my decision! Edward would have overpowered us if I didn't concede."

"We could fight him."

"With what army? With Bahadur across the sea and Greater Bearnas in the north, we don't stand a chance."

"It was a weak decision, Father. A decision not worthy of a king." Loris spoke in such a way that Adrina had never heard before. It frightened her, the glint in his eyes.

"You are a weakling who has no place to berate me. Compared to your brothers, you are nothing."

"You're comparing me to them? Me?" Loris laughed. "That's pathetic."

Adrina quickly glanced at her father. She tried to slink farther back, but the mirror was in her way. Jannik clenched a fist and advanced on Loris. "You dare speak to me in that way? You are nothing."

Joran laid a hand on Loris's shoulder. "Perhaps we should discuss this later. When we're all rested."

"No, let's talk now. It's just starting to get interesting." Loris turned to Joran and without any warning, took Joran by the neck and lifted him off his feet. As Joran tried to free himself, Loris kept talking. "I like you. Out of everyone, you're almost decent. I was going to give Father a present after the Gathering was all done, but maybe now's the time to do it." He took a pouch from his pocket and threw it at Jannik.

"How?!" Jannik's eyes went wide.

"Let Joran go, Loris," Ailene demanded.

"Not until Father opens my present."

Jannik untied the strings of the pouch and took out a finger with a big emerald ring still circling it. "What is this?"

"The right question to ask is—whose is it?" Loris prompted without letting Joran go.

"No...it can't be." Jannik said at almost the same time as Adrina realized whose finger their father held. It was her oldest brother's, Crede's. "What have you done?"

"You're always comparing me to my brothers. I thought it would be a favor for both of us if you didn't have to do that anymore." Loris turned to Joran. "I've always liked you. But you're in my way." Loris slit his throat with a small dagger. He let Joran's body fall to the ground. "There, Father. I've made a strong decision for our kingdom."

Jannik was aghast and rushed to Joran's side. "What have you done?"

Ailene kneeled beside Jannik, her eyes wide in disbelief. "He was a good brother to you."

"You see, Father, I've just eliminated everything that barred my way to the throne. Well, except you."

"What have you done?" Jannik whispered again.

"Just in case you didn't know, and I'm surprised the Tribunal hasn't caught on yet, all my brothers are dead. Casualties of war."

Jannik sank on the ground, hugged Joran to him, and wept. This seemed to anger Loris even more. "How can you cry for him? He was weak. All of them were weak. Crede begged me to spare his wife and children. You should have seen him."

"Enough!" Jannik raised a fist. Water from the pitcher by Adrina's side floated in the air. More droplets entered the room from the windows and under the door. Jannik flung his hand toward Loris, and the water enveloped Loris's face. Jannik unsheathed his sword, but before he could swing it, Loris was already there by his side, the water still covering his head, not letting him breathe.

Loris caught Jannik's hand and crushed it. As the sword dropped with a clang, the water on Loris's face cascaded off. "A petty trick, Father. You're not on the coast. That's too bad."

"Stop, Loris. Please," Ailene begged him as she took his arm. He shrugged her off, flinging her to the far side of the room.

"How to kill you. That's the question," Loris said in a taunt.

"Guards!" Jannik screamed as he nursed his broken hand.

When two guards came into the room, Jannik pointed at Loris. "Take him."

Instead of following his orders, the guards stood still and looked at Loris.

"You may go."

Adrina looked at Loris with dread.

"Yes, their loyalty is with me." Loris wagged a finger.

"You've been careless, Father, and too trusting for your own good."

"I thought I could trust my own sons."

"You've always underestimated me. Don't worry, Father. I won't kill you right away. I'll let you watch everything you've worked so hard for unfold to my glory."

"Don't be too sure of yourself." Jannik grabbed the sword from the floor and stabbed at Loris, but Loris lifted a hand and with a flick, the sword flew from Jannik's hand and into Loris's hand.

"I now have metalforce. Just in case you're wondering, I'm not the weakling I once was." Loris walked to Adrina. She didn't have anywhere else to go and when he grabbed her hair and pulled her, she yelped in pain. "Shall I kill her or maybe marry her off to the highest bidder?"

"Don't you dare harm her!" Ailene screamed.

"Oh, Mother. How can I forget that Adrina is your precious princess?" Loris sighed. "I do need her alive to be High Queen."

Adrina screamed when Loris pulled sharply at her hair. It felt like he was setting her head on fire.

"Quiet," Loris ordered her. "Fucking weakling."

"Let her go," Jannik demanded.

Adrina felt, rather than saw, herself being thrown. She slammed against her father. Dazed and out of breath, she looked up and watched Loris as walked closer to them. Loris cocked a head and smiled. "Goodbye, Father."

Adrina screamed as Loris swung the sword and sliced through Jannik's stomach.

❧

LEONA STAYED A FEW STEPS BEHIND TREVELYN AND IRENA as they entered the Great Hall. It was resplendent with lights, and everyone shone in their finery. Leona felt drab in comparison with the other women. She hadn't been planning to be here, but Jaworek hadn't shown up yet. Doyle, who was beside her, raised an eyebrow.

Leona shook her head, knowing she should try to look like she actually wanted to be here. As soon as they entered the Hall, Leticia greeted them.

"Your Majesty," Leona bowed. "I don't think I've seen the castle this way before."

"Thank you for the kind words. We've done a lot of work." Leticia led them toward the other side of the room, where a long table stood on the dais. High Healer Irena, always a bit odd, veered away and off to the left, with Doyle following her.

Edward stood just below the dais with a big group of people. His admirers were there as well. Typical, Leona thought.

Trevelyn approached Edward, leaving Leona behind with Leticia.

"Where's Jamie?" Leona asked.

"I don't know. I'm hoping he's picking a wife right now, before his father does it for him."

"You hope he picks a princess, and she proves to be a good alliance," Leona teased.

"He needs to take this seriously. When else will he be able to compare?"

"Compare what?" Jamie said from behind them. "I hope you were talking about horses."

Leticia rolled her eyes as Jamie bowed and kissed the back of Leticia's hand. "Mother, you've outdone yourself once again."

"Aren't you interested in any of the women?"

"I don't think I can decide just yet. Especially since Edward hasn't. I'm sure all the women in the castle swooned when they heard that he won't easily be forced into picking his queen purely for the alliance. I'm second fiddle, a mere prince. Don't you think so?" Jamie put an arm around Leona's shoulder.

"You're not second fiddle, Jamie. But if you don't take your arm off, I'm going to have to take you down."

"You're in a bad mood," Jamie commented, but complied.

"Children," Leticia said in a quiet voice.

"I think Trevelyn is signaling to you," Jamie told Leona.

Leona made the mistake of glancing at Edward first. His sharp gaze held anger before he turned away. She approached Trevelyn, who inclined his head toward the doorway. "Jaworek is here, but you can stay if you want."

"Thank you, but I think I'll go back to the temple." As Leona turned, Leticia put a hand on her arm. "Can I ask a favor?"

"Of course."

"Can you find a servant and tell them to look in on Jannik and my sister. I don't know why they aren't here yet. They know we can't start eating without them."

As soon as Leona was outside the Great Hall, she expelled a huge breath of relief. Maybe tonight she'd be able to fall asleep without thinking of Edward. A walk. That's what she'd do. Fresh air and the night sky.

She tried to flag down a servant, but they all looked harried and most were carrying plates and food into the Great Hall. Deciding that it was probably better for her not to harass a servant, Leona stopped one of them long enough to ask where Jannik's rooms were.

As she walked to the other end of the castle, she tried to recall if her aunt had ever visited Normundir while Leona was there. She'd always known that her aunt was married to Jannik, but she'd never seen her aunt before this. Her mother rarely talked about her. Jamie had once told her he'd heard a rumor that their aunt had wanted to marry their father. Whether that was true or not, they never asked their mother.

Leona turned a corner in the hallway and saw two guards standing in front of Jannik's rooms. She approached one of them. "Are King Jannik and Queen Ailene inside?"

"What is it to you?" the guard to Leona's right asked.

Annoyed at his tone, Leona crossed her arms in front of her. "I'm from the Tribunal. Queen Leticia has asked me to let them know that they're both needed in the Great Hall."

"We'll deliver your message."

Leona turned to go, but there was something that didn't seem right to her. The two guards just stayed at their post. She took a step closer, and they both immediately drew their spears across the door. "The king and queen will go when they're ready."

A woman's scream sounded through the door. When the guards just remained standing there, Leona knew something was indeed wrong. She grabbed both spears and, using a small bit of fire, she heated the handle. The guards yelped in pain. Leona knocked one of the guards off his feet with a sweep of a spear across his legs. For the other, she used the dull edge against his forehead.

She rushed through the door and stopped at the sight of Jannik. Shock was on his face as his hands tried to hold his entrails in. He fell to the ground as Adrina screamed again.

Loris turned and quirked a smile. "Trevelyn's guard. Now, this will be fun."

She looked into his eyes. "Loris, right?"

"At your service. Why are you here?"

"The banquet can't start without your father."

Loris barked in delighted laughter. "What a predicament we have. I suppose I should also kill you."

Leona kept silent and watched Adrina in the corner of her

eye. The princess was slowly creeping away from Loris and to the queen.

Loris tapped the bloodied sword against the ground. "Did you know I wanted to be adopted by the Tribunal when I was young? Never worked out because I didn't have any feru'talent. I had to find my own way. Of course, you're just a servant of the Tribunal. I realized that I wanted more than that."

"Is that why you killed your father and brother?"

"How else was I supposed to become king?"

Leona felt the pull of Edward's fire and tamped it down. She had ice in her ferum, but the small amount would only be good for one use.

Loris cocked his head. "I know what you're doing. You can't protect my mother and sister from me. I am their ruler now."

Leona felt the tug on her spear from Loris. He was a metalforce. A strong one.

"Get out," she said in Adrina's direction. Leona didn't have to say it again. Adrina hooked her arm through her mother's, and they scrambled for the door.

Leona let the spear pull her, and she blasted Loris with fire.

Adrina tripped on one of the guards and sprawled on the ground, bringing her mother with her. She picked Ailene up by the arm, but she wouldn't budge.

"Mother, please. You have to get up. We have to get away from Loris."

Ailene turned to the door. Her pale face was gaunt, and her eyes seemed to see right through the door. "He needs me. My Loris has been hurt too long. It's Jannik's fault. Loris is a sweet boy."

"We have to go. Please, Mother," Adrina implored as she pulled at Ailene.

"That woman is going to kill him. We have to help him."

Adrina hoped that that woman from the Tribunal would kill Loris, but she didn't say that. "We can't stop her. But we can find someone in the Great Hall who can help Loris."

"Yes. Yes, you're right. Yes," Ailene muttered as she let Adrina pull her up.

Adrina raced through the hallway as much as she could while pulling at Ailene. Once they reached the entrance to the Great Hall, Adrina stopped. She turned to Ailene and looked at her in the eyes. "We mustn't create a scene. I'll take you inside and leave you in the back with someone. Then I can go to my aunt and tell her what happened."

Ailene nodded.

Once they were inside, she found a servant and told him to stay with her mother. At his strange look, Adrina gazed down at her skirt and saw the splotches of blood. She took hold of her skirt and tried her best to cover up the blood. Turning, she straightened her shoulders and held her head high as she made her way to the dais.

She clutched at her skirt, willing her hands not to shake. Willing herself to keep walking. The dais came into closer view, and she saw Edward. He would know what to do. She forced herself to slow down, not wanting to attract any attention, when Jamie fell in step with her.

"Princess, you're fashionably late."

She shrugged him off. "I know. I need to talk to Edward."

Jamie sighed audibly. "It's not about this announcement that my father's about to make, is it? He's been trying to stall and decided now's a good time to tell everyone about some marriage that's to take place."

"For once, stop jesting." Something in her tone must have said something about her state of mind, because even as Jamie beamed at her, in an undertone, he said, "Smile, Princess. Or other people are going to wonder why you're upset."

Adrina nodded and mustered a smile.

"Does this have anything to do with why your father isn't here and your stepmother is in the back?"

She nodded again.

"Why don't you tell me and maybe it's something I can help with?"

It was as if she was seeing Jamie for the first time. The smile was the same, but he seemed less young. More capable.

"My brother, Loris...He—" She gulped some air. "He killed my brothers and my father."

"Where is he now?"

"Someone from the Tribunal came in. Trevelyn's guard? She's there fighting him right now."

At that, his stance completely changed, although the smile was gone. "Leona?"

"I don't know her name. She looked young but wasn't scared of him. She told us to get out. I didn't know what else to do. I couldn't help her."

Jamie moved in front of her, blocking her from view. He took her by the chin. "You're handling this well. Stay here and tell my father after he's done. Discretely."

Adrina watched Jamie walk away and felt lost. She smiled and went closer to the table on the dais, trying to get closer to Rikard. She noticed Edward looking at her curiously.

"Yes?" she asked.

"You have blood on your dress."

Adrina realized she'd been careless as she'd spoken with Jamie and hadn't covered all of the blood-splotched fabric. "Sorry." She tried to fold her skirt over, but Edward caught her wrist. He moved her hand and looked at the blood.

"What happened?"

"Jamie told me to tell his father."

"Tell me." His voice was a command she couldn't ignore.

"My brother, Loris, killed my father and brothers. He's dangerous."

"Where is he now?"

"Trevelyn's guard is fighting him. I don't remember her name."

"Where are they?" Edward demanded.

Once she told him, he got up and left the Great Hall.

Rikard stopped talking and turned to Adrina. She just shook her head. He turned back to his audience. "Well, it's good Jamie and Edward aren't the bridegrooms."

While everyone laughed, Adrina fought the growing nausea. Everything that had just happened was starting to come crashing down on her. She felt unbearably cold, and she could no longer stop the shaking. The only thing keeping her upright was the thought of her distraught stepmother. Even though she felt weak and guilty that she couldn't do anything, her stepmother needed her. There was at least one person for whom she could be strong.

❧

"Fire. How delightful," Loris exclaimed.

Leona slammed the spear toward Loris, but he was already gone. He was just off to her left. His face and body were covered in a layer of ice. He shrugged the ice off, and it melted in the air.

"You're a grabber." Leona would have been awed at finding someone like her, except he was trying to kill her.

"Now, I am. And it feels glorious. I have every feru'talent available to me." He blasted fire at Leona. Instead of avoiding it, she ran toward him. They crashed through the window and into the empty courtyard on the far side of the castle. Loris stomped on Leona's arm, and when she let the spear go, he froze it and shattered it in different pieces. He shot the shards at Leona. She ran in a zigzag, away from him, but a few shards caught her along with the strong wind that slammed on her back.

Leona faded into the shadow world, but he was there with her. She deflected his sword with the dagger from her leg. His speed and strength astonished her. Judging by his looks and the way he held his sword, he didn't seem to be a trained fighter. But with all the powers in his arsenal, along with the fading, he was more of a match than she'd expected.

Before she knew it, he'd pushed her dagger away and grabbed her one-handed by the neck. His grip was strong, choking her as she tried to pry his fingers away. She lifted her leg and tried to kick at him, but he just laughed.

"Let go of her. If you're wanting a fight, it's me you want," Edward called out.

"That's true. But fighting her is so much fun." Loris pressed the tip of his sword against Leona's neck. "Tell me, Edward, you'll show me your fire, won't you? I've heard great things about it."

Edward obliged with a strong blast that engulfed Loris.

Leona fell onto her hunches. She flipped her dagger and surged at Loris, but his metalforce repelled the blade. The flames died. Loris was covered in ice, but patches of his skin and clothes were burned. He frowned, and his skin started to repair itself.

A strong wind blew into the courtyard. It forced Leona and Edward onto their knees.

Loris cocked his head. "Listen."

Beyond the wind, the thundering sounds of footsteps resounded nearby. Loris's smile turned into a scowl when the clash of weapons and screams of fighting began.

"That's Jamie," Edward told Loris.

Soldiers appeared in their midst and quickly reported to Loris that the small contingent of soldiers they had had been attacked.

Loris lifted a hand and pointed it at Edward. "Kill him."

As the soldiers surrounded Edward, Leona lunged at Loris. He caught her, and using wind, he threw her up with enough force to knock her through the window of the soldiers' mess hall. She crashed through the window and slid on the table.

Leona knew she'd broken something. With every breath and every movement, the pain on her left side was a sharp, unbearable thing. She used what she could of Margret's ferum and numbed the pain. She jumped on to her feet. A small group of soldiers were eating at the table, and they all stood in surprise. Loris stabbed one of them from behind and threw his body aside

Leona grabbed the fallen soldier's sword. She faced Loris, and now they truly fought. He was too fast even for her, and she needed to get past his guard. She saw her opening and made a run for the doorway beyond the mess hall.

They ended in the training courtyard. What Leona lacked in Loris's speed, strength, and power, she made up in skills that had been drilled into her since childhood. Even then, he knocked her weapon down and forced her to her knees. Water lightly splashed from the muddied puddle Leona knelt on.

He crouched in front of her. "What a pity that it had to end this way for you. I thought the Tribunal would have done better." Loris brought the sword against her neck. "I won't make this fast. I want to watch you die slowly. My father's and brother's deaths happened too quickly for my liking."

Leona dug a hand into the puddle. She willed the water to take form and freeze. As the sword's edge dug into her neck to draw blood, she took the newly formed stake and stabbed Loris on the side of his face.

She caught his falling sword, flipped it over, and cut his hand off.

He caught her wrist and burned fire. "You bitch," he said, as his face started to heal.

The pain made Leona drop the sword. She felt the webs of connection between his fiery hand and her wrist. She felt the feru'talent surging from the strings of ferum he had layered on his neck. Leona pulled at them, grabbing power for healing. Emptying it out quicker than he could, she healed the broken rib. The skin on her wrist was coated with ice as water surged from the puddles in the courtyard. It couldn't heal completely, but it was enough for Loris to look in shock at her.

He closed his eyes and faded away, but Leona was there. Her hand was on his, not letting him go. She felt the tug of power coming from whatever was in him. Just as had happened years ago, she couldn't break the connection between them.

She felt his life force surging inside her. They reappeared, and Leona screamed as she used wind, water, and fire to break them apart.

Leona would have fallen to the ground had Edward not caught her. She leaned against him, breathing in ragged gasps.

"Can you stand up?" Edward asked.

"Yes. Just give me a moment." She stood up, but almost buckled. She'd never used that much feru'talent, except for when she'd killed that boy.

"Leona, how badly are you hurt?" Jamie rushed at her.

"It's worse than it looks. It's mostly his blood."

"Here, why don't you come with me? I'll take you to the healer." Jamie took Leona from Edward. As they walked away, Leona turned and looked back. She found Edward staring at her.

Leticia met Jamie and Leona inside the castle and escorted them to small room. Soon, the castle healer came in. Leona closed her eyes under the ministrations of the healer. She wished she'd brought the ferum that Margret had given her. It was back in the temple, and she could probably heal herself faster.

She opened her eyes when the doors opened to High Healer Irena and High Historian Trevelyn.

"I'll take it from here," Irena said as greeting. Her coarse black hair was pulled back in a severe bun high atop her head. Her dark brown skin gleamed in the candlelight.

"Thank you, High Healer," Leticia said graciously. "Since Leona's been hurt, I think it would be good for her to stay here and recover for at a few weeks until she heals."

"I understand, but that's not possible. And it's why I'm here."

They waged a silent battle until Leticia sighed and gave in. She turned to Jamie and the healer. "Come with me."

"But—" Jamie stammered.

"They'll help me now." Leona gave Jamie and her mother a reassuring smile.

Trevelyn closed the door while Irena sat down on the chair vacated by the healer. She took Leona's hand and immediately, Leona felt the skin on her wrist knitting itself.

Trevelyn made his way to the foot of the bed and linked his hands behind his back. "You're able to wield again."

"Yes, I told Priest Orin that it was starting to come back."

"It more than came back," Irena responded. "I can feel a pull from you. Subtle, but it's there."

Leona tried to remain silent. To admit fear in front of them was weakness. But the look of concern in Trevelyn's eyes made her feel as if he knew how to help her. "I don't like taking other people's feru'talent. What if I kill someone again?"

Trevelyn nodded in understanding. "Light wielders are rare. Society has put a stigma on them because they fear the feru'talent that you have. What did Edward say of this when you showed him?"

"He told me to use it to my advantage." Leona blinked at her answer. Why was she telling him all this? She stared at Trevelyn, and the impression of understanding melted away into stoicism. He was a whisperer. Somehow, Leona had always forgotten that.

"You wouldn't have fallen for my little trick if you were willing to wield," he admonished her. "That's why Loris almost beat you. He was a wielder too, wasn't he?"

"He said he wasn't born with it."

Trevelyn turned to Irena, who shook her head in consternation. "I've never heard of someone being given feru'talent like that. Only the Elders can bequeath and withdraw power." The last was quoted from the Prayers to the Weavers and Protectors.

"Did he say anything else?" Trevelyn asked.

"No." Leona looked down at her healed wrist. She could feel the other aches from her body fading away. She looked up and found Trevelyn staring at the fireplace.

"We must go to the Elders," Irena said in a low voice. For the first time in her life, Leona had a suspicion that they weren't talking about the carvings in the temple or the ixmus stone. She was almost certain that Irena wasn't talking about the High Priest either.

"Not yet." Trevelyn turned to face Leona. "I want you to come with me. We're interrogating Loris, and I'd like for you to be there. It might make him more angry—therefore amenable to answering our questions, if he sees you there."

Leona swung her legs to the side of the bed and stood up. She looked down at her clothes, drenched in blood, and noticed for the first time that the threaded bracelet that Edward had given to her was gone. His ring was still in the chain around her neck, but the bracelet reminded her of Storwood and what they had had for that fleeting moment in time.

Leona turned the blanket over and checked the floor.

"Did you lose something?" Irena asked.

She shook her head. "No."

Adrina tucked the blanket around her mother's shoulder. Ailene had just fallen asleep. Thankfully so. She'd been hysterical, insisting on seeing Loris.

Adrina left the room and went in search of Jamie. She needed to thank him and to find out what had happened to Loris and the Tribunal guard.

The hallways were crowded with people going to and fro. One of the servants told her that they'd seen him upstairs. Adrina found a nearby staircase and went up into another hallway. She caught a glimpse of Edward, who was issuing orders to some men. Mortification crept up and made her cheeks warm. She wanted to turn around, but he caught sight of her.

"Adrina, do you need anything?"

She squared her shoulders and walked up to him. "I was just looking for Jamie. I wanted to ask him if Loris is…dead."

"He's alive."

Adrina didn't know what else to say. She looked out the window and noticed something red up in the sky far away. "What is that?"

They both peeked out the window. As people rushed past them, they saw two horses with riders speeding away from the castle. Jamie was running through the hallway when Edward called out to him. "What is happening?"

"We're sending scouts to investigate the flare's source. It shot from the eastern part of the Borderlands." Jamie rubbed the back of his neck.

"Could be a mistake."

"We've tried to limit the access to the flares to a limited few. Don't want any kids just playing pranks."

Adrina dug her hands into her skirt, wanting to interrupt, but dared not to. When Jamie flashed a smile at her, she stepped forward. "Do you know what's happened to Loris?"

"Why do you ask?"

Coming from any other person, it would have annoyed Adrina, but Jamie had helped her earlier. "My mother's worried about him and wishes to see him before…" Adrina shrugged.

"He's going to be questioned as soon as he wakes up. I don't know if my aunt will be able to see him tonight."

"He's her only son. She's been good to all of us, but Loris was the only child she was able to birth. Maybe after he's questioned, she can see him? Just once?" Adrina implored to both Jamie and Edward.

"I'll see what I can do," Jamie replied. He turned to Edward. "Speaking of Loris, my father is expecting you in the dungeon."

"My thanks." Edward nodded to Jamie and Adrina before turning to leave.

"I should go back to my mother."

"If you need me, tell one of the servants, and they'll come find me."

Adrina left before he could say anything more.

❧

Leona led Trevelyn to the dungeon. She'd rarely gone there. The first time was when Jamie had snuck her down there. She must have been eight or nine. Leona nearly smiled when she remembered that he'd gotten a good thrashing after that.

The cold, dark, and damp seeped into her skin. A guard opened the door to a small room that had implements of torture hanging from the low ceiling.

Loris was in shackles, supported by iron bands that held him in place by the wall. A healer had already staunched the blood from the stump that was his hand. There was a gaping hole in Loris's face where Leona had stabbed him with the arrow. A healer was kneeling by Loris, a curved needle in one hand and thread in the other. A scowl from Edward had the healer scurrying away.

Rikard turned when they entered the room. Leona met his eyes as they roamed, seeming to look for injuries. Rikard gave a brief nod after his assessment. "You've recovered quickly."

"Irena's work," Trevelyn replied for Leona.

Edward glanced at Leona and also perused her, but he didn't say anything.

"How's Ailene?" Rikard asked.

"Incoherent. Irena will look in on her."

They heard a moan and turned toward the chained man. Loris's eyes blinked open, then closed again. He audibly swallowed, his Adam's apple bobbing up and down. His chains clinked as his hands tried to move toward his face.

"Awake? Do you see me?" Edward said.

"Yes," Loris looked at him blearily. His eyes went around from face to face, as if trying to figure out where he was. When he fixed his gaze on Leona, his eyes went wide with recognition. "Tribunal bitch. You'll pay for what you did. Fucking grabber." He closed his eyes and opened them once again. "Where is my ferum? What did you do with it?"

"You didn't think we'd let you keep it, did you?" Edward replied.

"Let me go. You have no idea who you're dealing with."

"Why don't you tell us?" Rikard demanded.

"You'll pay for this if you don't let me go. You'll all be mine before this all ends."

"Just like your father's kingdom, Varannis, is already yours?" Edward asked.

Loris cocked his head and smiled. "Yes. It's mine now. Let me go," he roared and struggled against his chains.

"Stop it," Edward ordered.

Loris calmed down. His eyes closed and he was unnaturally still, so that they all thought he had fallen asleep. Rikard moved closer and reached out when Loris suddenly reared forward and screamed. Everyone in the room jumped except Edward. Loris suddenly laughed. "You should have seen your faces." He smiled as if the pain didn't bother him. He looked at Edward. "Have you no sense of humor?"

Edward just looked at him.

"I guess not." Loris shrugged.

"How did you become a grabber? You said you weren't born with it," Leona asked.

Loris sneered. "I don't answer to you."

"Loris," Rikard said in warning.

"Uncle." He smiled widely.

"Answer her."

"I don't answer to any of you. I'm beyond all of you."

"You're the one shackled in chains," Rikard insisted.

"No chains can hold me." He pulled at his chains and the iron bent, alarming everybody.

"Enough. I can see you're strong," Edward said.

"Then set me free."

"We saw how you fought earlier. These chains will give everyone here the assurance that no harm will come to them. So, why don't you talk to us first?"

Loris considered it and shrugged. "It's too late. You can't do anything. The wheels I've set are in motion. Look in the skies. The flares will light the lands in red. Just like the river of blood that will flow if you don't bow to me." Loris moved his head forward, and the stakes that held the chains in place were partially pulled from their rock base.

Trevelyn stepped forward. "Who are you working with? Who helped you in Varannis? Who made you a wielder?"

"Everyone always underestimated me. Even now, all of you think you're better than me." He appealed to Edward. "Let's be allies, and I'll spare Greater Bearnas. As for my uncle and the Tribunal, there's no mercy. They have both tried to oppose me. I'm not a forgiving man." He looked at Rikard and Trevelyn. "You will all die."

"Fuck you." Rikard rushed at Loris, but Edward blocked him. "I want to hear him out."

Loris smiled at Rikard. "I wouldn't be so rash." Loris shook his head. "I have an army ten times greater than yours. I can crush your kingdom in a day. If you think you can just saunter in and take what's mine, then you're mistaken."

"Varannis has nowhere near the size of that army," Rikard said.

"Ah, my father doesn't, but I do," Loris smirked. "The Asshai has given his soldiers." He looked at Edward and ignored Rikard. "Ally yourself with me and declare me High King, and my army will spare your people, even my uncle's, if he does a good job of begging."

"Stop baiting him, Your Majesty," Edward said, emphasizing the last two words.

"Yes, I like the sound of that." Loris smiled. "My father and brothers have always thought little of me. My mother was the only one who truly believed in me."

"She knew about this?" Rikard asked.

"Enough to keep my father placated."

"You've spent a long time planning this," observed Edward.

"Yes." Loris was enjoying Edward's attention. "I was waiting for the right time. Thanks to you, you provided me with the perfect opportunity."

"The Gathering?"

"Couldn't have planned it better. And you traveling through the Borderlands...that temptation was too hard to resist."

Edward cocked his head. "How did you get the Greyfolk to ally themselves with your army?"

"They only needed permission to do what they've always wanted, and I gave it to them. And they're just the beginning. My army will storm all of Bearnas, and there will be no mercy for you."

"Where is the army now?"

"Watch the skies. When they turn blood red, then you'll know my army is coming."

"When did you get your first communication from the Shahan of Arshavir?"

"He's nothing but a servant," Loris scoffed. "I was the one who chose to ally with him. Who thought to conceal the army? Who was it that the Asshai has deemed worthy to lead them? Me. I was the one who woke him up from his slumber. I brought him back to life. The one who reminded him of who he was. Their own god has deemed me worthy above everyone else to let me call him by his name," Loris bragged. He cleared his throat and then coughed. His face turned red.

"Lord Dragomir," he choked out. He struggled against his bonds, rattling the chains against each other.

At the name, Trevelyn staggered back. Soldiers tried to hold Loris down, but his body convulsed in unnatural ways. He arched forward, his torso straining until a loud pop reverberated in the room. Loris broke his own back and died hanging from chains and restraints half pulled out of the wall.

"What the fuck," Rikard exclaimed.

Loris's head suddenly lifted up, and his eyes were all black. "You're all dead."

Edward put a hand on his sword. "What are you?"

"I am Dragomir of the Bruadar, the Asshai of Bahadur, and holder of the Mithruim. I will come for all of you." He turned his head unnaturally to Trevelyn. "Well, well, well. The Tribunal's pet is here. I can sense the mark of the Namtar coursing through your blood, and it reeks. Why don't you come here to me?"

Trevelyn's eyes widened in fear as he flung himself forward. Loris whipped out an arm and wrapped a hand around Trevelyn's throat. Loris pulled him forward and cocked his head. "Tell your masters I'm coming for them. I'm already here. I'm everywhere." Loris tightened his hold, and Trevelyn's eyes bulged. Edward swung his sword and struck at Loris's neck, severing his head.

"I thought the Asshai was just one of the gods they worshipped?" Edward turned to Trevelyn and waited for Trevelyn to stop coughing.

"Dragomir is a name I've seen in our books," Trevelyn sputtered out.

"Who is he?"

"Dragomir of the Bruadar was the one who started the great war a thousand years ago. Our Elders, the Namtar, sacrificed a great deal to defeat him." Trevelyn had to stop after every word to get his breath back.

"He was in the Bruadar?"

Trevelyn nodded as he held a hand to his throat. "He was a Greyfolk half-breed of great renown who lived in the Bruadar a thousand years ago, before he was banished for crimes against the Namtar." Trevelyn looked at the body of Loris. "This changes everything. We must consult with our Elders."

※

Leona followed Trevelyn into the Temple. She looked up at the carvings of the Elders. She'd never really paid attention before. Trevelyn had spoken of them earlier as if they were real. But then, she'd heard the priests, and even the healers, sometimes say that they needed to consult with the Elders—and they always did, in the temples, their arms up in supplication to those beings carved above them.

They walked past worshipers and into Priest Orin's study. The priest stood there, as if waiting for them the whole time.

"It has begun," Trevelyn said without preamble. "Dragomir is here."

"Are you sure?" Orin steepled his fingers in front of him.

"Tell him what happened, Leona."

Leona relayed everything about her fight with Loris, up to what he'd revealed in the dungeon and how he'd died.

"Who would have thought?" Orin finally said after a long silence. "This happens in our lifetime."

Trevelyn nodded thoughtfully. "Everything hangs on a balance. We can't afford to do anything wrong. I must go back to Midroska right away."

"I just received word." Orin took a small piece of paper from a pocket in his robes and handed it to Trevelyn. "It's not safe. Midroska is under siege."

"Is Doyle here?"

"Yes, do you want to send for him?"

"Yes."

As Orin left the room, Trevelyn turned his gaze to Leona. "You will have to go to Midroska and tell the Elders." Trevelyn took a ring from his finger. The round signet held the mark of the Tribunal—a circular pattern with lines entwined with each other. He handed it to Leona.

"Once Midroska is secured, do you want me to come back and escort you and the High Healer?"

"No, you are not to come back to Normundir. You're to go to Mandubrath. You'll be stationed there indefinitely."

Leona's heart pounded in her ears. She clutched her shaking hands into fists. "I thought my station here was permanent."

"It never was. You go where you are needed, of course." Trevelyn raised an eyebrow. "Questions?"

"Did Edward have anything to do with this?"

"He was so pleased with how you conducted yourself that he requested that you be assigned to Mandubrath. I agreed. After all, it is the most prosperous kingdom in Bearnas."

"And my father, does he know about this?"

Trevelyn raised an eyebrow at her questioning him. "We'll handle him when it comes."

Leona knew her father was going to be furious, but Trevelyn knew that already. "What are my duties in Mandubrath?"

"You'll protect the temple." When Leona didn't answer right away, Trevelyn frowned. "Understood?"

She nodded. "Yes, sir."

After she was dismissed, Leona went to her room and started to pack. In the past, excited to travel, she'd breeze through packing her things. But today, she trudged through it. Sure, she was looking forward to seeing Mandubrath, but not with the thought of Edward there. Or the permanence of her assignment. Edward wanted something she didn't, something she couldn't give him. If she agreed, people will eventually find out about them. And what would they do when they realized she's a grabber? Even within the Tribunal, some still sneered at her. And then there were her mother and father, who would be disappointed in her. Edward eventually needed to marry to have an heir. The thought of his getting married and being with another woman made her sick.

"Stop this," Leona said to herself—more to her racing thoughts. She couldn't go to her parents like this. Not when she needed to tell them she was leaving and would be gone for a long time.

Once she had her mind set, packing her things didn't take very long. After all, she didn't really own very much.

Leona carried her packs to the stable and prepared her horse.

❧

TELLING HER MOTHER AND FATHER WAS ONE OF THE WORST things she'd ever had to tell them.

Rikard sat wearily down in his chair. "Is it that bad you don't want to be where you belong?"

"Father," she implored, "it's not like that. I've accepted a long time ago who I am and what I do. Being a Chosen of the Tribunal is not a curse, it's a blessing. I won't apologize for following orders."

Rikard nodded. "Fine. Go." He gestured her dismissal, and Leona hated feeling like she had somehow disappointed him. She had stood up and turned to leave when Leticia called to her. "Be careful."

"I'll see you when I'm allowed to visit. Can you tell Jamie?"

Leticia nodded and stood to embrace Leona. "We should have kept you. I'm sorry we didn't."

"Thank you for saying that." Leona smiled through the tears that welled up in her eyes.

As she left the castle, she had this strange feeling that things were never going to be the same after this. She looked back and etched a picture of this moment in her mind and heart.

"Are you coming?" Doyle called out to her from just inside the gates of the kingdom. "Colm's waiting outside with our horses."

"Just saying goodbye."

"You'll come back," he assured her.

"I hope so."

As Leona rode away from her home, she didn't look back.

Instead, her gaze was to the road ahead. Flashes of red light twinkled up in the sky. Flares—and there must have been at least a hundred.

"By the Elder gods! What could this mean?" Colm exclaimed.

"War," Doyle grimly said.

Thank you for reading The High King's Protector. I hope you enjoyed it! Please help other people find this book by writing a review.

Get a free ebook of Golden Sands — a novella about Edward's adventure in Bahadur. Available at:

www.caklippert.com/book/golden-sands/

To get notified of new releases, giveaways and pre-release specials, sign up at: www.caklippert.com

ABOUT THE AUTHOR

C.A. Klippert is the author of The High King's Protector, the first book in the Bruadar series.

She lives in Seattle, but previously lived in Manila, Philippines. She loves adventure, travel, and would never turn down a good cocktail.

You can visit the author at caklippert.com.